CODE

AN INTERNATIONAL SENSORY ASSASSIN NETWORK NOVEL

MARY TING

Other Books by Mary Ting

ISAN, International Sensory Assassin Network, Book 1
Helix, International Sensory Assassin Network, Book 2
Genes, International Sensory Assassin Network, Book 3
Jaclyn and the Beanstalk
When the Wind Chimes

Forthcoming from Mary Ting
Redd Riding Hood
Ronin Witch

Awards
ISAN—International Sensory Assassin Network, Book I
GOLD MEDAL—Science Fiction & Fantasy
2019 Benjamin Franklin Awards
GOLD MEDAL—Science Fiction—Post-Apocalyptic
2018 American Fiction Awards
GOLD MEDAL—Science Fiction
2018 International Book Awards
GOLD MEDAL—Young Adult Thriller
2019 Readers' Favorite Awards
GOLD MEDAL—Young Adult Action
2018 Readers' Favorite Awards
SILVER MEDAL—Young Adult Fiction—Fantasy / Sci-Fi
2019 Moonbeam Children's Book Awards
FINALIST — Action Adventure
2019 Silver Falchion Awards

Jaclyn and the Beanstalk
BRONZE MEDAL – Juvenile / Young Adult Fiction
2019 Illumination Book Awards

CODE

AN INTERNATIONAL SENSORY ASSASSIN NETWORK NOVEL

MARY TING

Code
An International Sensory Assassin Network Novel

Cover Credit: Michael J. Canales
www.MJCImageworks.com

ISBN: 978-1-64548-067-9

VESUVIAN BOOKS

Published by Vesuvian Books
www.vesuvianbooks.com

Printed in the United States of America

10 9 8 7 6 5 4 3 2 1

TABLE OF CONTENTS

CHAPTER ONE – TOO LATE

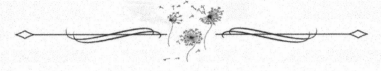

MITCH

"**W**hat happened?" Mitch pitched forward and anchored his hands on Russ's smooth metal desk. "Why is Payton's group still here? His team is supposed to attack the rebel base in Hope City. Gene gave Novak the coordinates."

Russ eased back into his leather seat. With a raised eyebrow, he looked from where Mitch gripped the desk and back to his face. Mitch retreated a step, falling into an at-ease position.

"I don't know." Russ skimmed his hologram screen. "According to the log, Novak sent teams from the west. He put Sabrina in charge at the last minute."

Mitch froze. "What?"

But he knew. Payton's team had failed to capture Ava at the black market, so Novak had lost confidence in Mitch and opted for another team instead.

Ava had become Novak's obsession. Mitch understood why he wanted her back. Ava had the ability to temporarily absorb another person's gift. At the black market, she had produced an electric current and zapped the life from one of the guards from a distance, with no weapon but herself.

Mitch had placed Nina and Cora on Payton's team—the two girls he'd convinced to join ISAN after they had been captured by

1

Justine and Payton. Nina had the ability to create an electrical spark from her fingertips, and Cora to turn invisible.

The girls were to go with Payton, defect and help the rebels defeat Gene, and then stay there. That was Mitch's plan at least.

Mitch slammed a fist on Russ's desk. The water inside the pitcher swished, nearly spilling over. "Do you think Novak suspects something?"

Russ flinched and his nostrils flared as he eyed the three empty glasses next to the pitcher. "Careful. And I don't know," he said with a steady tone. "I don't know why Novak does what he does."

Mitch inhaled the scent of lavender permeating the air. Russ had told him it helped him relax and think better. Well, it wasn't helping him on either count.

He shouldn't admit anything out loud. Russ had been sure his office wasn't bugged, but who really knew? Novak had a way of springing nasty surprises. Mitch uncurled his fingers. He wanted to knock the glasses or punch the wall—punch anything.

"Did Sabrina log in?" Mitch asked. "Do we know if they found the rebel base? I messaged Zeke as soon as I found out Gene could send Novak his coordinates. It was up to Zeke to get the message to Rhett."

Russ shook his head, his expression stoic.

That boy cared about Ava more than he should, so he must be apprehensive, too. Though if Lydia were in Ava's position, Mitch would probably die trying to kill Novak alone.

Mitch straightened when the door slid open, then eased his shoulders. Lydia walked in with a handheld TAB. She swung her arms to the stride of her long legs across the polished tile floor toward them.

"Russ. Mitch." She gave a curt nod, her long dark hair cascading down the side of her face. When she offered a small smile, she dimpled slightly.

Mitch's lips tugged at the corner. He melted in her presence, but tried not to grin too widely. She always looked sophisticated and put together no matter what she wore, even a ponytail and a plain gray training outfit, like the one she wore now. However, her eyes were shadowed with puffy, dark half-moons.

She cleared her throat, her long lashes lifting upward. "Mr. Novak sent me a message. He won't be attending today's meeting."

"Do you know where he is?" Russ avoided her eyes, folding the sleeve of his white lab coat.

When Mitch had told Lydia about Russ being on their side, she'd warmed up to him and pretty much told him everything. She'd even told him about being a spy for Councilor Josephine Chang, but not about her relationship with Mitch. No one could know *that*. It would make them too vulnerable.

"No. He didn't say." She swiped her thumb across the tablet, her brown eyes following the words across the screen.

"What about your source?" Mitch stood with his legs a foot apart and his hands behind his back. "Did she get back to you?"

That source was supposed to let the rebels into ISAN's secret base.

Her pink lips twisted. "No. Not yet."

"So then we don't know anything. *Anything.*" Mitch cleared his throat and tried again with a softer tone. "I meant, we don't know if the rebels even found the secret facility."

A muscle jumped in Russ's jaw. "Why didn't you tell me earlier about this plan? How much do you trust this person? This could be a trap. If Ava is there, she won't wait for anyone. She'll— she'll—"

"You don't know that. She might not even be there." Mitch curled his fingers on Russ's desk, his knuckles white from the pressure.

"You don't know her like I do." Russ cursed and raked a hand down his face, letting out a small sound of defeat.

"Nothing is going according to plan." Mitch fisted a hand in his hair, rage building inside him. "Novak is always a step ahead of us."

Lydia touched his arm, then dropped her hand. "There's something else." She glanced between Russ and Mitch.

Mitch's stomach churned. *Something else.* That was never good.

She scanned her TAB, patting the screen. "According to Diana's log, Payton isn't in class. He must be with Novak."

Mitch scoffed and shoved his hands inside the front pockets of his black training suit. "What else is new? Novak must have taken his favorite lapdog to the secret base."

Was this the first time? Mitch searched his memory, wondering if Payton had been to this secret base before and hadn't been able to tell anyone about it. He should have grilled Payton harder.

Lydia hugged her TAB to her chest. "Do you think the rebels who went to the facility have been captured?"

"My gut tells me Rhett and Ava split up," Mitch said. Restless, he paced to the sofa in the center of the office and then to the wall. "Rhett would have gone back to the base since those are his people. Ava probably went to the facility to ensure she doesn't miss the window of opportunity to get inside. And… and… Payton." It dawned on him with cold certainty. Heart pounding, Mitch planted his palms on the wall, needing to brace himself. "Ava went in. That's why Novak took Payton. I think she's been captured."

Russ poured three glasses of water with trembling hands. "I

4

need a drink."

"Water isn't going to help shit. I need a shot of whiskey." Mitch pushed off the wall to Russ's desk, took a glass anyway, and gulped it down.

Mitch's entire purpose in signing up for ISAN had been to find his father. His half brother Rhett was the only other person he cared about—and that had taken time.

That little slit in his heart had opened up even more. Now he worried for too many people. Lydia. Ava. Russ. Even Cora and Nina, the newest ISAN recruits. Mitch hadn't asked for this.

A ping chimed on Lydia's chip and she set down her half-full glass with a thud. She put her thumbprint on her TAB and paled. She swallowed hard. Twice.

Lydia, the master of deception, master at hiding her emotions—she literally taught the class on it—had fooled Novak for years. Strong and determined, she was the ultimate assassin. Not a brute force killer, but the kind that was quietly invincible.

When her eyes pooled with tears, Mitch's heart shattered. He knew that expression all too well—the one she tried to hide when an agent died on a mission.

Russ slowly rose from his chair.

"What? What happened?" Dread coursed through Mitch as his fists tightened. His pulse hammered against his temples. Mr. Novak switching teams had caused chaos in his plan and there was not a damn thing he could do to help the renegades.

"I'm reading Sabrina's log." Her hands trembled as she scrolled. "Gene is safe." Her voice cracked, and she paused to regain control. "Rebel base has been demolished. There is nothing left." She let out a shuddering breath. "We… we were… too late."

Mitch clenched his jaw. He didn't know when his butt hit the sofa. Disoriented. Numb. He felt nothing. Shock had rendered him speechless.

What of Rhett? And so many others?

Too late. Too late. Too late. The words echoed with devastating finality.

Russ fell back to his seat. Elbows on the table, he covered his face with his hands. Tears covered Lydia's cheeks as she stood motionless, staring at the screen.

Mitch rose and dragged his feet to Russ… to do what? He didn't know, but he planted his hands on the table, his chest rising and falling faster.

He'd lost the battle—the battle to be one step ahead of Novak—the battle to save the rebel base. And now he'd lost the battle to calm his fury. With one swift swing, he'd knocked the pitcher and the glasses off the desk.

They shattered into tiny crystal pieces, bouncing on the floor like hail, water pooling around the shards. Lydia and Russ flinched but didn't look up or speak.

Mitch let the horrible revelation ride its course. When he was capable, he would work on plan B. But plan B wouldn't take root if there was no one left.

CHAPTER TWO – WHERE AM I?

AVA

Mr. Novak's face hovering over me as I lay helpless on a hard bed, chained to the wall, was the last thing I recalled.

Goodnight, pumpkin. Pumpkin wasn't an unusual pet name, but that had been a special name my father had used for me. It had to be a coincidence. It *had* to.

I spun around at the center of an empty room I didn't recognize. My hands grew slick with sweat as I aimed my Taser at each of the four gray, featureless walls. I inhaled the scent of sterile lab. Then it hit me. I *did* recognize the room.

A few memories sharpened. I had entered the facility alone—the ISAN secret base. I'd left Naomi by herself near a pile of debris by the entrance. Hopefully she hadn't shot Janine—the source—the girl who let me in.

I tiptoed to the nearest wall. As I ran my hand along the length, feeling for something to push it open, I recalled seeing my mother wearing a white night gown, and then Gene. Or had that been a dream?

If Gene was here, I didn't want to think about what that meant for the rebels. I had to find my way out. I would pay dearly for being curious, for thinking I could snoop around an ISAN facility and walk right out.

No guards. No footsteps. Not even a voice outside the room.

Only the dim light keeping me company, and my heart thundering and blood rushing to my ears. But someone was watching me; I felt it.

"Who are you? Show yourself." I checked every corner for a bug or camera. My ISAN black suit, layered on me like a second skin, stretched as I turned.

My voice echoed in the room but no one answered. There had to be a door. With my Taser leveled, I marched toward the wall to my left.

It didn't budge.

I banged harder, and pain rippled up my arm. I tugged at my Helix to give me strength, but the wall must have been made out of something much stronger, only a dent the size of my fist remained.

"What do you want from me?" I said.

Whoosh, clank, and *click,* metal on metal. I braced against the smooth wall as the floor lengthened and widened. The room turned midnight dark, and then colorful neon city lights surrounded me. Apartment buildings, shopping plazas, restaurants, nightclubs, and even trees materialized from the darkness.

A simulation room?

Cool wind brushed my face and tousled my hair. Pedestrians strolled about in protective-bubble walkways with their families. Gliders flew in their orderly fashion, while speaking advertisements competed for attention along the faces of office building.

I peered past the skyscrapers and admired the pale moon and pinprick lights scattered over the night sky. The stars looked so lifelike. Too bad they weren't real. But I'd much rather have this view than be stuck in the stuffy hellhole.

I released a harsh sigh. A group of ISAN guards had marched out of the shadows by the office building to my right.

"Go ahead and do your worst," I hissed.

The concussion of firearms rent the peaceful air. Bullets whizzed at my forehead, and I whirled. They shattered a shop window and the others deflected off the brick walls. Tasers pelted at me, red tracer lights streaking toward me. I arched my back, twisted to the side, and did a backward flip to dodge them all.

The guards' footsteps pounded, their weapons firing. I crouched behind a restaurant and checked my side for a weapon. I drew a Taser and shot a few soldiers, but more kept coming in a black-suited flood.

One of me and dozens of them.

So not fair.

I did what any reasonable assassin would do—I ran.

I bumped citizens' shoulders down the sidewalk, not bothering to apologize. They weren't real anyway.

An unattended motor glider was parked up ahead by the bakery, so I skidded to a halt. I hopped over it and switched that baby on, its two wheels spinning on the road.

Guards jumped onto the same type of motor glider and gave chase. I tipped sideways and almost lost my balance to avoid bullets. One hit the sideview mirror, another ricocheted against the back.

One guard veered to the side and drew alongside me with a Taser drawn. As he aimed, I kicked his machine. It collided into another glider. I twisted to the side and shot twice at the front tire of another glider pulling close. It blasted apart like a mini bomb and the driver lost control.

I weaved between pedestrians, small street stalls, then into an alley, hoping to lose them, but the alley turned into a maze of branching streets that looked identical. I pulled up my map.

With a blueprint of the labyrinth in front of me, I turned left, and then angled right. Each corner I turned, I went with the confidence of knowing exactly where I was headed until the maze shifted and skyscrapers blocked my exit.

A dead end, created just for me. Of course it wouldn't be that easy.

I had two choices: get off my motor glider or go inside the building. I decided to do the latter. This was a mental mission after all, no matter how real it felt.

The two wheels slid into their slots and the machine became an aircraft when I tapped on the monitor. I banked straight up. Below, a handful of ISAN guards crashed into the structure, unable to pull up in time, but some stayed right on my tail. Fire exploded and flames roared up the edifice's surface behind me.

I soared up the length of the skyscraper, wind rushing past me, and my peripheral view blurred. Vibrant colors from the busy city light blended into white. When I landed on the roof, I debated turning back around but decided to have a little fun. I took off to the next office building.

Too bad motor gliders weren't made like in the olden days. I would have loved to throttle the engine, make that powerful sound, and traverse from one rooftop to the next.

ISAN guards gave a good chase. Taser pellets and bullets ricocheted. They missed and wasted ammunition. At the very last skyscraper, I pointed my glider into a nosedive. ISAN guards followed.

Faster and faster I plummeted, my hair flapping, my breath catching from the strong gale. But I felt a sense of freedom. Before,

I had been too frightened to enjoy free fall, even on mental missions. But the sensation of my stomach dropping and energy jolting through me must have been the reason Rhett loved to fly, to be one with the aircraft.

At the verge of losing control of the machine and myself, I reached a pivotal movement—would I allow myself to die and hope I would wake up in the room? We came out unscathed no matter what happened in a mental mission. Not a scrape, even if we had been shot or sliced by a sword. But I had no idea if that was true here. Novak had a way of changing the rules unexpectedly.

I would have taken that chance before, but I had so much to live for. Thinking of Rhett, my friends, and the possibility of my mother being alive, I braked hard, made a U-turn, and launched upward right at the point of no return.

Fires blasted below as the ISAN gliders crashed one after another. None had survived the daredevil dive. The city disappeared, my motor glider and Taser gone, and my victory smirk faded.

I stood in a… cave? No, not a cave, but a rocky tunnel.

"Ava? Help me."

My mother's desperate voice rang in my ears. I reminded myself this wasn't real. I planted my feet with no intention of moving, no matter what appeared. Going after my mother, who had turned out to be a hologram, was how I'd gotten into this mess in the first place.

"I'm very impressed with your ability to function without being injected with Helix." A man's voice, somewhat distorted, boomed around me.

"Who are you?" I placed my back to the rocky wall, but flinched when I realized the scenery had changed. I stood back in the center of the same room with no doors.

"Your brother wasn't as successful as you on the flight test, but let's see how you fare on the next one."

"I don't have a brother." I gritted the words through my teeth as I pushed back to the nearest wall.

"Now, Ava. Don't let him hear you say that. It isn't nice. You'll hurt his feelings."

"Oh, believe me. He doesn't care. He'd rather see me dead. I won't cooperate with your stupid tests."

"Then your friend waiting for you outside the compound dies."

How did he know?

"There's no one waiting for me. I came alone. Don't waste my time with empty threats." I ran my hand across from wall-to-wall, looking for a knob or a button. Anything to open this room.

"Is that so?" his said. "Janine was instructed to let you in. She has a gun pointed at Naomi's head. Do you want me to tell Janine to shoot her?"

How did I know he hadn't already killed Naomi? The thought made me sick. This had been a setup from the get-go. Who was Mitch's source? A traitor?

You were in one of the groups that escaped ISAN, Janine had told me before she'd let me inside the secret base. *Your group was one of the lucky ones. Our group was found out and guards stormed the halls. I pretended to be dead when they shot and killed my team... I swore if I could help the rebels, I would.*

Had Janine made up a story to get me to trust her?

"Fine. I'll do anything as long as you don't touch Naomi." I would cooperate until my backup got here.

What backup? If the rebel team hadn't made it out alive, no one would come for me. Rhett and Ozzie would be devastated, and they'd need to gather the survivors. Most likely they would head to the mountain base. Hopefully they had all made it and were on their way.

Something cranked, and metal screeched against metal all around me. The room quaked as it expanded.

No time to rest.

CHAPTER THREE – AFTERMATH

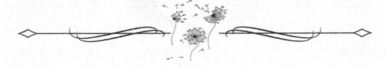

RHETT

R hett stood alone, three feet away from the lip of the massive crater, wondering what he could have done to prevent this.

Nothing. He had been at the black market when ISAN had attacked. And Gene… well, no one could have guessed he'd had an undetectable tracker inside him.

Rhett tightened the fabric covering his nose and mouth. Everyone wore a mask. The lingering particles floated like phantoms in Hope City—haunting—covering the sun, darkening what was left of the day. The aftermath of the destruction stung his eyes and poisoned the air.

Zen had ordered Rhett to take the survivors to the mountain base. So few of them had survived the attack. Half of Hope City had been destroyed.

Gone in a blink of an eye.

The already-dilapidated building had not only collapsed, it had sunk under, as if smashed by a titanic meteor. Metal, wood, plaster. Their personal things. Everything. All had turned to ash.

Hope City looked like death. Smelled like death. It stunk of something burnt and left a powdery taste in his mouth.

Rhett kicked a pebble and watched it tumble into the rubble-filled pit. He shoved his hands inside the front pockets, thinking of his friends.

Reyna had used her power to shield against the blast, with help from the two girls they had recruited—Mia and Ella. Mia, the tall redhead, and Ella, the petite one, had the ability to move things with their breath and could also change the temperature within limited space.

Rhett didn't want to think how it might've turned out without them.

Someone came toward him, but Rhett kept his gaze rooted to the pit of hell, so deep and massive. He couldn't stop staring. Everything they owned and people he knew had turned to ash.

Momo tugged at his shirt, snapping him out of his reverie. "Rhett. Jo told me to get you."

The destruction in front of him made him feel small. Vulnerable. ISAN had taken a piece of his soul. Hope City had been their home. Their shelter. A safe haven for those who wanted a better future.

"Rhett. *Rhett.*" Momo shook him again.

Rhett swayed, numb.

Then there was Ava, off God-knew-where. She was supposed to send him the coordinates when she arrived at the facility, but he hadn't received anything.

His sensible half said she had been delayed. She would reach out soon. Rhett hated being separated from Ava. Something must be wrong. Except Tamara and Naomi were with her—and that was the only reason he wasn't having a panic attack.

Ava better not have gone inside without backup. She had promised she wouldn't, but he knew her too well. He needed to be at the secret base with her. He had to hurry.

Something hit the back of his leg. No, not something, someone.

"Momo. Did you just kick me?" He narrowed his eyes at her and flicked the grimy cap she wore that said "Renegades."

The pale ash and dust coating Momo's clothes made it look like she had jumped into a barrel of flour. She crossed her arms in an attempt to look defiant, but then shrugged. "Well, you wouldn't answer me. You're spacing out. I need you to stop staring at the big hole. What's done is done. Don't think about what-ifs. You're creeping me out, and besides, we need to go."

Rhett brushed her shoulder and waved at the white powder that flaked off her. "Sorry, kid. I was just—"

"Thinking." She rolled her eyes. "Yeah, I know. Adults do that a lot. But us kids don't like to think. We want to dive into action. Come on." Momo rushed ahead to her group of friends without him.

As Rhett shuffled across the powdery debris, he flashed a weary glance at the destruction one last time. He would never forget what ISAN had done. Never forgive. Momo was right. He had to stop dwelling on what could have been and concentrate on getting the rest of the survivors to safety.

No sign of ISAN gliders in the dark sky or guards on the premises, but they might be back. Novak would want no survivors.

"Ready, Jo?" Rhett gave her a curt nod by the transporter.

"Yes. You shouldn't have any problems with the kids."

"Wait. You're not going?" Rhett had to be sure. Her voice sounded muffled under the fabric covering half her face.

"No. I'm staying with Marissa." She rested her hands on the little girl's shoulders—petite, shy little thing with blonde hair, blue eyes, and an innocent face. "Marissa will worry about being left behind and she won't be able to perform. You'll be fine."

Rhett didn't like the team splitting up, but they had no choice. Marissa had to stay and heal the soldiers who were too wounded to move. So much responsibility rested on this little girl. But she was the only one with a healing gift.

"I understand," Rhett said. "Keep your com on and keep me updated. I'm coming back for you when you let me know you're ready."

He gazed behind Jo to the group of kids waiting for her, all wearing "Renegades" caps. Cleo, Mia, and Elle had been keeping watch over them.

Their clothes were coated with dirt and ash, and their eyes sullen and red-rimmed. The devastation left them broken. Unsure. Weakened. Too many losses to comprehend. But Rhett was grateful for every survivor. It could have been worse.

"I'm counting on it." She lit a small smile and turned to the kids.

Something pricked at Rhett's chest. Not a warning, but... *No. They're going to be fine.*

Jo gave a last talk to her group and watched them get into gliders with Cleo, Mia, and Elle. Then hand in hand, Marissa and Jo trudged toward the structure that had been untouched.

Reyna, Ozzie, and Brooke walked out of the makeshift compound the kids had made. Had the kids not built it, some—if not all—of the survivors would have died.

Stop thinking about the past. You'll drive yourself crazy.

"Oz and Reyna, I'm putting you in command here," Rhett said. "Stay safe until I come back."

The three gliders were just big enough to fit most of them, a tight squeeze nevertheless. Rhett would have to come back and pick up everyone who stayed behind.

"You be safe too." Reyna poked his chest. "I'm ready to be Ava's backup, so count me in."

"You don't have to ask me. You know I'm there." Oz squeezed Rhett's shoulder and kicked a small bug out of the way.

"Me too." Brooke shifted, wincing.

"Feeling better, Brooke?" Rhett asked.

Brooke rubbed at her chest. "Still sore, but I think Marissa fixed all my cracked ribs."

The blue and green bruises on her face had disappeared within an hour. Thank God for Marissa, who had healed all of Brooke's broken pieces. A miracle child indeed.

Gene had beaten Brooke so badly she'd nearly died from internal bleeding. HelixB77 made the males do horrible things, but ISAN was able to manage the guys' behavior with HelixB88, which came from Gene's DNA. Perhaps getting dosed with it on top of producing it naturally made him psychotic.

Brooke jerked her head up, her eyes growing wider. She must have heard something. Ozzie and Reyna yanked their Tasers from their holsters, reacting at Brooke. Rhett's heart ricocheted against the walls of his chest and he pointed his weapon at the incoming glider. It had been invisible seconds before.

ISAN guards would have begun shooting already so Rhett eased his shoulders. Zen, Frank, and Vince were on a mission Zen would not disclose, so scratch them out. The sleek silver bullet-shaped glider, somewhat dusty, was too fancy to be one of theirs. So that left one person… Zeke.

Ava had forced Zeke to take her, Tamara, and Naomi to the ISAN's secret facility. They'd had no option but to go their separate ways at the black market when the news of the rebel base being bombed had come through Ava's chip.

The transport landed fifty feet away from him and a ramp dropped down. Someone came out, someone Rhett thought was

Ava for a second before he realized it was Tamara. She and Ava had similar short hair and they were about the same height.

Reyna gave a relieved sigh and lowered her weapon. Rhett held his breath, waiting for Ava.

No Ava and no Naomi. Why was he not surprised?

Tamara sprinted toward him, her features twisted in concern. She slowed when she turned her head to the destruction and covered her nose and mouth.

"Where are Ava and Naomi?" Rhett didn't mean to sound harsh. Tamara could have been hurt or in danger. He breathed out slowly, trying to calm down.

Tamara glanced at Brooke, who stood there in grimy, torn pants and bloody shirt, and then back to him. "We tried to reach you, but that place has no reception. We couldn't get through to you, so Ava sent me back with Zeke."

Rhett clenched his jaw. "Naomi is with her then?"

"Yes."

"Did she go inside?"

"I don't know. She gave me an order to come find you and give you the coordinates. The location you got from Gene was off. It's difficult to find the place if you've never been. It's out in nowhereland. A heavy, thick fog covers the dome entrance like a blanket, so it's easily overlooked."

Rhett inhaled a deep breath through the cloth. "Did Ava tell you anything else? Did she say she was going to go in without backup?"

Tamara lowered her head, and then met his gaze. "Ava told me to tell you…" She swallowed, her voice cracking. "That she loves you. Even when she didn't remember you, a part of her was missing you. Her heart is her map, and it leads her only to you."

Rhett's heart might have stopped. Those words... Ava's words... she left him those in case she didn't make it out alive.

Reyna squeezed Rhett's arm at the same time Brooke did. Ava's two best friends. He tried for hopeful thoughts. Maybe Zen would reach her before she decided to go in. Or the facility would be a dead end. Perhaps she would listen for once and stay put.

Yeah, right. He had to hurry.

"Tamara. You have room in your glider?"

Tamara looked over her shoulder, her hands still covering her nose. "Yes. What are you proposing? But Zeke is—"

"He won't be a problem. He has no choice," Rhett said, then turned to Ozzie and Brooke. "Get the rest on that glider now. Reyna, ride with me."

Rhett spotted something white by his feet. He picked up a dandelion in the mist of dead grass and dirt. That this single flower remained untouched amid the destruction boggled his mind.

Ava's words rushed through. *Dandelions put down deep roots and are impossible to destroy. It reminds me of us and what we stand for. They are strong and memorable. A reminder of us to be the same. Be resilient.*

Carefully, he tucked it between his palms as not to destroy the petals and walked up the ramp. Hope. Dandelions reminded him not just of Ava, but hope. All was not lost.

CHAPTER FOUR – SECTOR MEETING

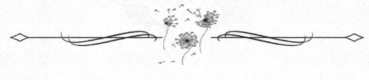

ZEN

After Zen made his assessment of the destruction and passed his duty to Rhett, he'd left the rebel team. He didn't want to leave them, especially after the devastation, but he had no choice.

It was imperative Vince, Frank, and Zen be present at the four-sector meeting to protect Councilor Chang. Citizens were allowed to attend, leaving the door wide open to assassins of all stripes. She needed more eyes than her personal guards.

There had been an attempt on Councilor Chang's life at their last meeting at the East Sector. She'd been lucky. Vince had stopped by to get his next assignment, and had spotted a shooter. He'd pretended to be a passing pedestrian and tackled Chang nanoseconds before the bullet struck. The guard nearest to her had been shot instead and had died at the scene.

Chang had to go into the meeting and pretend one of the men in front of her, Verlot, had not tried to assassinate her. She'd played her part well. Made him think she had no idea of his connection to ISAN. But the attempt on Chang's life indicated ISAN knew the rebels answered to her.

Zen wanted to be on top of his game to protect Chang, so he had injected himself with a small dose of HelixB88 when they had landed. Though, in truth, he also wanted to know what it felt like to be a superhuman—without the side effects. Zen hadn't told anyone. He had taken it before, but that had been before the serum had been perfected by Dr. Hunt.

At first, he'd wanted to vomit. The serum had made him queasy and nauseous. When the searing sensation undulating through his body subsided, he felt renewed. His body moved with ease, reflexes faster, and his mind was sharper.

He felt damn euphoric.

He also had to get used to brighter lights, louder sounds, and his olfactory senses being overpowered by perfumes and colognes.

Standing in a shadow to the left of the stadium, Zen tapped his earpiece. "Can you hear me, Vince? Frank?"

Vince hid on the right side of the arena, Frank in the back. The councilors' guards stood in various spots around the stage, and some hovered near the people on their aircraft.

"Yes," Vince said.

"I'm here," Frank said.

The grand, open platform seemed smaller from Zen's vantage point, but beautifully designed. Its architecture had classical-style white pillars and a high, domed ceiling. The ceiling had hand-painted depictions of Greek gods. Zeus, Poseidon, and Hades—thus the name Olympus Stadium. Fake vines outlined the platform with lights that twinkled as the sun went down.

"They're closing the gate." Frank's voice came through the earpiece. "The meeting is about to start."

The meeting was held in the West Sector, Chang's territory, and that gave them an upper hand. She had briefed Zen and his team on the layout of the stage and where to hide. She also had a hidden mic clipped to her so Zen could hear the conversations behind closed or open doors, no matter the distance. The other councilors had no idea Zen's team was there.

People gathered in masses, standing shoulder to shoulder. Young and old. Families came with their children. The stadium was full of eager faces. Anticipation hung thick in the air.

Timothy Jones from South District, clad in a fine navy tailored suit, stood on the podium and spoke into the mic. "Welcome ladies and gentlemen, and children. We"—he waved to his fellow council members—"have heard your concerns; therefore, we have convened this meeting."

He spoke about thirty minutes, addressing the topics on the agenda: the online school system, the recent hack of an app, transportation, and a few others. Then he got to the main topic for the assembled gathering.

"What you saw on the media, about those girls with supernatural powers, was a hoax. A completely manipulated video. I—we, your councilors—assure you that we will do everything to bring these women to justice."

Chang had informed Zen during the last meeting that the Council had agreed to tell the citizens the truth—or rather, Verlot's version of the truth. Pierre Verlot had informed the rest of the Council that his team had investigated a few of the captured girls and found nothing special about them.

Martinez and Jones had no idea what was going on behind their backs. Chang knew better but played along.

Loud murmurs erupted from the crowd.

Sylvia Martinez tapped her mic, the gentle breeze making her long red dress softly billow around her high heels. The assembly hushed. The last tap on the mic sounded like a loud drum pounding right next to Zen's ears. He groaned and winced.

"Please. Know that you are safe, and we are doing everything we can." Her tone—soothing, almost like a lullaby—did nothing to pacify the people.

"How can you guarantee our safety?" a man shouted near the front.

Verlot cleared his throat, the magnified sound echoing like thunder in the darkened sky. He pushed back his shoulders and straightened his navy suit jacket. "Didn't you hear what Councilor Jones said? What you saw was a trick. Do you actually believe these girls have some kind of superpowers?" He chuckled.

A chorus of laughter rose out of the crowd.

The man said nothing more.

"Does anyone have any questions?" Verlot ran his fingers through his dark hair. He followed protocol, but his tone dripped sourness, like he didn't want to be bothered.

"We haven't heard from Councilor Chang. What does she think?" a girl on the right side asked.

"Yeah. I want to know," someone shouted from the middle.

More murmurs joined them.

Verlot stiffened, but smiled and turned his attention to Chang, who stood at the podium beside him. When Chang raised her hand, her long black cloak shifted.

The people from her community seemed awed by her as they waited for her to speak. Even from the back, Zen could tell the public adored her. In dead silence, their eager expressions and sparkling eyes reflected her popularity.

How could they *not* adore her? She was a beautiful woman who carried herself with brisk professionalism. She radiated confidence and ability. Her photo was often on media sites, even those in other sectors.

They talked about her attire, her makeup, her speeches, and

everything and anything about her. She had become a role model. An excellent choice indeed.

"My people. My family," she began. The gentle breeze lifted strands of her short dark hair. "You may all rest assured you are safe. Had you been in danger, you would have been informed. Know that all of us put your safety first above all. Our nation has been through catastrophic devastation, but we have been recuperating. It isn't time to doubt your Council. You, the citizens, elected us. You put your faith and trust in us, so let us do our job. Doubting and pointing fingers will only separate us. As our forefathers have said… united we stand, divided we fall. May God bless you all."

Cheers sounded in a raucous uproar, the applause like beating drums.

Somewhere in the middle, a girl with red hair shouted, "What about ISAN? My sister is locked up because they said she has superpowers. They're holding her against her will and experimenting on her. What do you have to say about that?"

Zen wished he could speak to that girl. Who was she? He crept closer, but couldn't move any farther without being spotted. Verlot blanched, but raised his chin with a disdainful glare. Under the mask of arrogance, he was a coward.

"Young lady, I welcome you to our next private Council meeting and we will address this issue," Verlot said. "I would like to know more about this group you are speaking of. Now, I'm sure all of you would like to go home and spend your time with your families instead of discussing nonsensical theories. Enjoy the rest of your evening and have a wonderful, prosperous week. The meeting is adjourned."

Verlot turned toward Zen with uncanny accuracy. Zen

scurried to the darkness. He'd thought Verlot had spotted him, but instead Verlot pointed to the nearest guard on the hovering glider and spoke into his chip.

Zen read Verlot's lips. *"Find that girl and bring her to me."* Though from that distance, Zen wasn't sure enough to bet on it.

"I think that went fairly well," Jones said to Chang as they walked side by side to the back of the stage, toward the stairs.

Chang's gaze remained rooted to the crowd shuffling away toward the exit. She must be worried for that redhead, as Zen was.

"Zen. What do you want us to do about the girl? Should we look for her?" Frank's voice came through his earpiece.

"Stand down," Zen said.

Zen decided it was best to wait, though Frank brought up the same question he'd been mulling over. They would intervene only if the guards caught her.

When the stadium was completely empty, a whoosh tore through the air, and a flash of red caught Zen's eyes and a bullet whizzing by.

"For my sister, asshole. For ANS," the redhead's voice rang in his ears.

A girl flickered to life close to the platform, then disappeared, as if she was an apparition. At first Zen doubted his own senses. The guards still in formation hadn't seen her. She was too fast for human eyes.

Zen had spotted her because of HelixB88. Under normal circumstances, he wouldn't have been able to hear her words, nor see the girl. He almost lunged to cover Chang when the girl appeared, but halted before anyone could see him. The bullet wasn't meant for her.

Verlot collapsed. The councilors and guards gathered around

him in a rush of yells and pounding footsteps as the other soldiers encircled the remaining councilors.

Verlot had been shot in the chest, blood pooling on the cement under him. The bullet had penetrated the heavy shield under his clothing, which meant specialized ammunition. Someone would had to have known what kind of armor he was wearing. His suit jacket had a perfect hole to his left chest.

Chang pushed through the guards protecting her and straightened her cloak. "You." Chang pointed at the soldier talking into his chip, who was calling for help. "Stop. I've got this." Then she pointed at the guards nearest to her. "Put Councilor Verlot inside my glider now. I have a medical hub inside. Go."

Something about the way Chang took charge seemed fishy. Zen had a feeling Councilor Chang was behind the shooting.

CHAPTER FIVE – MY PRISON

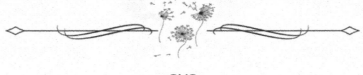

AVA

I jerked awake and sat up, my eyes opening to a blinding light. No shackles. No restraints. No one else in the room, as far as I could tell, but surely someone was watching through a hidden camera.

The gray, doorless walls were the same, but the room smelled floral, like spring, and my clothes felt different. Softer. Cooler. The ISAN assassin suit I'd worn coming in had been replaced by a pink silk pj set—long sleeve with buttons.

Someone had changed my clothes. The thought unnerved me.

I ran my hand from my neck to my collarbone. My necklaces were missing. I didn't care much for the necklace Mr. Lee had given me, but the one from Rhett was precious. The pendant was a small, pressed dandelion, encased in a flat see-through locket. I would get that back.

How many days had passed? I tried to pull up my map, but the dimensions of the walls only flickered. This room might have some kind of power deflecting mechanism. That had to be it, or they had injected me with something.

A single chair was stationed in a corner, on it a fabric doll. Chills prickled my skin. It couldn't be. It couldn't be the same doll my mom had given me when I'd turned thirteen. I'd lost it when she was taken from me, on the night she had supposedly died.

That day I'd run out of our apartment after we'd fought over something trivial. When I'd come home, the ambulance had been there. I had lost my mother and my doll that day.

I swung my legs off the bed and my feet met a warm, soft, white rug. Standing, I surveyed the walls, the corner, the ceiling. Not finding any cameras, I bolted for the doll across the chilly tile floor. When I picked it up, a familiar warmth enveloped me. I felt like a little girl again.

My mother had handmade the doll. She had used a too-small beige sweater of mine and stuffed it with the leftover materials. Then she'd taken one of my pink T-shirts and made a dress. She'd used buttons for the eyes, but the nose and lips had been hand-embroidered. Black thread for the nose, and red thread for the lips.

This was my doll. It even had a small ketchup stain on the front of the dress.

I dropped the doll back on the cushion and spun around when the door whooshed open—the door I hadn't seen because it blended with the wall. My brother entered, dressed in a dark suit with his hair sleeked back. He remained in the center of the room, keeping his distance. Glacier chills racked me and it took all my will not to pounce on him.

"Hello, sister." His tone was upbeat but his sharp glare told me he wanted to cut me open.

Standing in the far corner, I had no way out. I could probably bring him to his knees, but I stood straight and laced my fingers through my hair. *Play smart.*

"Are you going to just stare at me? No greetings for your brother?" He leaned slightly, looking past me. "I see you found your doll, or rather it has found you. Mother told—"

"Where is she? I want to see her." I wrung the silky fabric of my pj pants to tame the blazing rage ready to explode.

I had to see for myself if this so-called mother of ours was real. The last I recalled, I had followed a hologram into this trap. Was *he* even real? I should punch him and see for myself.

"Soon. I promise, little sis. By the way, did you know I was born a few minutes before you?" He shoved his hands inside his front pockets and shrugged, trying to act all cute and innocent.

I wanted to throw up.

I slumped on the edge of the chair, hopeless. The Helix had made me think I was invincible. I knew better. Nothing was ever certain, never guaranteed, especially going up against ISAN.

"Tell me, Gene, am I the only prisoner?" I tried to be inconspicuous. I didn't know what to trust.

"Prisoner?" He sounded appalled, blinking those beautiful dark lashes he didn't deserve. "Look at your wrists and your ankles. You're not shackled. You can move freely about this room." He extended his arm in a grand gesture.

I tried to give him the benefit of the doubt for about two seconds, but he was crazy. Beyond crazy. Psychotic. I walked toward the door I couldn't see, Gene watching my every step.

"If I'm not a prisoner, why won't the door *open*?" I slammed my fist on the wall.

He flinched. "All in good time. But first you need to speak to our father. Then he will decide if you're ready to move out of your chamber."

Father. *Finally*. Maybe he would give me some answers.

"I don't understand. Why did you get to see and talk to our mother and father, and I was left in the dark?" Something sliced my heart.

Gene's features twisted, the corner of his eyes crinkling like he felt sorry for me. He reached for my shoulders, but I backed away until my legs hit my bed. I'd seen his true self. No way did he feel sorry for me.

Gene frowned, his silver eyes darkening. "Because you sided with the rebels. I used to blame you, but I don't anymore. I understand everything now."

The buttons on my pajama top pressed into my skin when I crossed my arms. "Why are you trying to sound nice? Cut the crap. You wanted to kill me back at the rebel base. You said you wanted to *dissect* me."

"I don't anymore. I feel sorry for you. You were grossly misled. Rhett made you abandon us." His nostrils flared, jaw clenching. "He's at fault, and he will pay dearly for taking you away."

"You don't touch him, understand?" I raised my voice.

I searched around the bed for something to use as a weapon. Something sharp or hard. But of course I couldn't find anything. ISAN was thorough.

I recalled the question I'd wanted to ask him. Actually, I dreaded asking. Whatever the answer, it would crush me.

"How did you get out?" I planted a hand on the edge of the mattress to brace for the answer.

Gene's gray eyes shot to the ceiling, and then back to me. His lips curved in amusement. "Oh, that's right. You don't know."

"Tell me." I balled my fists on the comforter and ground my teeth together.

Gene retreated a couple of steps. "You and I have special gifts. Unlike you, I know what I'm capable of. I made you think I was this quiet boy, nothing special about me. In fact, I'm the most dangerous assassin you'll ever encounter." He walked to the chair, picked up my doll, and stroked her hair.

31

I scowled with the need to protect her.

He tossed the doll back to the chair like it was trash. "Mr. Novak put a tracker on me, the kind that can't be detected by any machine or tech. On the day of your escape, you and Brooke had been injected with HelixB88. I made sure to be where you'd see no choice but to kidnap me to help you." He paced back to the wall, where he had entered. "Tamara was a surprise. Never expected her to go against Novak, but then again, she did seem a bit obsessed with you."

"Then what?" I snarled and squeezed the blanket harder.

"I made you think you had the upper hand. Manipulated you to take me where there was reception. Then my exact location went straight to Novak."

I wanted to punch him. No, I wanted to *mutilate* him.

"Go on," I encouraged. I was afraid he would change his mind and stop sharing.

He rested his back against the wall and steepled his fingers. "Then boom."

"Boom?" I shuddered.

"Then *more* boom." He made the same gesture again. "It was beautiful… the way the ceiling dropped, smashing their bones to dust. I wish you could have seen the little ones' powers. Too bad they had to die. Don't worry, sister, a handful of ISAN guards went down too, but not as many as yours. But they're not your people now. You belong to us."

I don't belong to anyone but to myself.

Defiance faded as his story sank in. I went weak at the knees and swayed on my feet. I'd done this. I'd fallen right into his trap.

A little part of me had thought our relationship was salvageable, that he would finally see the light if I gave him an inch.

I had been a fool. He'd taken a mile from me. My mind filled in unspeakable images of destruction raining on the people of Hope City.

Rhett and Ozzie had gone back and found—what? What was left? A few survivors, maybe, if any at all.

"Oh, by the way." He cleared his throat. "You know that friend of yours, Brooke? I caught on she had the gift of hearing but it wasn't enough to save her."

"What do you mean?" I reached for Helix even though I knew it was to no avail. Like a candlewick at the tail end, it had fizzled out.

"She challenged me after I punched out the 'unbreakable' wall. I broke every one of her ribs." Gene dusted something off his sleeve and adjusted his tie. "Then I hit her hard enough to make her bleed internally. She was good as dead, as I am sure the rest of your underground rebels are. Our weapon not only destroys the building—it reduces everything inside to dust."

Until that point, I'd endured his taunts with my head high. But I stopped breathing. I stopped hearing. I lost any remaining control.

Not Brooke. I had never told him about her. I had purposely kept everyone's name out of our conversations.

He rocked on his spit-polished dress shoes with a smug grin. "By the way, in case you're wondering, Brooke came down to see me. I didn't know how much she meant to you then, but she made it clear you were her best friend. I was going to go easy on her, but she kept coming at me, and I might have lost control."

Lost control? I'll show you what losing control looks like.

Rage was an entity of its own. It took control of my mind and body. I couldn't see anything but my target. I had no thought but to destroy. Heat flamed in my chest like a bomb ready to detonate.

"I hate you," I seethed. "You're a monster. I'm going to kill you with my bare hands."

"Careful, sis." He dangled something in front of him.

My necklace, the one Rhett had given me. "Give it to me." I placed out my hand.

"Does this mean that much to you? I think I'll hold onto it a bit longer, or maybe I'll burn it." He shoved it inside his pocket.

That was the last straw. Not only had he stolen something precious from me, he was using it to keep me compliant. He hurt everyone I cared about and killed others. Many had died because I'd wanted to give my psycho brother a chance. No more. Never.

I pounced.

I should have landed on him, but instead I dropped to the floor on my hands and knees like a wounded deer. An electrical sensation zapped through my middle and wrapped around me like invisible arms, holding me in place. Hundreds of needles pricked me all at once.

Excruciating pain seared from head to toe. I couldn't move. I couldn't even blink. I had been wounded many times on missions, but nothing I'd felt in ISAN compared to what had just hit me.

Immobile, a foot from my monster of a brother, I'd never felt so vulnerable. My muscles simply shut down. A whimper escaped me, but it could have been only in my head. Worse, a tear slid down my cheek. I felt humiliated beyond measure.

"Aw, sis. Are you crying? Does it hurt?" Gene took his hand out of his pocket and showed me a metal trinket, a circle about the size of his thumb.

"I thought it was best to have it handy in case you lost control." He came dangerously closer and lowered, his warm breath brushing the shell of my ear. "Now you know, sis. I can contain you. You might want to show me some respect if you don't want to be on the ground, helpless and weak. I might accidentally hurt you. We don't want that do we?"

Oh, the pain. Every tiny movement—every blink—hurt so much.

He ran a knuckle down my cheek to wipe away another teardrop, and then grazed his index finger slowly across my neck, savoring my weakness.

"Next time it won't be so soft," he said. "You should get some rest. You look like hell."

I screamed in my head. Peering up under my eyelashes, I watched him walk toward the sliding door. I wanted to rip out his throat, stomp on his heart, but I couldn't move. Even a fraction of movement felt like a knife slitting deeper into my spine.

I couldn't win. At least not this time. But I would find a way. There *had* to be a way.

Gene's back to me, he held up that metal circle trinket and clicked. Just as the door blended into the wall, he released me. I thumped my head on the tile floor and wept for Brooke and the rebels who had died because of my stupid mistake.

Groaning, I crawled like a worm, my knees and elbows digging across to get to the rug, each movement agony. I refused to lie on the cold ground like I was nothing.

I'd never felt so small. No—I had, when my foster father beat me. Where was he now? Locked up. That would be Gene's fate, too.

Just you wait, big brother. Just you wait. Karma is a bitch.

CHAPTER SIX – MOUNTAIN BASE

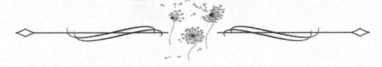

RHETT

Everyone got into the glider.

Rhett checked the monitor displaying the aircrafts' location.

He led in the front. Two other gliders skirted on either side of him, and Zeke's trailed behind. Rhett glanced at Reyna, who was gazing out the window, then stared at the vast ocean and the pink and purple clouds streaking across the day sky.

Rhett's mind spun with all the things he had to do. First and foremost, he had to get everyone to safety and get to his girl. He'd left a message for Zen with the ISAN facility's new coordinates, but there had been no answer.

Whatever Zen was doing must have been important. Imperative enough to put Ava second. Rhett couldn't be mad at him for putting duty first, though Zen would have made a different choice if it had been Cleo.

As they headed toward the mountain base, Rhett messaged Nick, his first captain, and Katina, his second, briefing them on the destruction and the number of people set to arrive. Rhett had instructed them to clear things on the west side to make room for a lot more people.

Rooms would have to be shared, duties carefully planned in shifts. So much to do and so little time.

Rhett looked over his shoulder and caught Momo's eyes, and

then Coco's. They gave him smiles—weak smiles—but smiles nevertheless. Some kids had fallen asleep. So had Reyna sitting next to him. He didn't blame them. They were all exhausted and spent.

As Rhett checked the monitor, something tugged at his heart. They were missing Bobo, the other member of their trio. Momo, Coco, and Bobo had always been together. His absence seemed to represent all the other absences, the lives lost to ISAN. Rhett recalled the first time he'd run into the kids in the alley. That seemed a lifetime ago.

Renegades forever, Bobo. You will always be remembered. Rest in peace, buddy. Keep your friends safe from above.

Grassland appeared, and then the mountains. Rhett had never appreciated the view, but he did now. Somehow, losing so much—almost everything—made him open his eyes.

Rhett thanked the universe for allowing them safe travels. They could have run into ISAN guards. He glanced at the single dandelion, placed for safekeeping inside a cup holder to the side of the door, and thanked the universe for that too.

"We're almost there," Rhett said in a singsong voice. He didn't feel the optimism he projected, but the kids had to have something to look forward to after what they'd been through. "You're going to love your new home."

"Yay," some of the kids said halfheartedly.

Rhett tapped the buttons to command the glider to land and called in to Nick. He turned his attention to the kids. "Want to see something cool?" When no one answered, he told them to look out the window.

A second later, a door that looked like the part of the rocky mountain structure slid open.

Momo pointed out the side window, her eyes wild. "Did that

mountain… no way. Did you see that?"

Her loud voice startled the kids who had been sleeping awake.

"Wow." Coco pressed her forehead to the window.

Rhett grinned, watching the kids' expressions as one by one, they made their way to the window and gawked. After all the transporters were inside, Rhett called Nick to seal the door. Throwing another thankful prayer out there, he released the ramp, and the kids filed in line to exit.

Rhett got off last and took in their slack jaws. His dusty boots thudded on the smooth concrete as he headed to the front of the gated entrance. He couldn't let everyone in at once, so he waited for Nick and Katina to give the orders.

"This is awesome," one kid said, gazing at the rocky walls.

"Why didn't we come here in the first place?" another grumbled, peering at the domed ceiling with recessed lights.

Rhett had offered Zen sanctuary here, but he had refused. He had said it was too far from Cleo's Bakery, and there wasn't enough space here for everyone anyway.

Zen had been right on both counts.

"So this is where you've been hiding." Zeke ran his hand through his dark curls, standing next to Rhett as if they were old friends.

Rhett let out a low growl, glancing at Zeke's pendants—one a spear shape made from jade and the other an onyx cross. "I'm trusting you because Zen and Mitch trust you. You mouth a word to anyone about this place, you're dead."

"Whoa. Hold on, Rhett." He stepped back and bumped into Coco. "Sorry, kid," he said and turned back to Rhett. "You don't need to get all crazy on me. I'm on your side."

"Fine," Rhett said.

"And if Rhett goes soft, I'll go all crazy on Zeke." Tamara twirled her pocketknife so fast, Rhett couldn't follow.

"However you want to play it. I'm all yours." Zeke waggled his eyebrows.

Rhett ignored the banter between them when a familiar voice called out. Nick sprinted over with Katina and a handful of their friends. They had all been ISAN subjects once, until they'd escaped. Sometimes Rhett forgot that most of the soldiers here were younger than him.

Nick patted Rhett on the back, but Katina squeezed him hard. She moved on to Reyna, Cleo, and Ozzie. Rhett quickly did the introductions. There were a few new faces—Zeke, Brooke, and Tamara.

"It's so good to see you all," Katina said, looking from person to person. About thirty kids and twenty slightly wounded soldiers had gathered behind Rhett. "Nick told us what happened. I'm so sorry."

"Thank you for taking us in," one of Zen's soldiers said. "We're very grateful."

"Of course." Nick rested a hand on a young girl next to him. "This is Jill. She'll feed you first." His eyes roamed over the kids' dirt-caked clothes. "Then let's wash and change your clothes. Afterward, she'll show you to your rooms and get you all settled."

"Know that we're safe here," Rhett said to the kids. "No one, and I mean no one knows this base exists, and I would like to keep it that way. Your rooms will be tight, spaces limited compared to where you were. You'll also have duties. Here, we all lend a helping hand to make our system work. Any questions?"

They shook their heads.

"Follow me." Jill waved a hand and led the way, her ash-blonde

39

ponytail bouncing with her steps.

"Be safe, Rhett," Coco said. "I'm sending you positive vibes. I'll tell everyone to do the same."

"Yeah. Bring Ava and Naomi back safe." Momo adjusted her cap.

If Ava went inside and hadn't come out, Rhett's team was going to need all the help and then some. Vince had told Rhett his team in the north was ready for war. Rhett just needed to let him know. He hoped he never had to.

"Are you sure you don't want us to tag along?" Momo flashed all her teeth in exaggeration. "We can be your backup."

Rhett smiled. "Thank you for putting your life on the line, but if I really need your help, I'll ask. Go before you get lost." He jerked his chin toward the group already crossing the plank that led to the entrance.

They saluted him and ran off while Ozzie, Brooke, Cleo, Tamara, and Reyna, headed to the meeting room.

Rhett inhaled the cool mountain air, taking in the scent of soil and earthy things. If he listened carefully, he could faintly hear the water rushing nearby. Home. He was home. He'd missed this place. If he'd had a choice, he would have brought Ava here, but they'd needed to be close to Zen.

Time was essential. Rhett needed to hurry. Every second counted. He rushed forward.

"How many of us do you need?" Nick matched Rhett's fast pace.

"I'd rather not take any of you. To be honest, I have no idea what we'll be facing."

How could Rhett pick a team knowing they might not make it out alive? He would rather not have Reyna, Ozzie, and Brooke go, but they wouldn't take *no* as an answer. Like him, their hearts were invested in saving Ava and Naomi.

Rhett's boots thumped on the metal plank. He stole a glimpse of Mia, Ella, and the kids eating at the cafeteria, while listening to Jill's instructions. When Rhett and Nick reached a meeting room, plates of food had been set on the table. Fruits and vegetables mostly, thanks to the garden, though also some boiled eggs and bread. Rhett had never been more grateful for food and water than when he took his seat at the head of the table.

Reyna's chair scraped on the concrete floor as she scooted closer to grab a piece of bread. "Rhett. You and I don't need to have this conversation, right? I'm going with you."

Rhett rubbed his temples, where a headache had blossomed. "Yeah, I know."

"Ozzie and I are going, too." Brooke reached for eggs and passed one to Ozzie, who sat next to her.

Rhett grabbed an orange and peeled it. "We're taking one glider, so Zeke will take us."

Zeke stopped chewing a long carrot. "Wait. I took Ava and her team there because she put a gun to my head, but don't I get a say in this?"

"No." Rhett savored the orange's sweet citrus juice.

Zeke cracked a boiled egg and peeled the shell. "Tamara has the correct coordinates. You don't need me. I have a business to run. I need to get back. My men will worry about me."

"No, they won't." Rhett scoffed and bit through another piece of orange. "Eben couldn't care less. If you're not around, he's the boss."

"Fine." Zeke bit his egg in half, and parts of the yolk crumbled on the table. "But time is money. And you're using a lot of my

41

time."

"Are you seriously telling me I need to pay?" Rhett grabbed a roll and squashed it between his fingers.

Tamara, sitting across from Zeke, stabbed her pocket knife on the wooden table in front of him, her eyes burning. "Is money all you think about? How about doing what's right?"

Zeke bristled, not looking at her, and said nothing.

Rhett nearly dropped the bread in surprise and snorted. He hadn't seen Zeke speechless and submissive before.

"Hurry and get your fill. We need to get going." Rhett pulled apart the bread and shoved a small piece into his mouth.

"Where's Zen?" Nick rested an elbow on the table, holding an apple.

"My father is taking care of business with... Councilor Chang." Cleo hesitated, dipping her head.

She knew where her father had gone and hadn't told Rhett. Zen must have instructed her not to say anything. Why?

"With Chang?" Nick's voice rose. "There was an open meeting in the eastern territory. It was all over the media. It's over now, but a redheaded girl from the audience mentioned ISAN and how they have her sister locked up."

Ozzie spoke with his mouth stuffed with eggs. "Remember, there was an attempt on Councilor Chang's life."

"There was?" Zeke shifted to Ozzie.

"Not a word. Nobody knows about this." Rhett pointed at him to stress the point.

"Okay. But if you want me on your team, you need to tell me everything."

"What changed your mind, Zeke?" Rhett hiked up an eyebrow.

"Nothing." He scoffed, but his gaze floated to Tamara.

Rhett gulped down his water and thumped the cup hard on the table to get everyone's attention. "It's time to go. I also need to make a call to Jo and see how Marissa is doing."

"I'll round up a team." Nick paused, assessing Rhett as he rose from his seat. "If it'll make you feel better, I'll ask for volunteers first."

"Thank you." Rhett walked around the table. "Only volunteers. No more than ten. It'll be tight in the glider."

Zen's priority was Chang at the moment, so Rhett was Ava's only hope. Hopefully she was waiting for backup. Their little team, about to face unknown monsters. God help them.

When Cleo began to stand, Rhett pressed her back down to her seat. "Where do you think you're going?"

She crinkled her forehead. "With you. Where else?"

"Nope. Your father gave me specific orders. You're not to come with me. He didn't let you go with Ava, and that was probably a good thing,"

She crossed her arms and scowled. "I'm my own person. I only listened the last time because *I* thought it was best I stayed behind. But now, I'm going with you. I might not have special powers, but I've been trained to fight since I was a little girl. It's all about playing it smart, anyway. If I were a guy, my father wouldn't try to stop me. So pretend I'm a guy. That's not too hard, is it?"

Rhett shook his head. She was right. Regardless, he stood his ground. "You're not coming."

She arched her eyebrows so high, her nose scrunched. "Watch me," she said and stormed off.

Zeke coughed, almost choking on the carrot. He hiked a thumb at her. "Are all the women like her here?"

"Yes, we are. So you better watch it." Reyna swayed her neck in a way only she could, displaying her don't-mess-with-me attitude.

"Anyway." Rhett reached over and grabbed another piece of bread. "Before we go to the facility, we need to stop by the black market."

"Why?" Zeke furrowed his brow. He must have guessed it had something to do with him.

Rhett smacked his Zeke's back and knocked him forward. "To pick up some of the gadgets you graciously offered. Don't you think that's nice of him, Tamara?"

Tamara stopped flipping her pocket knife. She was confused at first, then her face cleared.

"That's so thoughtful of you, Zeke." Her tone became sweet and lovely, and she literally fluttered her eyelashes at him.

Rhett had a feeling it wasn't all fake, and the attraction not one-sided. Zeke grinned like a besotted schoolboy. Desperate times, desperate measures. If Rhett guessed right, Zeke had lot of cool toys he hadn't shared yet, ones Zen couldn't afford.

Using Zeke's interest in Tamara wasn't his proudest moment, but Rhett intended to exhaust all his playing cards.

Hold on, Ava. I'm coming for you with everything I've got.

CHAPTER SEVEN – THE TRUTH

ZEN

"**C**ouncilor Chang wouldn't, would she?" Frank asked. He sat on the edge of an old black vinyl sofa with his legs apart, his hands clasped in the middle.

While the doctor and a couple of nurses operated on Verlot, Chang had taken Martinez and Jones to another room to tell them about the world of ISAN. Frank, Vince, and Zen had retreated to a waiting room where they discussed if Chang had influenced the redheaded girl to go after Verlot.

"If she did, good for her." Sitting on the opposite sofa, Vince scowled, an angry muscle jumping on his neck. "That bastard deserved it. He tried to assassinate her."

"Chang doesn't know anyone in ANS, does she?" Zen looked at Vince next to him, who was running a hand through his dark hair.

Vince glared at him. Zen had indirectly accused Chang of premediated murder. Probably not a good idea to say as much out loud, especially since Vince and Chang had been working together to shut down ISAN before he came into the picture.

"Remind me what ANS is again?" Vince asked, tapping his feet on the cracked tile floor.

Was he kidding? Zen had thought Vince knew more than he did.

"Advocacy Network for Superhumans," Zen said slowly, but it came off more like a question.

Frank got up, carefully avoiding the section of the uplifted tiles, and poured himself a glass of water.

"What do we do now?" Frank drank and wiped his mouth.

The sound of his gulps made Zen's mouth feel like sandpaper. "We wait until Chang is finished, but I need to get going." Ava would need backup, and he had a feeling he was already late.

Knowing Rhett, he'd leave without Zen after dropping off everyone at the mountain base. Zen should have acted sooner. He turned away from his friends by the door and called Rhett on his chip.

Rhett's face popped up immediately, like he'd been waiting for the call. Guilt pulled at Zen's conscience for not being there for Ava.

On the projection, Rhett sat in a sleek, black leather chair. When Rhett shifted, Zen glimpsed the inside of a familiar shiny, polished glider, with wood trim on the dashboard.

Zeke.

"Tell me you're with Ava." Rhett sounded desperate, his amber eyes glinting in the reflection of the sun.

"I'm sorry. I'm not, but I'm on my way. I promise."

A heavy sigh filtered through Zen's earpiece.

Rhett dipped his head and peered up. "I know you're with Chang. I know about the meeting. It must be important."

"You have no idea, Rhett." Zen rolled his aching shoulders. "I'll fill you in as soon as I can, but I'll be leaving shortly."

"You take care of what you need to do. I'm on my way with a team. Everyone is safe at the mountain base. Marissa is doing a great job. Jo has told me there's been no sign of ISAN."

"That's good. They're off our backs. Now, when you get there, don't go in without me. Where's Cleo? She's not with you, right?"

Rhett jerked to the side like someone had pushed him. Cleo's face appeared as she tucked strands of her red hair. Zen burned with rage. Why was his daughter with Rhett?

"You can't tell me what to do." Cleo's voice was level, but her eyes darkened. "I'm an adult. I'm not sitting around while my friends are out there risking their lives. If I were a boy, you would want me to join you."

Zen shook his head. So stubborn. So much like her mother it scared him. They even had the same fiery red hair and sky-blue eyes.

Zen wanted to scold her, but he had to face the fact she wasn't a child. She had practically raised herself. He'd had no idea how to raise a child on his own. He'd tried his best, but felt like he failed to be a good father at times.

All he had ever wanted to do was protect her from this wretched world, especially from ISAN. So he'd dosed her with CH20, the same formula in the protein drink the ISAN girls drank every day to dampen their abilities.

Yes, it was a horrible thing to do, but he'd had no choice. Cleo was only five years old when she'd first manifested her gift. No one knew of her powers, not even her mother. No one knew what he had done, or continued to do.

Zen clutched a hand to his heart. One day he wouldn't be around to protect his little girl. With their lifestyle, his death might be sooner than he'd hoped. So he let his shield down.

"You're right, Cleo. I can't tell you what to do. You are your own person."

Cleo blinked in surprise, and her face lit up. "Okay, Papa.

Thank you. I'll make you proud. Be careful. See you soon."

Something inside Zen crumbled. She hadn't called him Papa since her mother had died. Zen smiled, his words coming out not sounding like his own. Softer. Warmer.

"I'm already proud of you, princess."

She rubbed at her eyes and pressed her quivering lips together. "I love you, Papa."

"I love you, too." He shut his chip off and placed a hand to his face.

How long had it been since he uttered those three simple words to her? He didn't know. It shouldn't have been like that.

This war had taken a toll on everyone, and not just physically. It had not only taken lives, but innocence. In their fight for justice, they had forgotten to take time to breathe, to spend time with families. They had forgotten to live.

ISAN had to be brought down so the girls like Cleo could be free.

When Martinez and Jones stepped out of the meeting room, their pale faces drawn, they seemed to have aged ten years. Chang came out with sweat beaded on her forehead, but her smile said everything was resolved.

Everyone followed her to the Verlot's private room, where he was recovering. It didn't take long for the operation, and with the high-tech equipment available, he wouldn't even have a scar.

Too bad. He *should* be marked to remind him of the monster he was.

"The bullet is out. He'll be just fine," said a doctor with no nametag. Like the two nurses, he had a cloth mask covering his entire face, except for his eyes. They weren't hiding their identities from Chang, but from everyone else.

"Thank you." Chang gave him a nod. She waited by a dented file cabinet and a scratched up wooden desk with no chair. "I'll be in touch soon. If you don't need to do anything else, you and the nurses may see yourselves out."

The doctor and the two nurses scurried away as if they couldn't get out of there fast enough.

"What do we do with that monster?" Martinez gripped the monitor tube and snarled.

What if Martinez pulled it out? Zen reached out to stop her, but lowered his hand when Martinez let go of the tube.

"Nothing for now." Chang took off her cloak and draped it over her arm. "When he wakes up, he'll have to answer for his crimes." Chang cocked her head to the side, beckoning Vince.

Vince opened the last file drawer and took out four circular metal devices that looked like handcuffs. If Verlot tugged hard enough, the device would shock him.

After Vince clipped those to Verlot's wrists and ankles, he closed the thick see-through medical hub door. "He's all yours, madam. Do your worst."

"Vince," Chang said. "Please escort Counselor Martinez and Jones back to their gliders. Frank and Zen will join you momentarily."

Vince gave a curt nod, stepped over a raised cracked tile, and backed away to the door.

Zen had sworn he wouldn't ask, but he had to know. "Councilor Chang, do you know the assassin who shot Verlot? Are you in contact with ANS?"

Zen's rebels played mostly by the rules, but ANS didn't. They'd even tried to kill Ava, thinking she would never leave ISAN. Chang must be desperate, especially after Verlot's assassination attempt. He wouldn't put it past her to reach out to ANS.

She gave Zen a wry smile. "Zen, thank you so much for what you have done today."

There was Zen's answer. He didn't know if he should respect her even more, or be afraid of her.

CHAPTER EIGHT – MR. NOVAK

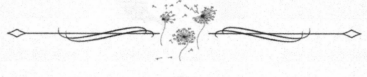

AVA

I pushed myself across the cold tile floor to the rug with wobbly knees and elbows. After seizing the edge of the mattress with trembling hands, I swung one leg over and sat.

The effort made my forehead bead with sweat and left me breathless. The pain dissipated and my muscles loosened.

Mind—focused.

Pride—damaged.

Anger—searing like never before.

Revenge—my new name.

Rage consumed me. I thought about the many different ways I could kill my brother.

Running my hand along my arm, my chest, and my neck, I searched for anything out of place, anything bumpy, but of course the device wouldn't be an easy find. Gene had pressed a controller to zap me with electrical current. I'd felt as though I burned from the inside out. Worse, I hadn't been able to move. I couldn't let it happen again.

Something slid out of the wall across the bed. A thin metal platform. A bedside table of some sort? Meal time. Then *click... click... click* went the heels. The sound of Mr. Novak.

My pulse raced, my mind reeled in all directions. Alone. No one could help me.

Mr. Novak entered with a tray in his hands. The door closed behind him, blending with the wall. I sucked in a breath, the reaction I always had when I saw him alone.

The aroma of roasted chicken with rosemary, garlic, and honey hit me first and I greedily inhaled. The seasoning reminded me of my mom—it was the same she had used. I refused to see what else he had brought.

Nothing had changed about him. Polished. Refined. Like he was going to a business meeting with his gray tailored suit and tie. Not a hair out of place on his sleek, dark head. He was even quite handsome, I realized as I boldly stared at him, taking in every inch of his sharp features.

What had happened to make him such a monster?

I held up my head high. "Come to kill me?"

He placed the tray on the metal table next to the bed that had popped out of the wall.

"Why would I do that?" His tone was smooth and warm, unlike the dangerous vitality in his dark eyes and in his ISAN resting stance—feet apart with hands behind his back.

"What do you want?" I flexed and unflexed my fingers, working my muscles to get back to full strength. I was astounded by how quickly my body had recovered from the torture.

"Why would I want to hurt you, Ava? I want to help you." He unbuttoned his suit jacket, revealing a black and blue pin-striped dress shirt underneath.

"You want to help me?" I scoffed and pushed off the bed, my feet warm on the rug. I stood dangerously close to Novak. He smelled like lavender and mint. "Why? I know everything. The protein drinks. How you took our memories, or at least tried to take mine. Killing our parents and experimenting on them.

Turning us into killing machines. I'm sure there are other things I'm missing."

"You're wrong about everything." His tone was nonchalant.

I wrung my fingers on the soft comforter, close to losing my level head. How do you communicate with a lunatic?

"Explain," I said.

He paced toward the chair in the corner, his hands inside his pockets, his back to me. "You don't remember *every*thing. I might not have been successful for the latter part of your life, but your childhood memories are lost. You don't even know what your father looks like. You can't remember that this…" He extended his arms and faced me. "This remarkable place was your home. *Is* still your home."

"What?" Stunned, I couldn't get my tongue to form words.

"Yes. You lived here with your parents."

"I don't believe you… you… you manipulating beast."

Novak ran a hand down his face and stretched his neck from side to side. "Ava. Watch your words. Lydia taught you better manners than that."

Shuddering, I almost knocked the tray. *Steady, Ava. Get more information. Your life depends on it.* I lowered my eyes to my expensive pj's, pretending to be ashamed, and looked back up with a newly calm expression.

"Sorry. You're right. I should know better."

His eyes widened a little, then narrowed with suspicion. "As I was saying, this was your home until it was time for you to leave with your mother."

In one of my dreams when my mother and father had argued, I'd been in a lab. And in other dreams when my father had read me my favorite book, he'd smelled like… like this room. Sterile.

I compared his words to my fragments of memory, trying not to fall apart. "You faked my mother's death. How?"

"ISAN had been watching you your whole life." He picked up the doll and sat in the chair. "We'd been waiting for an opportunity as soon as you turned thirteen. When you left your mother that morning, we took action. You were young and callow. You believed everything the social worker told you. Your mother was brought back here, her home, and you were taken to a foster home of my choosing. I made sure to pick a family that wouldn't treat you well."

"Why?" I snarled.

"It's simple, Ava. You had such a pathetically weak heart. Your emotions were all over the place. You would have been useless as an assassin. I needed a killing machine. You needed something to fight for—and to fight against."

I shook my head. "I can't believe you're saying this."

He continued, "Had you killed your foster father, I would have taken you straight to ISAN, but instead I had brought you here. That was when you met your brother. I wanted to see what you were both capable of. We put you both under rigorous conditions and training. You don't remember, do you?"

When I didn't say anything, he went on. "I trained you and your brother together. I prepared you to be a fighter before you were sent to juvie, but I also took those memories away. It seems I was pretty successful."

"Why go to all that trouble? You had me under your control."

He rose and tossed my doll to the chair. "We had our protocol. I'm not the only person running ISAN, but you already know that, don't you? You see Ava, I'm not going to kill you. You're—"

"You gave me HelixB88." The words rushed out of me as if

he'd hurt my feelings, and I pounded a fist on the mattress. "You tried to kill Brooke." I remembered Brooke was dead. Gene had killed her.

My chest felt like cement—heavy and hard. My throat like a rock—blocking my air.

His nostrils flared. "You needed to remember who was in control, so Brooke had to be disposed of. Tamara, on the other hand… I didn't know she had it in her. She surprised me. Perhaps I should have studied her more."

"Do you hear yourself? They're people, not things."

He let out an irritated sigh. "See what I mean? You feel too much. You're not seeing the bigger picture. As for you, I gave you HelixB88 as a warning. Only because I knew you could fight it. Your body always prevails. Always. Anything given to you, you've bounced back. You're practically indestructible."

He came closer and I climbed on the bed. Realizing I didn't want him near me, he halted at the center of the room.

"You and your brother have so much in common, so much strength, so much endurance," he said. "You're both remarkable. And yet you each have a unique power the other one doesn't have." His whole face lit up with something like pride. "Yes, you were conceived, but your father made you. You were named Ava for a reason, just like your brother's name has a purpose. Gene. Genetically Enhanced Neo Entity. Ava stands for Acquired Viral Advancement. You were engineered by a vision. Can you imagine if we had soldiers with your talents? ISAN would not only conquer our nation, but the world."

I shifted far back to the mattress, near the tray. I didn't want to hear what this psycho had to say anymore.

Novak loosened his tie as if he needed more air, his dark eyes never leaving mine. "You were doing so well in ISAN. Only the memories I wanted you to have remained intact. Your drive. Your ability to lead. So perfect. But then you allowed yourself to have such unnecessary emotion, and then you got weak." He paused with a shuddering breath. "Everything went spiraling down when they kidnapped you. It was my fault. I had too much hope and faith in you. I thought without your memories you would pick ISAN over that… boy. Now you're back, and I have to fix you again."

Fix me? Icy chills racked my torso.

I didn't want to talk about me anymore. He spoke as if I were his project. I needed to shift the subject to something else. Anything. So I said the first thing that popped in my head.

"What about Justine, your daughter? Why not fix her?"

The crease on his forehead deepened and his voice softened. "You know about that? Of course you do. Justine told you, didn't she? Well, that was a mistake."

Since he answered so freely, I thought to ask about Naomi.

"What about my friend? Where is she?"

He peered down at his fingernails, and then regarded me again. "Oh, that friend. Don't worry. She's fine."

"What is your definition of *fine*?"

"Locked up for now. Whether she lives or dies is up to you. Your actions determine her fate."

"Where's my mother? I want to see her." I brought my knees to my chest, feeling sick to my stomach, my courage wavering. I might not get out this time.

He came closer and stood at the edge of the bed, still keeping his distance. "In good time. I promise, pumpkin. She has missed you very much. I showed her pictures of you and shared your progress every step of the way."

"Don't call me pumpkin," I seethed. "Who told you about that?"

"Your father, who else? We're longtime friends. He's done so much for our cause. I'm sorry he had to be absent. He has so much important work to accomplish."

"I want to see him," I said.

"You will, but first you need to eat. You'll need your strength. Your friends will be here soon."

At the thought of my friends, I went rigid and brought my fingers back to the buttons. "What are you going to do when they come?"

He gave me a sidelong glance. "What would you like me to do with them? You have several options. One, I could have them killed. Two, put them in a cell. Three, send them on a wild-goose chase. They wouldn't be here to help you, but at least they might be safe, though I can't guarantee that."

I peered down and focused on my toes. I hated him. I want to claw at his triumphant grin. I want him to feel all the pain and agony he had caused others. Even hell would be too good for him.

"Well, what's it going to be?" He tapped at his empty wrist.

No dirt under his manicured nails. No calluses. It sickened me. While the rebels scrambled for food and supplies to help others, he lived in luxury and destroyed lives.

Fury crept up again and all my ferocity poured through. "Why did you bomb the rebel base? Why did you kill all those people?"

I wanted to fall on my knees and weep for my friends. Saying it out loud made it real... so real. I yanked the comforter tight around me and squeezed. It took all of my will not to break down.

He strained his eyes and tilted his head. "Why do you ask such an obvious question?" He peered up to the flat low ceiling, and then back at me. "It was either them or us. They took you. They took Gene. We had to fight back. This is war. Don't think Zen wouldn't have done the same if he had the opportunity to land the blow on us. Everything I did was for you, pumpkin."

I grinded my teeth, my jaw twitching. "I told you not to call me that."

"Such temper." He shook his head, disappointed. "You must learn to control your emotions. So what's it going to be?"

As much as I wanted my friends to help me escape, I wouldn't put them in danger. Novak gave no empty threats. He would make them suffer, even kill them in front of me. He would make me watch.

Worse, the team had no chance of survival, especially coming to a place they'd never been with hostile forces expecting them. It was a maze in here. Perhaps Novak spoke the truth and I had lived here. Everything about this place screamed déjà vu.

I shoved my fingers through my hair and let out a defeated sigh. "Send them off on a wild-goose chase."

"Good. A wise choice. I plan to keep them busy. I promise, you'll see them when you're ready."

Something cold slithered through me at his words. *When you're ready.* I didn't want to know what he meant.

The door slid open.

"I must go to a meeting now. After you eat, I will keep my word. I'll arrange a meeting for you to see your parents this evening."

I watched him leave and let out a long breath of relief.

I finally looked at the tray he had brought in. Baked chicken quarter, white rice, vegetables. A glass of water and the damn protein drink. There was no spoon. No fork. No utensils at all. Not even a plate. Although, the food was nicely arranged and well prepared.

My mouth had watered at the aroma when he had brought the food in, but I'd refused to so much as a glimpse in its direction. I hadn't wanted to give him the impression I was hungry.

I picked up the chicken by the leg bone and bit into the tender meat. My stomach rumbled and welcomed the flavor. I tasted rosemary, garlic, and honey. Definitely Mom's chicken. I ate every last bit to keep up my strength. I gulped down water, but didn't touch the other glass.

After I finished eating, my skin felt hot to touch. Not a fever, but... I examined my palms. They twitched, and then my veins protruded and wiggled like worms in dirt.

What was happening to me? What was in my food or the water?

My body had been changing. Adapting. Assimilating. Mr. Novak had no idea of my recent findings.

I'd discovered I could absorb the power of others. The first time it had happened had been on a beat-up glider that wouldn't fly; I'd directed the energy from Coco to ISAN guards. A similar incident had happened at Crystal Tower Casino. Mia hadn't cooperated, so I'd become the lightning and taken on Mia's power of wind.

I planned my escape and counted how many different ways I could murder Novak and my sick brother.

CHAPTER NINE – BLACK MARKET

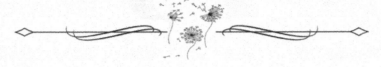

RHETT

Rhett couldn't lead his team into battle without a proper arsenal, or he might as well take them to their graves. He had no choice but to go back to the black market.

Saving Ava was all he could think about, but his friends and fellow rebels relied on him to execute the mission with his head screwed on right. Still, it was extremely difficult having to push his girl aside.

"Are you sure you're going the right direction?" Rhett studied the hologram projecting the map toward the black market from the passenger seat before admiring the dark wooden trim around the dashboard and the silver polished knobs on the monitor.

Zeke frowned. "You do recall I practically live there, right? I'm not driving. This baby knows where to go."

"All right. How much longer?" Rhett snickered, thinking of how many times Momo and Coco had asked him the same question. Then his thoughts returned to the task at hand.

Zeke flashed him an annoyed glance and went back to the map. "Geez. Are you a child?"

"Look. It's a grown-up question. I'm worried about Ava. I'm in no mood for your humor." Rhett didn't know why he bothered to defend himself, only this guy got on his nerves all the time, and his pride wouldn't let him give an inch.

Zeke murmured something under his breath, and then a little louder. "Fine. Ten minutes." He pointed at a dot on the hologram. "See… we're right here. We need to go there." He stabbed a finger at the destination point.

"See. Was that so hard?" Rhett caressed the leather seat. Yup, just as he'd thought. Top-notch quality.

"Are you two arguing up there?" Cleo hollered, sounding like a mother. "Cause if you are, we can trade places."

Cleo, Ozzie, Brooke, Tamara, Mia, Ella, and the ten rebel soldiers from the mountain base sat belted in the back.

"We're fine," Zeke and Rhett barked at the same time as they twisted to look over the seats to their friends.

Brooke and Ozzie had their eyes closed. Reyna had her face turned to the window. Tamara tilted her head, looking confused.

Zeke stared at Tamara a bit longer, and then back to the window. The onyx cross and the spear-shaped jade pendants clanked on his chest.

"Don't even think about it." Rhett shook his head.

"What?" Zeke's face colored. He half raised his arms. "I didn't do anything."

Ten minutes. Grab what they needed and get to Ava. But ten minutes with Zeke would feel like an eternity.

"Why the dragon tattoo and what does it mean?" Rhett asked, eyeing the ink peeking out from under Zeke's long-sleeve shirt.

Zeke released a long sigh. "My mother committed suicide after my father left us when I was ten years old. My uncle, whom you call Mr. Lee, took me in. I was so angry at my parents and at the world. I got into trouble more times than I can count. I found comfort in a group called the Imugi. They were all about brotherhood. Hence the dragon tattoo."

Rhett shifted, placing an elbow on the armrest. "I've heard of Imugi. Korean dragon?"

"Yes. Korean folk mythology. Most dragons were originally Imugis, known as lesser dragons, until they became full dragons. That's how our group operates. You have to work hard to move up. Imugi are benevolent beings and their sighting is associated with good luck. So I'll bring you good luck."

When Rhett rolled his eyes, Zeke shut his mouth.

"I doubt that people think of Imugi members as good luck," Rhett said, resting his back against the seat and staring out the front window. Nothing but the vast blue water and the clouds, such a large contrast to the previous view earlier of hollowed buildings and debris left from the meteor's devastation. "People are afraid of them."

"*Were*," Zeke stressed. He ran his fingers through his dark, curly hair and checked the monitor. "There were a few members who gave us a bad name, but this new generation helps people too."

Rhett checked the map and glanced back at Zeke. "Eben and his men have the same tattoo. Why?"

Zeke lowered his eyes to his arm, then to Rhett. "It has to all look the same. It's a symbol. Unification. I saved his ass when a deal went wrong, and because of that, I became like his big brother. It's going to sound strange, but he's bound to me. We're a family. Think of it like a fraternity, big bro and little bro. Through the Imugis' contacts, I got my position. I import and export what you'd call goods."

"Legally or illegally?"

Zeke rubbed at his forehead. "Both. My uncle doesn't understand. He only sees me in a gang. Just because my organization has tattoos doesn't mean we're bad people. He wants me to wear a suit and tie."

"Your uncle is too old to be working. With all the 4Qs you're making, you should put him in a nice, comfortable place."

Zeke pushed buttons on the monitor, getting ready to land. "I don't get to keep all my earnings—that was the deal when I got the job. I have to split my share. You really think I'm an asshole, don't you?"

Rhett sighed. He supposed he should play nice. "I didn't say that."

"Look. I don't have to prove myself to you, but… my uncle is very stubborn. He won't take my money. He thinks I make dirty 4Qs, so what's a guy to do? And that is all I'm going to share. I'm only telling you all this so you can relax and trust me."

"You can't blame me, especially when you're reluctant to help."

"Hey." Zeke flashed another sideways glance before focusing on the skyscrapers through the front window. "Look, I'm a businessman. I'm not a fighter. I wasn't trained like you. I've never killed anyone in my life." He lowered his voice. "It's kind of embarrassing when the girls can kick my ass. I wish I was one of them."

"You don't know what they've been through. Just be grateful." Rhett narrowed his eyes, then gazed at the abandoned broken city below. No bushes or trees, just buildings with no faces, some crumbled to the ground. Streetlights bent, car windows smashed, and dust and litter tumbled with the breeze.

Silence fell between them. The rest of the crew was deep in conversation as the sleek glider descended—smooth like a bird with its wings spread out.

"I don't know what beef you have with me," Zeke began as he monitored the building they were headed toward, his tone even.

"But I did nothing to you." He turned on the headlights when the parking structure turned dark. "Sure, I might be a little difficult to deal with, but that's business." Then he turned off the auto drive and took over. "Besides—"

Rhett was out of his seat before Zeke could finish. He told Cleo, Mia, Ella, and the ten soldiers from the mountain base to stay put, while Zeke, Tamara, Ozzie, and Reyna got off the glider with Rhett. Too many people caused unwanted attention.

They went through the back entrance, which was accessible only to the vendors. The smell of soil was overpowering even before they entered the underground market.

Six tank-sized men carried guns by the vendor entrance of the rundown building. They watched every step Rhett and his team took, their hands on their weapons. Rhett wished he could take these men with him to get Ava.

"Hey, Cory." Zeke gave the security guard a high five.

"Zeke. What's up, man?"

"In a rush, so I'll catch you later with some good stuff." Zeke jerked his chin at Rhett. "These are my friends. They're coming with me."

Cory narrowed his eyes, then gestured to the door. "Sure. Go on in. But everyone is packing. We're going to sector B tomorrow. Your uncle is already out."

Zeke escorted them through a hallway and then up the stairs. Just like Cory had said, the vendors were packing and there were no customers. Inside a tent, Rhett stood by a sofa, while his team went around a tea table, steering clear of a low table that held a few bowls filled with smoking incense.

A young girl with dark skin and a long ponytail walked in and bowed. "Zeke. You're back. Would you like some tea?" Her eyes rounded when she saw the rebels. In one swift move, the girl drew out two swords from her back, ready to attack. She might have, had Zeke not intervened.

Zeke placed out a hand. "Tiana. Stop. It's okay. They're with me."

Clad in a black warrior suit, Tiana had additional weapons holstered on both hips. At Zeke's command, she relaxed and sheathed the swords.

"Sorry." Tiana's small smile accentuated her high cheekbones.

Rhett gave a curt nod. "Let's get what we came for."

"What's that smell? It's stinks in here." Brooke waved a hand in front of her nose. "Ohhhh. Now I know why Zeke's brain is all messed up."

"What is it you need? Tasers? Guns?" Zeke said with a bite, frowning at Brooke.

"We have guns and Tasers," Ozzie said. "You think we came all the way here to get something we already have?"

"Please, Zeke." Tamara softened her tone, but the sharp angles of her features gave a different expression. "We're up against a formidable enemy. This is serious."

"Fine." Zeke's shoulders slumped. "But someone has to pay the Imugis, and it's not coming out of my pocket. Follow me."

They went inside to an adjacent black tent, even smaller.

"There." Zeke pointed on the cemented ground with five long, brown duffle bags. "Take what you need."

Ozzie unzipped one and lifted a metal object. "What is this?"

Zeke stood at the opening of the tent. "Be careful. It's called the glove. You loop it through your fingers and strap the band around your wrist. When you squeeze your fist, a powerful air blast shoots out. It's like punching someone without contact."

"Cool. I'll take this one." Ozzie handed one to Brooke and slid his set on.

"What's this?" Reyna held up a twelve-inch metal rod.

"Here. Let me show you." Zeke grabbed one from the open bag, hit the end of the rod on his thigh, then held it up. Both sides extended with ends as sharp as spears. When he tapped the rod's middle, it closed itself back.

"Show me how this works." Tamara strapped a small square gadget around her wrist.

"Touch the home base and you'll see," Zeke said with a soft tone that seemed to be reserved only for Tamara. "I named it the bomb."

When she did, four clicks resonated, and four small throwing stars slid out from a compartment and hovered over her head.

"Wow," she squealed, peering up. "What do they do?"

Zeke pointed at the colorful lights. "When you touch the yellow dot, they track body heat, and you'll get a hologram image. Tap green, they fire. But you'll have to be careful at who you aim. These are mini bombs."

"That's pretty cool, but I'll take the stick," Tamara said.

Brooke let out a wolf whistle. "I'm surprised ISAN hasn't invented these types of weapons. They had Kendrick, but he was all about creating the arsenal around clothes and fashion to preserve a disguise."

"Why does he have that *I know something* look?" Looking murderous, Ozzie pointed at Zeke. "Don't tell me ISAN…"

Zeke raised his hands. "I didn't make the deal, okay. At my last meeting, we were told some big company purchased some of our high-tech weapons. I don't know who."

"Was it ANS?" Rhett asked.

"ANS. SAN. Sass. My ass. Who the hell knows?" Zeke shrugged. "They all sound alike. As long as you guys know I didn't make the deal, we're good."

"Good? Did you say good?" Reyna's face twisted. "Your idiot friends shouldn't be selling this kind of artillery to any group. This is how bad things happen. Can we just hurry up and get the hell out of here?"

Rhett's thoughts exactly. He grabbed one of the same gadgets from Tamara and said, "Take whatever you can."

CHAPTER TEN – INTERROGATION

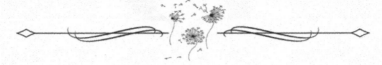

JOSEPHINE CHANG

Josephine Chang stood in front of Verlot, who was recovering inside a medical hub. Mr. San from ANS had founded this abandoned office building in the West Sector and created a makeshift hospital for this specific, carefully planned occasion.

Josephine knew the organization existed, but never in her wildest dream had she expected an offer to work with them. She had lied to everyone that she knew who they were. That was one of the conditions Mr. San had given her.

ANS was a separate entity. Josephine didn't tell them what to do, and they didn't give her orders. They had a common goal, and that was enough for her to keep in contact and share information with Mr. San.

With her gun pointed at Verlot, she pressed her finger on the cool metal trigger. It would be so easy to shoot Verlot and tell the world that the assassin had slipped through the guards at the end of the meeting and killed him. People had witnessed the shooting. Martinez and Jones would back up her story as far as the assassin, but would they if she killed him? Josephine was no cold-blooded murderer. She had to push the cruel thought out of her mind.

Footsteps shuffled outside the door—two pair by the sound of it. Josephine shoved the weapon inside her cloak pocket. She had released Zen and his men, but not her soldiers. They were stationed at the entrance.

"Here. I brought you some tea." Martinez handed Josephine a recyclable paper cup, steam rising and filling the room with the scent of chamomile.

"Thank you." Josephine graciously took the tea. The warmth of the first sip wrapped around her like a cozy blanket.

Jones placed his cup on the table and stood beside Josephine. He unbuttoned his suit jacket and loosened his tie.

"Did the doctor tell you when he'd be awake?" he asked.

Josephine tapped on her chip to look at the time. It had been a least a couple of hours since the surgery. "He didn't say, but it'll give us time to figure out what to do."

Josephine shifted from side to side, digging her toes into the tip of her high heels. She wanted out of her dress and her shoes, into something more comfortable. She could change later.

"An attempt on your life is treason." Martinez's eyes darkened with anger. "He needs to be put to trial and be executed in front of the citizens."

"Josephine doesn't have proof," Jones said.

Josephine inhaled a deep breath. "Vince is the only one who saw one of Verlot's guards aiming for me. It happened at our last meeting at the East Sector. I can't bring him to the forefront. He's wanted by Verlot and ISAN."

Jones gave a sidelong glance. "How do you know Verlot and ISAN want Vince dead?"

"Vince is a good man," Josephine said. "He was an ISAN guard in the north. When he found out the job was not what he'd signed up for, he helped facilitate an escape. The north facility trained male teens at first. When the HelixB77 serum kept failing, they brought in the females, and planned to get rid of the males."

Jones bared his teeth at sleeping Verlot. "Our country has been through so much, and now this? How do we fix this?"

"Many have escaped." Josephine took a mouthful of her tea. "But many are still active. If we try to bring down ISAN, they'll send their highly trained soldiers, along with their guards. If we combine our soldiers, we'll have the numbers, but we won't have their power. We'll have no chance."

"How about the rebels you spoke of? The ones who escaped?" Martinez gripped her paper mug tightly.

"They are training and growing their numbers, but Zen's group took a big hit recently. They lost more than half of their people in an ISAN airstrike."

Jones placed his tea on the table and pounded once on the hub, his eyes blazing. "He doesn't deserve to be treated like royalty. We should force him to wake up."

"What's our next step?" Martinez walked over to the other side of the hub, opposite Jones, her long red dress pooling around the ankles, sweeping up the dust.

A loud beep resounded from Verlot's machine just once and stilled, like a hiccup. Holding her breath, Josephine stole a glance at his chart.

Steady.

Alive.

"To have him surrender," Josephine said.

As if Verlot had heard her, he opened his eyes. Josephine stilled and waited. He couldn't possibly have heard through the humming from the medical hub, and Josephine had switched on "No sound" to conceal their conversation, but still...

Verlot peered up at the ceiling, and craned his neck forward. His eyes rounded in surprise when they locked on Josephine, and

70

grew bigger when he tried to lift his arms and couldn't.

"What is the meaning of this?" he snarled, yanking at the cuffs around his wrists, then stopped.

The electrical current had shot him when he tugged. The shock wasn't long, but it was enough to stop him from acting out.

When Verlot's chest settled, his breathing steadier, Josephine reached over and touched her finger on the pad. His medical hub cranked and hissed, moving him in a sitting position. Verlot's nostrils flared when Martinez and Jones came into view.

"I wouldn't move much if I were you, unless you like the feeling of getting shocked," Josephine said. "You were shot by a girl. Do you remember?"

"I remember, but why these?" He rattled the metal cuffs. "You better have a good explanation or I'll—I'll—"

"You'll what, Councilor?" Jones came face-to-face with Verlot, the glass the only barrier between them. He looked utterly disgusted. "Call ISAN? Call your scientist? No one knows you're here. Yes, Martinez and I know everything. You're not fit to represent our nation."

Verlot made a low, animalistic growl. "I don't know what you're talking about and neither do you, apparently. I'm not associated with any group. I got shot, for crying out loud, and why do I feel pain? The machine should have fixed me." He looked down to his chest, which was covered by a hospital gown.

Verlot was a smart man. He knew what could happen to him locked up inside the hub. With one brush on the hologram monitor, Josephine could have the laser lights tear him into pieces, muscle by muscle, and bone by bone. Then put him back together again only to repeat the torture.

Verlot's shoulders eased and he relaxed into the pillow. "What do you want from me?"

Martinez's lips twitched and tightened. "You should feel lucky we didn't execute you on the spot."

"Execute me? For what?" The corners of Verlot's eyes shifted to Josephine. "Chang lied to you, and you fell into her trap. She's been working with ISAN, not me. Who do you think gave the coordinates for the attack that killed so many innocents recently?"

"You have two choices." Martinez jabbed a finger on the glass. "You resign with or without a public speech. Either way, you're going to be locked up forever. You're lucky you even get a choice."

Understanding crossed his features. "You don't want the world to know about ISAN, do you? You don't want people asking questions and causing chaos. Well, it's too late. I don't understand why the meteor affected the females mostly. But what you saw on social media… those girls with powers… that's just the beginning. More and more will come forward, and they'll eventually figure out what they are capable of. Yes, I know about ISAN, but only because I had to research to try to stop Chang." His eyes darkened. "You have the wrong person locked up."

Verlot was so desperate he was willing to say anything. He didn't realize he wasn't making sense.

Josephine looked at her colleagues. "I think we've heard enough. The three of us should make a decision and get this over with."

Verlot banged on the hub, his voice rising. "It's not me. It's Josephine. You will be the makers of your own doom. You're all fools. When I get out of here, I'll remember this. No mercy for all of you. How do I know you're not all in this together with ISAN?"

"Seriously, Verlot." Josephine shook her head. "Goodnight."

"Josephine. I was willing to spare your life, but I've changed my mind. My men will be coming for you."

Josephine offered him a grim smile and slapped a button. "They have no idea where you are. This place doesn't exist."

Mist streamed out from his hub, covering him up entirely. When the fog cleared, Verlot was sound asleep.

"Well…" Josephine faced Martinez and Jones. "I have work to do, but first I'm going to change into something comfortable. His threats are empty. His men don't know where we are. I'll get in touch with you in a few days."

CHAPTER ELEVEN – FATHER

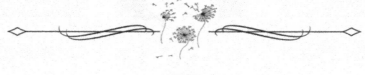

AVA

Still holding my doll, I examined my free hand. It had stopped twitching. The drug had worn off. Had it been in the food or the water? I had to be sure, but there was no way to test it unless I stopped eating or drinking.

The wall opened, and I dropped my doll back to its place and jumped back from the corner chair. Polished black shoes peeked through, then a man wearing a fine suit. When Novak entered, I placed my hands behind my back.

"Hello, Ava." He met my gaze and his dark eyes went to the tray. "I see you finished your dinner. If you're ready, we can talk about your father." He glanced about the gray walls while scrubbing his clean-shaven jaw, then loosened his tie.

I pinched my eyebrows together. Had I been reading him wrong? He seemed nervous, edgy. He raked his hair back and even rubbed his hands together. He'd always stood straight, his hands inside his pockets or to his side. Never had I seen Novak like this. I walked to the bed and eased on the comforter.

"Talk about my father?" My voice rose, my jaw clenching. "I don't want to talk about him. I want to see him. You said if I ate, you would let me see him."

Novak picked up the corner chair. "Yes, of course, but there's something I want to show you first." He set it three feet from me and tossed my doll on the mattress.

There was no use fighting him on the small things. I had to get the upper hand, so I listened for any clues or information I could gather between the lines.

He tapped at the chip on his arm. The lights in the room went out and a hologram he'd projected from his chip flickered to life. A life-size little girl with two side-ponytails held a woman's hand.

"This isn't my memory, is it?" But it was. I recognized my mother's heart-shaped face—her perfect nose, and those beautiful eyes that always seemed to smile.

"No. We're not that sophisticated. It's a home video of you and your mother."

I wanted to ask him how he had gotten it, but changed my mind when my mother opened a door, and my little feet squeaked across the floor on the projected movie. Those were the same hallways I had passed before I had been kidnapped. I shuddered a breath as the video continued.

My mother opened another door with gray walls and a small bed with pink comforter, and nothing else. My bedroom, I realized. *Me*. Memories rushed to the forefront of my mind.

"Why are we here, Mama?" The little me with curious eyes peered up at Mom.

"It's your birthday today. You're four years old," she said.

Mom's excited, animated tone made little me smile.

"My birthday. Do I get a party?"

"I don't know," she singsonged. "Somebody might be hiding somewhere."

The little girl clapped. "It's Daddy." She ran around the outside of the room, touching the wall. "Where are you, Daddy? Come out. I know you're in here somewhere."

A wall slid open like a door, and closed back when a man wearing a white lab coat appeared with a cake. The camera, focusing on the cake, didn't show the man's face.

"Happy birthday, pumpkin," the man said cheerfully.

The four candles burst into life, flames dancing, sparkling. Little me could hardly contain the excitement, covering her mouth as she bounced on her toes. They sang "Happy Birthday."

I wondered where Gene was, then I recalled from my father's journal that he had been sent away when he was an infant. My mother had thought her firstborn was dead at birth.

"Blow out the candles." My mother's tender gaze on the little girl was full of love.

My eyes stung. Seeing and hearing her, my heart broke all over again. How I had missed her, even after all these years. These videos didn't help. Overwhelmed, I didn't know whether to cry or be happy.

My little self blew out the candles. As I coughed, my mother guided me away and waved at the smoke.

"She's fine." The lower half of Father's face showed and he held a prideful grin. I could tell he loved the little girl very much. "She'll have to learn to protect herself."

"She's only four." Mother sounded defensive.

The mood in the room suddenly changed from light to dark. The little girl's eyes darted from her mother to her father, back and forth, noticing the tension.

"This is the best birthday," my younger self cooed, bringing them back to her. The little girl wrapped one arm around her mother's neck, and the second around the man she called Daddy.

What I saw next fractured my world and I suppressed a gasp. She kissed her mom, the gadget recording them had tipped when she kissed her father's cheek.

"No," I whispered, the past colliding with the present.

The hair color was lighter. His eyes gray. But the face—thick eyebrows, the sharp nose, high cheek bones. Squared jawline. That face... almost a duplicate of Gene's face.

My heart thundered. It couldn't be. My mouth couldn't form words. Surely it had been a trick of the mind.

Novak raised his chin higher, the light from the projection highlighted his face. "Now you know. I couldn't just tell you I'm your father. You wouldn't have believed me. I had to give you proof."

Something inside me broke into a thousand pieces and I felt myself falling... falling... falling and there was no bottom. This was my hell, but I wouldn't stay in it. He was *not* my father.

I matched his gaze—fierce and cold—like he had always given me. "You're lying. We have the technology to manipulate anything, so you altered this video. I don't believe you. Where is Dr. Hunt? I want to see him now."

Novak released an agitated sigh and tapped on his chip, pulling up another video. My little self was sitting in a black pod-like chair, hands strapped against the arm rest with a square flat metal plate over her forehead. Beside her, Novak stood in front of a table.

"Is this going to hurt?" Tears formed in the little girl's eyes.

Mother lowered herself in front of her and slipped a finger to her daughter's hand, still strapped. "No, pumpkin. It won't hurt at all. I promise."

"But why do I have to have that thing on my head?" The little girl trembled.

Father stood beside the mother. "Pumpkin, you have nothing to worry about. I want to test what you know. Do you remember what we did yesterday?" Father asked, but it was clearly Novak. There was no denying the fact.

My little self shook her head, squeezing her mother's fingers tighter.

"She's so strong, Victor. Hurry."

"We celebrated your birthday," Father said in a loving tone. "You blew out your candles. Do you remember?"

"No." Little me cried from frustration, and sparks flew about the room. My little self shrank in terror. I had done that. Four-year-old me had power.

Mr. Novak's face scrunched. "Ava, you won't remember this conversation when you wake up. Know that your mom and I love you very much. We are only doing this to protect you from the bad people. You'll be leaving with your mom and you won't remember me. It's better this way."

"No, Daddy." Tears fell faster down the little girl's cheek, then the girl went still with her eyes closed.

"It's done, Avary," Novak said. "You need to go now. Get your bags. I'll carry Ava."

Mother stroked the little girl's hair and kissed her forehead. "You're sure she's going to be fine, right?"

"Yes. We have no other option. No one can know. You can't trust anyone. No one, do you understand?"

"Yes," she said with conviction.

"I wish there was another way, but I have to stay. We have to sacrifice for our little girl."

When he kissed my mother's lips, tears ran down her face. Without looking back, she rushed out. Novak released the square flat metal plate and picked up the little girl, her body limp in his arms. He cradled the girl tenderly, and his endearments nauseated me. But something about the way he looked at her with adoration broke something inside.

"I promise you, pumpkin, we will meet again when the time is right. The family will be back together again. Me, your mother, your brother, and you. Know that whatever I do, it's for you and our family. I love you."

Novak kissed the little girl's forehead, and the hologram projection shut down and the lights came back on.

I squinted from the brightness and faced Novak.

"Do you believe me now?" He smirked. "As you can see, I've dyed my hair black. I have contact lenses on. I took a serum to deepen my voice by damaging my vocal cords. A few simple alterations can change a person's appearance in a dramatic way."

I didn't want to believe it. I so did not want to, but the evidence was irrefutable. The faces. The words. If I weren't already sitting on my bed, I would have fallen to my knees.

What joke was the universe playing on me?

I croaked out a weak laugh, a pathetic noise to attempt to sound tough. I clutched the top button on my pj's, fighting my rage. Drained beyond exhaustion, I had no energy left. My voice left me like a ghostly whisper.

"It makes sense... why you spent so many hours with me, training me, giving me your attention in ISAN. You told me I was special, that I stood out from everyone one else. You planned out everything."

"I did what I had to do." Novak's eyebrows knitted in the center, as he rose and dragged the chair back to the corner. "When you have children of your own, you will understand. And I have a feeling you will one day."

Had he forgotten girls in ISAN couldn't bear children? What

was he talking about?

I clutched my shirt in the middle, trying not to lose control. I needed more answers. "Why are you a monster?"

"It was all for you, Ava." His voice was serene, and yet so full of malice. "You and your brother are my masterpiece, one I tried to create again."

Create again? Oh, God. It suddenly came to me. I had forgotten.

"Justine…" I shoved back on the bed, my spine pressing on the wall. "She's my half sister." Bile rose up my throat. I had a psycho brother, and Justine wasn't far behind him. Shoot me now. "You had an affair with another woman and had a child? Justine is my age, so that must mean…" I couldn't look at him.

"It's not what you think." He strolled to the center of the room as if he needed to keep his distance. "I love your mother very much. She doesn't know about Justine, between you and me. It's better that she doesn't in her frail condition. And Justine didn't turn out like you."

His disappointed tone only made me angrier.

"You think so little of her, but she knows that. You knew Justine was jealous of me, but you put us together in the same team. Why?"

"I'd thought she would be inspired by you. I was hoping her powers would transform into something like yours. Not exactly, of course, but something close. She was placed with other teams before, but I kept her with you because she performed the best on your team. She seemed to thrive on her jealousy."

I shook my head, my palms planted on my face. "You're not my father. My father is dead." I recalled the video I had watched, the one where Dr. Hunt and my thirteen-year-old self had talked at the park. I lifted my head and said, "Dr. Hunt doesn't exist to you. Do you understand? Do you recall what you said to me?"

I couldn't believe we were having this conversation, that I'd pacified my rage. When you're beyond fury there is only tranquility, like the calm before the storm.

He shoved his hands inside his pockets, still standing in the center. "You're older and your mind is stronger. Your inner power won't let me even if I wanted to. You've managed to remember everything else I tried to make you forget."

"Rhett." I immediately regretted saying his name.

A special kind of madness entered his eyes. I wrung my fingers around the doll and brought it to my side.

He dusted something off his suit jacket sleeve. "You were supposed to be my best weapon, along with your brother. I was molding you to be indestructible, preparing you one step at a time, but then that boy came along." His tone intensified. "You let your emotions get to you. You became weak. You couldn't focus. I wasn't going to let him ruin what I'd worked so hard to build. You were mine to create, and mine to destroy. No one else."

I shuddered. He was beyond helping.

I squeezed the doll tighter, grinding my teeth. "I'm nobody's property. I don't belong to you. I belong to myself."

Novak stiffened and then squared his shoulders, his voice softer. "You're right. I suppose no one really belongs to anyone. But enough has been said between us and we have so much to do. Your brother is anxious to see you again. And I know you want to see your mother."

"Keep Gene away from me if you know what's best for him. I swear I'll kill him if he enters my room. He used some kind of device on me and I won't take it again."

81

His lips curled a bit, humor in his eyes. "Huh. You said *your* room."

"I didn't mean it," I snarled.

"Well, that's a baby step, pumpkin. I'm so proud of you." He sauntered to the door.

"Don't call me that. You're not my father."

He looked over his shoulder as the wall opened. "But I am, and now you know everything. If you want your mother alive, you will do as I say. We will be a family again, and this time, no one is leaving."

The finality in his voice made me quiver. I grabbed the chair and hurled it at Novak, then jerked to the side to avoid it hitting me on the rebound. My chest heaved. Had I been a second faster, I would have hit my target. But I had hesitated.

I reprimanded myself for being soft. The videos had resurrected emotions I had locked away. He might be my father, but he was Mr. Novak to me.

When you become a parent you give your children wings to fly, not to clip. I planned to regrow my own and escape with my mother.

CHAPTER TWELVE – NEW MISSION

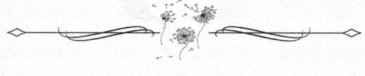

MITCH

Justine marched into Russ's office with a scowl, but sat, cross-legged, next to her team, minus Payton, Nina, Cora, and Tessa.

Justine laced her fingers through her blonde hair. "Why is our next assignment to No Man's Land? And who is our target?"

Mitch stood in front of her, his legs a foot apart, his hands behind his back. "What page are you on?" he said and Lydia, who stood beside him, hiked up her eyebrows. He rolled his eyes and tried again with a politer tone. "What is No Man's Land? That's not your destination."

"Yes, it is." Nina's brown eyes sparked with electricity.

"Nina, what did we say about control?" Russ said from his desk.

Good. Mitch didn't have to be the bad guy this time.

"I—I'm sorry." She placed her hands on her lap as the light in her eyes dulled. "I'm just saying that nothing exists in Pearl Valley."

"I've never heard of such a place," Tessa said. She played with the hem of her gray training outfit top and cast a glance at Lydia, who was scrolling through her TAB.

Mitch glared at Tessa for speaking without permission. A newbie shouldn't talk without being spoken to, but Ava's team had never understood that rule. Apparently, this team didn't either.

"Justine is right. They're both right." Cora stroked the two braids draped over her shoulders. "Pearl Valley is called No Man's Land."

"And you know this because…" Mitch encouraged her to continue by spinning his hand like a wheel.

"Nina and I have been there before. We wanted to know why it was called Pearl Valley." She shrugged sheepishly. "We thought maybe they had pearls."

"Because of the name?" Mitch shook his head.

"We needed money." Nina crinkled her once-pierced nose. "We were running away from… from… people like you. People from your network."

Something softened inside him. He shouldn't judge. He had no right. "Sorry."

"Wait." Justine uncrossed her legs and straightened her spine. "Did you just apologize?"

"No." Mitch craned his neck to the side, avoiding her gaze. But it was too late.

"Oh. My. God." Justine snickered, her blue eyes beaming. "Yes, you did."

There was something innocent and sweet about her laugh. He would have never thought that a year ago. Lydia had made him softer. Mitch loved and hated his new self.

"Enough," Mitch snapped, walking a circle around the four of them. We need to leave in…" He looked at his chip. "Twenty minutes."

Tessa raised her hand, then put it down. Her gaze went from Lydia to Russ. She sighed. "Never mind," she said.

She reminded Mitch of Tamara. Her shyness, her uncertainty. He missed the old group. He missed provoking, threatening, and enlightening them. Ava's team was one of the finest he'd ever worked with.

"What is it that we're doing exactly?" Justine tilted her head, wringing her hair round her finger. Always playing with her hair. "I don't understand our mission. And where is Payton?"

"I guess it's your lucky day, Justine." Mitch patted her shoulder behind her, then went around to face her. "Payton is out with your…"

He'd almost said *daddy*.

He needed to keep track of what he was supposed to know and shouldn't know. One day, it might get him killed.

"With whom… Mitch?" Justine tapped her feet like a drum.

So impatient, like her father. Like Ava.

"Um…" Mitch rubbed his temple.

Lydia lifted her brow in concern.

"I meant…" Mitch cleared his throat. "I have no idea where Payton is, so you're the lead."

Justine's eyes grew bigger, and her lips extended wide. She had never looked so happy and proud. "Thanks, Mitch. This means a lot to me."

Mitch gave her a curt nod. Well, what do you know… a moment of mutual respect from Justine. Who knew how long that would last, but it felt good. When he stole a glance to Lydia, she rewarded him with her best smile, deepening the dimples he loved.

He had to turn away before anyone noticed him grinning.

"Who is our target?" Russ's fingers danced in the air, typing on the hologram keyboard.

"See, even Russ is confused," Justine said with a mock smile.

"Wait. Let me log into…" Lydia pushed down on her TAB. "I skimmed it earlier and I thought I saw…" She paused and lifted her eyes to Mitch.

"Who?" Mitch said, his pulse spiking.

She tried to sound nonchalant about it, but he heard the tremor in her voice.

"Rhett," she said.

Mitch cursed. He had been worried sick wondering if Rhett was alive. But what about the rest of the rebels? Ava? Mitch hadn't signed up for this. This emotion, this overwhelming emotion that made him lose focus. He had to shut it down.

Mitch clapped his hands once. "Okay, so this is the new plan. We're going to assess and see if the mission is worth staying for."

"What do you mean?" Justine squinted her eyes. "We can't just leave. That's not the protocol. Are you afraid of Rhett? That rebel team? Are you afraid you'll come face-to-face with Ava? Well, I'm not. I've been waiting for a chance. Ava is a traitor. Novak will realize I'm the star."

Just when Mitch had thought he could like her a tiny bit, she reminded him how fixated she was on Ava.

"Seriously, Justine?" Mitch snapped, still standing in front of her, and then added in a gentler voice, "You are already a star. You don't need to prove yourself to anyone. If you would stop comparing yourself to Ava, you would realize it too. And so would Mr. Novak."

Mitch couldn't believe what he'd said. His father had fed him those exact words when Rhett had entered his life. It was the speech that had hit home, made him realize his father wouldn't love him less. Mitch didn't have to prove he was better than Rhett. It was then he'd decided to stop being a prick and actually treated his half brother like one of the family.

Justine blinked, her eyes glistening. She parted her lips to speak, but closed them instead.

Russ and Lydia dropped their jaws. He shrugged at them.

"Anyway, anyone have a problem with my new plan?" Mitch asked, looking from Tessa, Cora, and to Nina.

The team shook their heads.

"Good," Mitch said. "Go get geared up. You're excused. Nina and Cora, stay behind. We'd like a few words with you."

When Justine and Tessa left, Mitch and Lydia took the empty seats.

"Girls, you know what to do, right?" Lydia asked.

Cora nodded, her braided hair bouncing.

"Stay behind Mitch and do as he says," Nina said. "And I get to put on my nose stud, right?"

"Exactly." Mitch gave a thumbs-up.

Mitch's plan was to get these girls to help the rebels, and have Cora and Nina go with the rebels to their new base. The girls knew they would be marked as traitors, but they didn't care. They wanted out of ISAN and that was the only motive they needed.

Lydia pulled up something from her TAB. "Novak sent a second message to the south. Looks like your team won't be the only one. Novak said meet Team East at Pearl Valley with the new arsenal."

Russ walked to Lydia and read her message as if he needed to see it for himself. "We don't have anything new," Russ said.

Lydia closed the TAB, scowling. "Novak had to have purchased them through the Imugi network. They sell illegal stuff to anyone for the right price."

"Why don't we have them?" Nina scrunched her rosebud lips together.

"That's a good question."

Perhaps he was being paranoid. Maybe Novak wanted Team

South to test the weapons first. Sometimes he had single teams test things out before the rest of them got theirs.

"I'm sure everything will be fine." Lydia always knew what to say, and her soothing tone pacified the thick tension in the room.

"Well, we won't know until we're there." Mitch shrugged, waving off the concern. "No use worrying about something we don't know about." He turned to Russ, who stood on the other side of Lydia with his head down, looking at something on the floor with heavy concentration. "Russ, ready?"

He answered with a defeated sigh that didn't inspire confidence.

"Well then, Lydia." Mitch gave a curt nod. "I'll see you soon, love." His neck blazed with heat. "Sorry about that. I didn't mean *love*. It was a slip of the tongue."

"It's fine, Mitch." Lydia laughed and tried to salvage the situation. "See you soon, Russ. Lovely ladies, good luck and see you soon. Be safe."

"Well, then, stop wasting time smiling and get ready." Mitch glared at everyone and left.

He had to be more careful.

CHAPTER THIRTEEN – PEARL VALLEY

RHETT

"**A**re you sure we're going the right direction?" Rhett asked Tamara.

Tamara angled her body to face Rhett, who sat behind her. "The facility isn't in the city or near habitable area. It's somewhere in the south.

"Dude. I'm right here." Zeke waved a hand from where he sat beside Tamara, looking at the hologram map in front of him. "I'm the driver. You can ask me. Stop pestering her."

The glider jerked, and Rhett grabbed the back of Tamara's headrest.

"Not my driving. Turbulence." Zeke tapped the touchscreen on the monitor. "The wind is picking up. You should seat belt yourself."

The glider aggressively bolted high and then low like a roller-coaster ride. Then it sailed smoother and the ruins of a lost city materialized through the thick clouds. A whole section of a freeway tilted sideways. Office buildings and shops destroyed with smashed windows. Overturned cars and street signs littered the faded asphalt. Homes and trees were flattened to the dirt.

"Wow. This is spooky." Cleo pressed her forehead to the window. "It's completely deserted."

"This is the face of apocalypse," Brooke said, who sat beside

Ozzie. "And Ava is down there somewhere."

Rhett squeezed his eyes, trying not to go to that place where emotion took root. His girl was down there and she needed him.

A chime came through the monitor.

Zeke swiped at the screen. "I got a message. It said Ava has been moved to another location. I received new coordinates. Everyone, hold on, I'm turning this baby around."

"Wait." Suspicion waved through Rhett. "Who sent you the message?"

"It didn't say from whom, but it has to be from Mitch. He's my only contact placed high enough to know Ava's whereabouts. Hold on, let me try something." Zeke drummed his fingers across the keys. "Strange. It's from Zen. Satisfied?"

Not really. Not that Rhett didn't trust Zen. He didn't trust Zeke.

"Do you know where we're headed?" They were losing time.

"It looks like… according to my map… Pearl Valley."

"Pearl Valley?" Tamara's voice went an octave higher. She gripped the arm rest. "That's No Man's Land. There's nothing there. It used to be a resort with hiking trails and hot springs, but that was back in the old days."

"Well, there's nothing here, either." Ozzie hiked his thumb to the window. "Why do you call it No Man's Land?"

"It's exactly what it means." Ella bit down on her bottom lip.

"My father mentioned it before," Cleo said.

"I don't like the sound of it." Mia crossed her arms and tilted her head on Ella's shoulder. Her red hair fanned over her face.

No one had gotten any rest since ISAN had bombed Hope City. Everyone was exhausted.

"I heard no one leaves that place," one of Rhett's men from the

90

mountain base said.

"I heard there are creatures, alien-looking things," another guy added.

Reyna scoffed. "Those are rumors to keep people away."

"Are they?" Mia blew out a long breath and tucked her red strands. The air inside the glider shifted from cool to warm from her power. Sometimes she didn't know her strength. "If people like us can do unimageable things, then couldn't there be such creatures?"

Ella, sitting next to Mia, chimed in, "The human species has evolved. The world is changing. Why not animals? Something to think about."

"Well then, it looks like we have monsters to kill." Zeke veered the glider in a U-turn.

When they arrived at Pearl Valley, the section looked similar to the place they had left. Nothing but destroyed buildings and trash. Heavy fog loomed, masking what was behind the veil.

Zeke stood when his seat belt released. "I sent a message to Zen, but there's no response. We're at the right coordinates, though. I've released the ramp, so everyone out."

"Wow, it's like we never left." Brooke patted her gear, and helped Ozzie put on his glove.

Reyna handed Mia and Ella the metal rod and did a quick demonstration before heading out.

Rhett focused on positive thoughts, because doubt that they'd find Ava had risen to the surface. He patted his gun and Taser on their holsters, then shoved his fingers through the loops and wrapped the glove strap around his wrist. He flexed and unflexed his fingers. The gadget felt strange, like second thick skin, but if it would save him, he would use it.

As Rhett headed for the door, he said, "We'll wait for Zen outside, but we'll scout around. Cleo, stay with me. If you have your mask with you, use it."

"Hey." Zeke tugged on Rhett's shirt before he reached the ramp and whispered. "Remember I told you I never killed anyone. It's the truth. You're not going to tell anyone, are you?"

Rhett furrowed his brow. He had no idea what to say, but Zeke's embarrassment was sincere. "Just stay close to me and don't get in my way." Rhett lowered his gaze at the gun in Zeke's hand. "But you better use that weapon of yours and watch my back."

A gust of air whipped Rhett's face as he went down the ramp. He pulled on a cloth mask, and the others did the same. Zeke shadowed Rhett while Cleo stayed beside him.

Rhett pointed his team east and directed the rest to scatter toward west in pairs or threes.

"Anything unusual?" Rhett spoke into his chip and surveyed the grounds near Zeke's glider.

"Nothing. Just the usual wrecked and busted things." Reyna's voice echoed in his earpiece.

"I found… is this an old cell phone?" Ozzie said. "I can't believe people had to actually hold this piece to talk to others."

The mist became thicker, cloudier, making it difficult to see the sky and the ground. An eerie chill prickled down Rhett's arms. They would have no way of detecting a glider until it was close to landing.

Something crunched under Rhett's feet. He looked down to see… bones. Human bones?

"Is that…?" Zeke gasped.

Cleo's eyes rounded and her lips parted to scream. Rhett gathered her in his arms and covered her mouth, but his glove gadget made it difficult.

"Shhh. Don't say a word." He didn't want to awaken anything. "Cleo," Rhett whispered harshly in her ear. "I'm here. Hold on to me. I'm going to let go. Don't scream, okay?"

When she nodded, he released his hand. Rhett kept treading carefully with measured caution as more bones rattled underfoot. When he kicked something hard and solid, he shuffled his feet to clear the path and get a better look, then wished he hadn't.

Skulls. Dozens and dozens of skulls.

Cleo whimpered and tightened her grip on Rhett's arm.

"Tamara? You feel anything?" Rhett asked through the chip.

"Rhett. There's something coming. A lot of them. I feel them. It's not good."

Her petrified tone was enough to validate his own instinct. So he felt he had no choice. "Everyone, retreat. Go back to the glider. I repeat. Go—"

Deafening screams from his mountain team resonated through the earpiece, as the sounds from guns firing echoed through the air.

"Retreat. Retreat," Rhett hollered, desperation taking over him.

Taser beams and bullets whizzed through the mist. One bullet stuck the ground an inch from Rhett's foot.

"Zen?" Rhett called out. He thought Zen might have confused them with ISAN.

A person appeared, stepping out of the fog. Rhett raised his hand, informing his team not to fire. Not Zen. Mitch. Mitch in ISAN combat suit with a mask that covered his entire face. Rhett missed that equipment.

Mitch kept his distance, his face contorted in concern, and lowered his gaze to Rhett's hand. "I gave you a warning shot. Get out of here. Why on earth would you come here? And why is Zeke with you? Don't tell me you've kidnapped him."

Even with a mask on, Mitch's voice projected loud and clear.

"I didn't kidnap him. He's... never mind. He's of no importance." Rhett considered Mitch's words. "We got a message from Zen that Ava had been relocated here. By any chance, would you know anything about that?"

Mitch frowned. "Ava isn't here. This is a trap. Get out now. There's too many of us. I won't be able to save your asses this time. I'm sending two girls with you. Their names are Nina and Cora."

"You're recruiting now?"

"Hey, whatever it takes."

Something about those words twisted Rhett's heart. He didn't know whether to hug Mitch or... "Thanks. I'll—"

More screams. Gunshots boomed consistently.

Mitch's eyes went wild, his arm going skyward, firing away. "Get out, Rhett!" he hollered and then ran back to his team.

Rhett whirled and leaped behind a chunk of cement. Zeke and Cleo hid next to him as something sharp impaled the dry earth. Not a missile. A giant insect about two stories tall. A mix between spider and something else he couldn't discern with eight legs and eight bulging, nasty-looking eyeballs. A hard shell, like a turtle's but covered in fine hair, protected its body.

"They do exist?" Zeke grabbed Cleo's shoulder with his trembling hand. "The girls were right."

Rhett leaped over the cement, pointed at the abomination, and squeezed his fist. The force of air from his glove shot out. A person would have been thrown far back, but the tank-sized beast only tilted with no damage. Rhett hit it again and again.

The beast screeched in rage, its cry piercing the air. Rhett hoped it wasn't calling more friends.

"Reyna, Brooke and I got you." Ozzie's voice boomed through Rhett's earpiece. "We're firing from behind. We're coming."

Brooke's voice came through the chip. "This giant thing won't go down. Can't you huff and puff it away?"

She must have been asking Mia and Ella.

In the distance, two smaller hideous creatures were tossed into the air.

"I told you. I warned you about them." Ella or Mia. Rhett couldn't tell their voices apart.

Then out from the mist, about fifty yards from where Rhett stood, Tamara thumped on the beast's back, speeding upward like an ant along its shell. With incredible speed and dexterity, she soared into the air and landed on its head.

With a flick of her wrists, she used her favorite weapons and did what she did best. She speared her pocket knife into its head repeatedly until blood oozed out. Tamara took out the rod shoved inside the back of her waistband, tapped it open, and plunged the sharp edge in the middle of its skull.

Atta girl.

The beast got onto its hind legs, shaking its head, blood spattering out. The knife Tamara had spiked through its exoskeleton held her in place for the time being. When the beast finally collapsed, she somersaulted and landed behind it.

"She's my hero," Zeke said.

"Everyone back," one of Rhett's men hollered. "Incoming bomb."

Something flew in the air, coming toward Rhett.

"Shit. Run. No, hide." Rhett yanked Zeke and Cleo with him and leaped into the nearest section of debris for protection, behind a flipped car.

Rhett had thought they were good as dead until a girl with a diamond stud nose ring stood in front of them, her eyes and fingers sparking with electricity like Coco. She had created a shield with her power. Reyna appeared beside her and pushed her hands up, sending the bomb skyward. The bomb had to have come from ISAN soldiers.

The girl with a sparkling stud nose ring and brown eyes stood in front of Rhett. "My name is Nina, and this is my friend, Cora. Mitch told you about us. He told me to come find you."

At first, Rhett thought Nina was out of her mind, introducing someone he couldn't see, until a girl with neatly braided hair—Cora—materialized.

"Sorry," Cora said, "I forgot I was invisible."

Rhett reflexively ducked when another bomb went off nearby, uplifting debris and smoke. "This way to the glider. Follow me."

Only half of the mountain rebels had made it back to the meeting point. Rhett second-guessed his decision to bring his team along. The fog blinded Rhett's view. He couldn't tell where the ISAN soldiers were. Mitch said there were too many of them, indicating more than one team.

"ISAN. They've found us." Nina yanked Cora to the side. "We can't be seen. Sorry. We'll help you from the side."

"The ramp is open. Get in," Zeke said. "I'll get the glider started."

"Oz," Brooke hollered his name in panic.

Ozzie flew skyward, but halted in midair. Mia had exhaled, causing air to wrap around Oz, and brought him down without a scratch.

Brooke's features contorted. When she planted her hand on the ground, the one without the glove, her body trembled, but her eyes were focused.

Brooke inhaled. "I found out something else I could do when I thought of how much I wanted to hurt Gene."

The ground quaked and cracked open around her hand, and then a straight line tore the earth, splintering in all directions as far as Rhett could see. Brooke became one with the earth and it listened.

Creatures screeched and backed away. When the ISAN guards scattered, Rhett got a good look at them. The ISAN team was made up of kids, around Momo's age judging by their height, but their combat suits were different. Sleeker. Resilient. Perhaps more comfortable and bulletproof.

"Rhett. Oz. Cleo. Get inside," Reyna demanded. "Let us handle this."

Rhett ran up the ramp, grabbed Zeke and pointed at the girls. "Look. Your people did this. They sold their weapons to ISAN."

Zeke lowered his eyes at Rhett's hand and drew his lips into a frown. "Like I said before, I didn't. The Imugis don't know anything about ISAN. They're just doing their thing to survive."

Cursing under his breath, Rhett released Zeke and watched the battle before him in awe. Zeke, too, was mesmerized.

Mia and Ella, back-to-back, spun their sticks like windmills. When they blew, the sticks twirled faster.

Brooke cartwheeled to dodge Taser pellets. She used her glove to knock the kids to the ground. Tamara twirled her stick the same way she twirled her knives, and instead of impaling the kid challenging her, she hurled the stick at the beasts that had creeped without a sound behind ISAN's team.

Too late. Its leg had pierced four ISAN girls' backs.

"Run!" Brooke yelled.

Rhett dug through the weapon bag in search of something useful. There. The weapon he needed. He took off the glove and grabbed the one Zeke called the bomb.

Rhett bolted out. "Everyone inside!"

The metal around his wrist tightened. As the four disks from the gadget slipped out and hovered over him, he recalled Zeke's words. *When you touch the yellow dot, they track body heat, and you'll get a hologram image. Tap green, they fire. But you'll have to be careful at who you aim. These are mini bombs.*

Rhett pressed the green one. The throwing stars spun. He directed the stars to the four monsters attacking the ISAN kids.

When the last of Rhett's band was in the glider, he charged inside as the creatures blew up. He heard the explosion but didn't bother to look.

"Go. Go. Get us out of here." Rhett directed Zeke, the aircraft already in the air. He did a quick check of who was present. "Are Nina and Cora in here?"

"Here." Cora flickered into existence, sitting at the back with Nina.

In the chaos, Rhett had almost forgotten about them. He did a quick introduction and thanked Mitch for the new recruits. Words Rhett never thought he would say. How Mitch had managed to talk the girls into joining the rebels was beyond him.

"What the hell was that?" Brooke slapped the window, gazing out. Panting, she fogged up a section of the glass her nose touched.

"That was insane." Ozzie scrubbed a hand down his face, sitting beside Brooke.

"I can't believe that," Cleo chimed in, clutching her chest. "Maybe they ate a piece of meteor, who knows?"

"Maybe," Ella added. "Those things didn't even seem real at first. I felt like I was watching a movie."

They hadn't seen all of what had happened to the ISAN teams and the creatures from the mist, but Rhett's heart went out to those soldiers. ISAN or no, they were just kids.

"Is everyone okay? Is anyone hurt?" Still standing, Rhett swayed a little from a sudden jerk of the aircraft.

"It's not me. It's the turbulence," Zeke hollered from the front.

When no one said a word, Rhett plopped down next to Mia. Gripping fistfuls of hair, he inhaled a deep breath and exhaled an even longer one. With his legs spread a foot apart, he pitched forward, his elbows on his thighs.

Rhett couldn't believe any of them had made it back in one piece, though five of the soldiers from the mountain base hadn't. If it hadn't been impossible, he would have looked for them in case they were injured. There'd been no time to do anything but survive. But still, he couldn't stop seeing the faces he'd left behind. Considering how deadly the creatures were, he doubted any had survived.

Then there was the issue of Ava. She hadn't been there and neither had Zen. Zen hadn't sent Zeke that message. Then who had? Novak?

"Did you see the ISAN soldiers?" Tamara said.

"Um yeah." Reyna groaned an agitated sigh. "They were about Momo's age."

Tamara twisted in her seat to face Reyna behind her. "Something was different about them. There was no life in their eyes. I didn't feel *anything* from those kids. I usually can feel fear or pain, but I didn't get that vibe from them."

Nina and Cora were quiet but listening.

"So what's the next plan?" Ozzie said. "Because we're not going home. Not without Ava."

Rhett stood to get a better view of everyone. "First, we're going back to the mountain base to drop some of you off. Zeke needs to go back to the black market. As for me, whoever wants to join me, I'm going back to get Ava."

"But you don't know where they've taken her," Reyna said. "I want to go with you, Rhett, but we can't waste our time. It's like chasing your own tail."

"Go where, Rhett?" Oz said. "You sound like she'll materialize wherever you go."

Rhett looked at Tamara, only because no one else would understand what he was about to say.

"My heart is my map, and it will lead me to her."

Everyone looked at Rhett like he was crazy, but not Tamara. She offered a soft, understanding smile and then stared out the window.

CHAPTER FOURTEEN – ABORT

MITCH

Mitch shot at the creature clawing into the dirt, who was salivating and ready to eat Rhett for lunch. He fired like there was no tomorrow, and then ran back to his team.

"Abort. Abort. Abort this mission," Mitch yelled into his com. He spotted his team near a beat-up school bus, about a hundred yards from their glider.

Russ spun around Mitch to cover him.

"I thought we here for the rebels. I don't understand." Justine fired her Taser, barely nicking the giant insect. Her feet scuffled in the dirt as she moved around Mitch and Russ.

"I'll hold them off," Mitch said. "At the count of three, run back to the ramp."

"It's too hard to see in the fog. Which way is our glider?" Tessa swung her arm from left to right when the beast squealed.

The roar pierced Mitch's eardrums. Mitch trembled, his heart racing. In all the years of training and all the missions, he'd never been so scared for himself and his team.

"The creatures sound close," Russ shouted and turned on a mini flashlight he must have taken out of the emergency pack. "Follow me. I'll guide."

"Mitch, where are Nina and Cora?" Justine bellowed, bumping into Mitch.

"I told them to find you when the three of us scouted ahead. They didn't come back?"

"No," she said.

"Shit. I don't know." Mitch tried to sound genuinely worried. "I'll go look for them."

Justine grabbed his arm just as he pivoted. "No. You and Russ go in. Tessa and I got this. We can buy them some time to find us. Go."

Mitch had never seen Justine act like a leader, and she had never put his safety over hers. He liked this side of her. Mitch ran, Russ beside him.

Inside the glider, Mitch turned on the transporter's headlight, a beacon for his team, long enough to give them direction, and then turned it off before it could attract the creatures' attention. As he waited, he watched in terror as one giant creature made its way toward Justine.

Justine somersaulted and hid under the monster's belly. As the beast continued to stomp through the dirt and at the bus, she fired her Taser in rapid succession. Tessa climbed on top of the bus, jumped on its head, and pulled the trigger. The monster collapsed. Dust lifted like clouds, the dried earth soaked up the blood, and the girls ran toward the light.

"Hurry," Mitch murmured, his fists curled. "Hurry." He pounded the dashboard.

"There's another one." Russ spoke into his com, his voice frantic. "It's behind you, Justine."

The wounded monster behind Justine dropped, kicking up a dust cloud, providing more view of the perimeter. Five assassins geared in head to toe high-tech suits that might as well have been from another planet appeared beside the creature.

Mitch realized they were not only ISAN assassins, but they were kids—like maybe thirteen years old. The monster wailed a high-pitched sound, most likely calling for aid.

Five kids surrounded the beast. Two assassins held up their fists and the gadgets they wore made the beast stay still. An invisible ray of some sort. Each took out a short rod and tapped it on their hip. When they hurled the weapons at the creature, they lengthened into long spears, impaling the beast.

One girl touched a gadget on her wrist and something small and airborne went spinning toward the creature. When it attached to the beast's leathery skin, they ran for cover.

The monster exploded, crimson liquid spewing like rain. Organs and body parts thumped on the ground and on the bus. Flesh, muscles, bones, and guts laid out for a scavenger buffet.

"That is one messed up motherfu—" Mitch snapped out of the movie-like scene, back to reality. "Justine. Tessa. Where are you?"

"We're coming," Justine said, panic in her voice. "Did you see what they did? Why don't we have those weapons? The girl told me they're from ISAN South. They're just kids, Mitch."

"I know. Get here, now. Do not speak to them."

"Okay. Flash your headlights again. I'm disoriented from the blast."

Mitch did as he was asked but caught one of the beast's attention.

"I see them." Russ pointed at two figures appearing and vanishing between the mist coming their direction.

The creature that had been curious about the light tailed behind them.

"Take the reins. Get ready to fire when I say," Mitch said to Russ and dashed out of the glider. He stood guard at the front.

"Justine. Tessa. Don't look back. Keep going as fast as you can. I've got your backs."

Mitch fired, kept firing, wishing he had cool toys like the south girls. Bullets rained down on the beast but it wouldn't die.

"I see you," Justine said out of breath.

"I'm right beside you," Tessa said to Justine.

"Don't talk, just run." Mitch didn't mean to sound mad, but the creature was right on their tails.

The beast hollered a mighty roar. Must be the queen. It was bigger than the others. One giant impaled a leg through Tessa's head. Mitch's blood turned to ice and brought a mouthful of bile into his throat. And for the first time, he didn't know what to do.

"Mitch. Get Justine. Get Justine," Russ's voice rang urgently.

Mitch snapped out of it and rushed toward Justine, but he was too late. One of the legs whipped her aside and she smacked into a crumbled building.

"Now, Russ. Fire," Mitch shouted and ran in the direction Justine had fallen. He searched frantically through the debris.

Mitch shoved the chunks of concrete he could lift aside, one after the other. *Come on, Justine. Where are you?*

"Hurry Mitch. More are coming."

"I can't find her." His breath left him in spurts, sweat beading his forehead, his mask fogging. Then finally a hand. He moved more pieces of cement, revealing an ISAN combat suit.

Justine was unconscious in the amidst of chunks of concrete, wet blood coating her head. He released a sigh of relief, hefted her over his shoulder, and sprinted. Getting back to the glider wouldn't be easy. Mitch stayed low to keep out of Russ's firing range and avoid attracting the creatures' attention.

Every step seemed impossible, the roars sounding closer. He

trusted Russ to watch his back and kept going.

"We're in, go," Mitch said, out of breath. He laid Justine across the seats with trembling hands. He held on to her as the transporter soared to the sky.

Out of danger, Mitch's heart ricocheted, his adrenaline still pumping hard. He opened the cabinet above him and rummaged through the medical bag. He took out a needleless syringe and shot her up with a dosage of painkiller.

When they reached the clouds, Russ put the glider on autopilot. "How badly is she hurt?" he said.

Mitch looked her over from head to toe. "Blood on the side of the temple. No broken bones as far as I could tell. She's resilient. Her body is different than ours, so I think she'll be fine, but Tessa is dead." He couldn't get the image out of his mind.

He didn't mean to sound stone cold and uncaring, but he was used to seeing agents killed during the missions. Mitch couldn't let his emotions get the best of him. He would not break in front of Russ—or anyone for that matter.

"I know. I saw." Russ's shoulders sagged.

Mitch slumped on the seat, stared at the wall, and breathed… and breathed. Another one of them, dead. Another life gone for Novak. Tessa hadn't been with them long, but a life was a life. She'd deserved better. They all deserved better.

"Why was the rebel team there?" Russ asked, breaking the silence, sitting across from him.

Mitch shoved his palms to his face, then let go. "Rhett was told Ava was there."

"She's not, is she?" Russ paled.

"No," Mitch said, stretching his legs. "I gave Zeke the coordinates. Ava found the secret base. Novak has to be behind it.

He sent Rhett's team into an ambush, hoping these creatures would do his job. That's my guess."

"Lydia is on the line," Russ said. "Novak wants an update. What should I tell her?"

Tell her I love her. Mitch realized more with every day how much she meant to him.

"Novak can kiss my ass. That's what you should tell her to tell him," Mitch spat.

Russ sighed. "You've held yourself together all this time. Don't lose control for all of our sakes. Think of Lydia. If you go down, we all go down."

"What do you mean, think of Lydia?" Mitch tugged the belts around Justine to ensure she was strapped in and retook the wheel. They had gotten out of there safely—but barely. He welcomed the reprieve.

Russ flushed when he sank into the passenger seat. "Come on, Mitch. We've been working together for a while; I can recognize a co-mance when I see one."

Mitch snorted. "Co-mance? Never heard of it."

He furrowed his brow. "You know when your coworker becomes a love interest. Coworker romance."

"That's lame." Mitch stared at the fluffy white clouds in front of him.

"But I'm right, aren't I?"

Mitch didn't answer. He felt strange opening up to Russ. Until recently, they had never seen eye to eye on anything. Russ was by the book and Mitch was a free spirit, and Mitch freely admitted he was a prick sometimes.

"Tell Lydia to tell Novak things went as planned. That is all he needs to know."

Mitch wanted to hear her voice, but he was afraid he might get a bit emotional. He checked the hologram map and leaned back, allowing the autopilot take control.

He didn't want to think of Tessa, or the creatures, or Rhett, or anyone else. But he did, all the way back to their base.

CHAPTER FIFTEEN – THE GARDEN

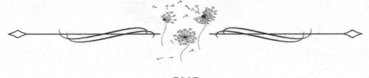

AVA

My palms twitched after I had breakfast the next morning. It happened every time I ate, but the side effects were shorter. Again, I kept this from Novak.

The reaction caused no pain. It had freaked me out when it happened the first time, but now I spent half my time wondering why this was happening to me. It could be a reaction to the serum meant to sap my powers. Or was maybe my body adapting.

My heart jolted when the door opened. I slid off my bed, expecting Novak or Gene, but I was quite surprised by my visitor, who wore an ISAN gray training outfit.

"Payton? What are you doing here?" I didn't know whether to hug him or kill him.

He lowered his amber eyes to my hands and my feet, then up to my face.

"I'm not going to hurt you." I crossed my arms.

Not yet at least.

"I came to take you to shower, then to see your mother."

At those words, I wanted to kill him.

"You knew she was alive all this time?" My angry voice bounced off the walls. I took a step toward him with my fists rounded, and he retreated a step.

"No, Ava." He placed out a hand. "I swear I didn't know she

was your mother until today. Mr. Novak never told me."

Only because he looked genuinely sorry did I yield.

Calm down, Ava. Get him on your side. Payton had been on my team. He had watched my back as many times as I had his.

"Fine. I believe you," I said in a softer tone.

He eased and gestured to the wall that had closed. "Follow me. Please don't try anything or I'll have to push this button." He showed the same gadget Gene had used on me.

Recalling the pain, I decided to comply and stay quiet.

"Listen very carefully," he said when we exited the room and turned right.

Cool air and sterile scent accosted me. The corridor was wider and brighter than I remembered. His strained voice was a cue he needed to tell me something, something we'd used on missions together. He planned to give me information indirectly.

I gave a curt nod, my bare feet cold on the tile floor. "How long have I... I mean, you been here?"

"Recently." He flashed three fingers by his side then curled them inward.

That meant three days had passed.

"Where are you taking me?" I asked and tugged and yanked Helix inside me.

The map of this facility flickered and died before I could grasp the layout. I couldn't even do that a day ago, so it felt like a triumph. I had to keep trying.

"You forget so easily. I'm taking you to bathe. There's nothing there except for the showers and toilet. So don't bother looking for mirrors. You can't see yourself. They're just walls."

They wouldn't have mirrors since they might be broken and used as weapons. But the walls... he was telling me there might be a spy on the other side.

"Fine." I spoke bitterly to keep up the pretense and kept a steady pace with him down the gray hallway, which reminded me of the ISAN facility I had once called home.

"We're going to turn right. Don't think you can escape. I have this, remember?" He held up the gadget again.

Left equals escape. I mentally noted that.

"We're down at the basement level, so don't try anything." He poked my biceps three times.

Three. Three levels?

We banked right to another hallway and stopped.

Payton jerked a chin at an arched entryway. "This is it. There are clothes on the counter to change into. I'll wait for you out here."

The small bathroom had four stalls and two showers. I stripped off my pj's and stood under the warm water. After I washed up, I put on the clothes laid out for me. Loose, gray cotton pants and a button-up shirt.

I slipped my toes into a pair of tennis shoes—soft and fluffy. The most comfortable shoes I'd ever worn. If I weren't in prison, I would actually love what I was wearing.

"Are you ready to see your mom?" Payton asked when I came out.

"I—it's been ages." My voice cracked as I walked beside him at a slower pace. It was unlike me to get emotional with a member of my team, so I was a bit surprised how quickly I opened up to him. "I thought she was dead and now I'm told she's not. She's been here all this time. Novak took five years from me and my mother. He had no right."

Payton couldn't meet my gaze as he escorted me down another

hallway.

"Why are you here?" I asked. "Shouldn't you be with your team? Last I heard—or should I say last I saw—you were the lead."

Payton cleared his throat, hands behind his back. We rounded another corner and stopped in front of a sliding door. "Novak sends me here often. I can tell you this because Novak said I could. I can tell if you're telling me a truth or a lie. It has something to do with your body temperature, which I'm able to gauge. Also, I can soothe a person's anger. Sadness. Even make someone happy."

"You can control our emotions?" I parted my lips. I knew about the first, but not the second. "Have you... have you ever—"

"Never," he said with conviction. "I never manipulated anyone's emotions in ISAN. The first power is my strongest. I'm still perfecting the second."

"Really?" I arched my eyebrows.

"I swear it. Although there were times when I wanted to with Justine, I didn't."

"Well, I have to give you credit, because I would have." I snorted, and then cut it short, reminding myself where I was.

He gave me a tight-lipped smile. Novak couldn't see us interacting like friends.

"There's something I need to tell you about your mom," he went on. "She's not stable. Most of the time, she's in a world by herself. She doesn't seem to distinguish reality and fiction. There were a few times she tried to hurt herself, and that's the reason I'm here."

I was suddenly grateful for his gift.

"Mr. Novak, your father." He hesitated when I rolled my eyes. "I found out today. Sorry." He lifted his gaze to the upper corner where I assumed a tiny camera was mounted. "Anyway, I'm told to go in with you. You're a new face to your mom. I mean, you're not, but she… You're grown up. She might not recognize you."

A part of me wanted to cry. Mom hadn't become like this on her own. Her husband, who had vowed to love her and protect her with his life, had done this. Payton placed his hand on the square scanner and the door slid open. I inhaled a deep breath and entered.

My eyes were drawn first to the broad, domed ceiling. The painting of the sun and the sky looked so real. No, not a painting, but a hologram image, complete with white puffy clouds. It reminded me of the garden in the West region. In fact, the layout was the same.

Plumes of flowers colored the ground. The smells of roses and honeysuckle hit me in tender spots, of my mother's garden. Off to the left were vegetables—carrots, squash, and tomatoes. To the right were more flowers—lilies, daffodils, carnations, sunflowers, and even a section of dandelions. A narrow path divided the two halves.

I searched for my mother among the flower beds.

"There she is." Payton pointed to the far back by the rose bushes and walked toward her.

My pulse thundering, I tiptoed beside Payton so as not to spook her. When I stood in front of a crouched woman, I nearly fell to my knees.

"Hello. You have a visitor." My voice squeaked out of me.

The woman stood, but kept her eyes on her feet.

I shuddered a blissful breath in recognition, my heart slamming into my ribcage. Not a hologram. Real. She was real. I bit my tongue to suppress a scream.

Oh, Mom. You're alive. I see you. I've missed you so much.

She wore a beige sunhat, like she always had to keep the sun from her face. But there was no sun here. Her attire was simple— loose khaki pants and a baggy T-shirt. What she'd worn at home when she worked in her garden. Her skin was paler without exposure to real sunlight.

"Hi. I'm Ava," I said. Tears pooled in my eyes and I swiped them away before they could fall.

I hated talking to her if she were a child with my voice high-pitched and sweet, but I didn't know how else to do this. I couldn't flat-out tell her I was her daughter. A shock to her system could be traumatic. Everything Payton had told me made me tread carefully.

Payton patted my elbow, encouraging me to continue.

"You have a lovely garden," I said.

Mom ever so slowly raised her eyes, locked them on mine, and took off one glove.

I went weak at the knees as I sucked in another breath. It took every ounce of my will not to break apart, to embrace her. Her tender beautiful eyes like the moon, her sharp nose, her perfect mouth, her porcelain face, exactly how I remembered. Though her hair was short like mine and I was now as tall as her.

For her to stand in front of me and not recognize me utterly killed me.

Mom, it's me Ava. Your daughter. Why don't you recognize me?

"Hello there." Her gaze extended over me, as if she spoke to someone behind me. "My garden is lovely. Yes. It is. Would you like to see? Come. Come."

I followed her down a path, Payton beside me. We passed between the tall pink rose bushes. She squatted at the far back corner, picked something up, and showed it to us.

"Dandelion." She placed it in front of my face. "People don't

113

like them, but I think they're pretty." Her voice dropped lower. "They are the strongest flower. So resilient, as we all must be. Ava, be resilient. Always be resilient."

I sucked in a breath. *Did* she recognize me? I thought she might have, but my hope faltered just as fast. She clearly remembered having a daughter, or at least knew the name.

Mom held up the dandelion still pinched between her thumb and forefinger. She placed it front of an imaginary person and said, "Ava. Blow and make a wish."

The words I recalled so clearly shattered my heart. My eyes burned, throat parched.

"That's a good girl," she continued, and then she yanked a red rose. "Red roses symbolize love." She rubbed the petals against her lips. "So soft. I love roses. I love Ava. I love Victor." She paused and squinted as if recalling something. "No, not Victor. Victor tells lies. Lies. Lies. Lies. All lies." She chanted *lies* as she plucked out the petals and kicked at the daffodils, one flower after the other. Each word getting louder and more indignant.

I backed away, trampling on dirt and carnations as my body trembled. I didn't know what to do.

Payton rushed to her from behind. He placed his hand over her forehead, the other arm wrapped around her. Not even a second later, Mom dropped her hands. Payton backed away. Mom lowered herself to the bed of sunflowers.

I placed a hand to my mouth and released a long relief sigh. The last thing I wanted was her out of control and hurting herself. But Payton helped Mom so fast. I was grateful.

"I'm sorry you had to see that," he said. "This is why I was told to come. Your fa... I mean Novak has me spend time with her. To monitor her progress. She had never said your name until recently.

114

I think she's starting to recall the memories Novak erased."

"He what?" My blood boiled.

Payton flinched and hiked his eyes to the fake sun. "I think I'm going to get questioned for that slip."

Maybe a slap on the wrist. I wondered if he had done it purposefully. He wasn't careless like he claimed to be.

"Come. Come. Come to see the vegetables." Mom stood and waved a hand as if nothing had happened.

As we tailed her to the other side, passing the lilies, I surveyed the perimeter. One way in and one way out.

"Does she have her own room?" I added as we passed a small water fountain.

"Sorry. I can't disclose that information." Payton blinked once.

First floor? Or did he mean the basement. Or maybe he meant nothing at all. Getting information was beyond frustrating.

"Look. Look." Mother pulled out two carrots and used her shirt to wipe off the remaining dirt. She handed Payton one, but when she placed the second in my hand, she gripped it tightly.

Either she didn't know her strength or she was trying to tell me something.

"Eat now, children." Mom clapped. "Carrots are good for you. Good for your skin."

Her words tugged a heartstring. Something she used to say to me when I was little to get me to eat them.

Payton crunched down on the carrot. "Novak is your father, then Justine is—"

"Don't say it." I took a bite and pointed at him. When he looked away in apology, I said, "Please don't remind me ever again, and please keep it between us. People will eventually find out, but I'd rather delay it as long as possible."

"Sure. I'll never tell."

I heard the honesty in his tone. I wished we weren't on opposite teams.

Mother knelt on the ground and shuffled dirt with a small pitchfork.

A ding chimed on Payton's chip. "Sorry, Ava, but it's time for me to take you back."

"This is too short." Rage burst out of me. "I want more time with my mother. I know you're listening. You owe me for what you took from me."

Another chime from Payton's chip. "Ava. You need to calm down."

"Or you'll what? Make me?" I didn't mean to explode on Payton, but he was Novak's messenger.

"Ava, please. Don't make me do this?" Payton's plea softened me, if only for a second.

I put my face to his. "Don't make you do what? You have a choice. I suggest you choose wisely before you end up dead like Novak will be soon."

I immediately regretted my words. Novak would punish me. No, not me. Someone I cared about.

"Now, now, children. Don't fight." Mom rose and wrapped her arms around me and patted my back like she had when I was a little girl.

Oh, God. I nearly collapsed in her arms. *Oh, Mom.* The warmth of her, the smell of garden in her hair, everything I lost came crashing in on me. *Do not cry.*

I bit my tongue to keep from sobbing. The ache in my mouth reminded me the pain I would feel if I didn't cooperate. Payton held the gadget and kept his distance.

"Fine. I'll leave," I said when Mom released herself from me and lowered to the dirt.

"Look at this tomato. So red and plump." Mom tossed one over Payton's head, forcing him to chase it. Then she yanked me down with her so hard I nearly tipped over. "Look. Beautiful. Aren't they?"

I shouldn't be annoyed at her. I should be grateful she was alive, but the fact that she couldn't recognize me had me exasperated.

When she twisted her wrist, I saw two tiny scribbled words on her skin. Not tattoos. She had written it herself, or someone had.

What did it say? I had to know, but it wasn't a good idea to grab her arm at our first meeting. But I read the one word she had carefully marked on the dirt with a carrot. That was not a coincidence, nor a mistake.

Help.

CHAPTER SIXTEEN – UNWELCOME VISITORS

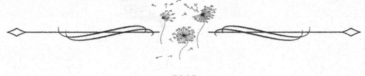

AVA

Hope was not all lost. My mother was not lost. Mother had written "Help" in the dirt and even erased the evidence. Someone whose mind was not all there wouldn't do that.

I had to keep seeing her. I had thought Payton was my key out; perhaps with both of their knowledge of this place, the three of us had a chance.

Then what?

I had to work on getting a glider. *Payton.* Payton could do it. We could plan and escape when Novak visited other ISAN sites.

I pushed off the mattress when the door whooshed. My shoes thudded on the tile floor. Novak and Gene entered and stood an arm's distance from me; two evil-minded souls in the small space seemed too much to bear. Suffocating. And intimidating.

Novak and Gene were dressed alike in formfitted suits. Novak had dyed his hair to the original brown and had taken out his contact lenses to reveal gray eyes.

"How was your meeting with your mother?" Novak asked. "I know it wasn't the reunion you expected but—"

"You poisoned her." I poked Novak and, surprisingly, he didn't stop me, so I pushed again. "You poisoned her body. You poisoned her mind."

Gene gripped my wrists. "Stop. You don't understand. Dad is

trying to fix her."

I yanked my arms away. "Fix? There was nothing to fix. She was happy. We were happy without you." I jabbed Novak again, then pointed at Gene. "And you should have stayed dead to me."

Gene shook his head, frowning. "You don't mean that."

"I mean it with every breath I take." I pounded my chest once, hitting a button at the same time. "You two should just be together and go rot in hell. You deserve each other."

A muscle twitched in Novak's neck, his face turning red. "I'm going to pretend this conversation never happened and you weren't disrespectful. I understand seeing your mother in that condition was a shock and caused you to react irrationally. As your brother was trying to tell you, there are two reasons why I took your mother away from you. First, she wasn't mentally sound. While you rushed out after your squabble, she tried to commit suicide."

"Liar," I spat.

"She tried, but I intervened. Your mother had contemplated it before, but hadn't followed through with action. That day she did."

"Wait." I shuffled backward to my bed. "How did you know I left or what she did? How could you have possibly known?" It hit me. "Oh. My. God. You watched us? There were cameras in our house? You monitored... us." Everything clicked in place. "She told me she didn't have pictures of us. She never would talk about you. I thought it was too painful." I narrowed my blazing gaze at him. "You're a sick man."

Gene slapped my face and I jerked to the left, my cheek stinging.

"Don't you dare call our father that," he snarled and stood beside Novak again.

I scoffed and wiped the metallic-tasting smudge of blood on my lip. "Like father, like son. You must be big and tough to strike an unarmed woman."

Gene reached for me to strike again, but Novak grabbed his wrist.

"Enough. I didn't come here to upset you, Ava. I came to explain why your mother is the way she is. It must have been a shock to see her like that."

I raised my chin. No one was going to lessen my dignity, especially not the people in front of me. "Your favorite, Payton, already explained it to me."

Gene stiffened and scowled.

Ah… and there it was. His weakness. My older brother was jealous of Payton. Why wouldn't he be? Novak adored Payton. I'd just added one more playing card to my deck.

I crossed my arms. "Why didn't you have Gene take me to see Mom? She would have loved to see her children together. Oh, wait, is it because Gene doesn't have the power to pacify her when she gets out of control? Or do you favor Payton more? Payton is like a son to you, right? I mean, he does spend a lot of time with you. Everyone in ISAN wondered about that."

Novak scrutinized me with a glare. He knew the game I played. His smirk told me he would volley back.

"It is true Payton has a special gift, but he is no son of mine." He patted Gene's back. "My son, my only son, has proven himself to be worthy in many ways. No one is powerful as him… or you. My two proudest joys and accomplishments."

Gene's grin and gleaming eyes made my stomach fill with acid.

"What about Justine?" I said. "Does she know I'm her half sister and Gene is her half brother? Does Gene know?"

120

"Of course I do." Gene shifted awkwardly, his dress shoes tapping on the floor.

I hate that sound.

Gene glanced at Novak and continued, "Justine isn't the only half sibling."

I think I stopped breathing. "What did you say?"

"It's none of your concern right now, no concern of either of you." Novak frowned at Gene. "But when I feel you're ready, Ava, I will show you."

"Show me what?" I rounded fists at my sides.

Gene held up the coin-sized metal gadget and I went rigid.

"Don't make me hurt you again, sis." He clenched his jaw. "Stand your ground."

"Don't give me an ISAN bullshit order." I pressed, anger propelling me forward as Gene stepped back.

"I'll do it." He held it in front of me. "You'll feel a lot of pain."

I took another step toward him and another as something hot bubbled inside me. "I felt a lot of pain the second I found out you were my brother. It's like being told the devil shares your blood. Do you even know what that feels like? Do you have any feelings at all?"

Gene's chest rose and fell rapidly, his body trembling in rage. "She's not fixable. We should put her down."

"Put me down?" I gripped the classy lapels of his suit and shoved him to the wall.

I only used half my strength, but even then, I was surprised at what I had just done. Helix? Impossible. The food and the drink should have suppressed it.

Turning, I fixed Novak with a deadly stare. "You. You ruined my life. You're the one who needs to be put down."

Novak flicked lint off his jacket sleeve as if I hadn't threatened him. Calm and collected. I didn't know how he lived with what he had done. But when he set his eyes on me, he looked scared.

"Don't bother trying to regain your natural Helix. I have figured out how to suppress it through sonic vibration. But don't worry, the serum is also in your food, which you know by now. I had to be careful and cover all bases, especially with you. Don't want to punish your mother for your insubordination."

At those words, I steadied my erratic breaths. What I was about to do next wasn't to punish my mother, it was to punish me for a very good reason.

"I don't think Mom will mind as long as I hurt you." I rushed toward Novak, purposely lessening my speed.

Before contact, I went stiff and dropped to my knees, hunched over and shaking violently as electricity coursed through me. The pain. Oh the pain, like thousands of knives stabbing me at once.

I screamed, but no sound escaped.

"For the record." Gene appeared in front of me, holding out the coin gadget. "Just so we're clear on this. When Father is done with you, you will be submissive. You will be fixed. You will be just like me."

"Enough, Gene. Release her." Novak stiffened, as if he were the one in pain.

Novak's snappish, urgent voice made Gene flinch, and he put his head down like a child who had been scolded. "Yes, of course. I'm hurting my sister without your permission."

Novak relaxed the tight lines on his face, but something cold and spoiled replaced it. Inside that deranged heart and mind, he held a soft spot for me.

They didn't know what I was doing. They didn't see my fingers flexing, the movement so small that they didn't notice.

When Gene clicked the gadget, I thumped hard to the ground with an oomph, every inch of me weak and unable to move.

"That should teach her a lesson."

Gene's satisfaction repulsed me, and I used that anger to give me one last burst of strength to absorb the energy petering away. I managed to peer up at Novak, my neck wobbling. I'd hoped he would show me something. Instead, his lips were straight, his eyes as icy as ever.

Not the Novak who had looked at me tenderly just minutes ago, but the Novak I recalled from ISAN.

CHAPTER SEVENTEEN – ISAN EAST COMPOUND

MITCH

"**M**eet me at the medical station," Mitch said frantically to Lydia through his chip as Russ followed him.

Mitch carried Justine in his arms and rushed down ISAN halls. He placed her on the Dr. Machine hub and slapped the button. The top sealed, then the red and blue laser lights crisscrossed her body to diagnose her wounds.

Mitch slumped on a chair, and Russ did the same beside him.

Lydia came rushing in, her chest heaving. When she saw Mitch, her eyes gleamed and she released a long, relieved sigh.

"You're okay. Russ is okay. Who's in there?" She marched over and gasped. "What happened? Where's Tessa? Where's Nina and Cora?" Her eyes widened in horror.

Mitch raked his hair back and began the story from when they had been attacked by the creatures while searching for the rebels, altering where necessary in case cameras had been installed at the medical room without his knowledge.

Lydia dropped to the seat beside Mitch, her hand over her mouth, her eyes glistening. She'd had a soft spot for Tessa from the start. Mitch hadn't understood at first, but the more he got to know Tessa, the more he had.

Lydia had told Mitch that Tessa reminded Lydia of herself, from her tall frame to her shy demeanor. Tessa had never been outspoken, but she focused on her task, determined and confident.

"It was a quick death for Tessa." Mitch pinched the bridge of his nose, pressing harder when he continued with the next lie. "Nina and Cora never made it back to the ship. I don't know what happened to them. They either got kidnapped by the rebels or the creatures got to them."

Though Lydia knew the truth, he had to be careful of what he said.

Lydia shuddered a breath and lowered her hands to her lap. "That's horrible. What did these creatures look like?"

Mitch showed her the footage Russ had recorded.

Lydia backed away in terror. "We have to inform Mr. Novak. Those monsters need to be exterminated."

"Justine doesn't have a team now." Russ walked over to the hub and stared at Justine.

"No, she doesn't," Lydia said. "But it doesn't matter."

The stern undercurrent in her voice indicated she had more to tell them.

"What is it?" Mitch met her gaze and curled his fingers on his knees because he itched to touch her.

Later. Later they would have their time.

"Justine has been assigned to another territory, but it didn't say where. Top secret." Her voice dropped down to a whisper as she murmured, "I don't have a good feeling about this."

Novak wouldn't kill his own flesh and blood, would he? Yes, he would. The sick bastard had done plenty of crazy shit. Mitch suddenly felt protective of Justine. Even though she'd acted like a spoiled brat since the day he had met her, he felt sorry for her. It couldn't have been easy having to live up to his expectations, all the while rated second to Ava. Perhaps her outbursts were to get

Novak's attention.

Novak sometimes acted as though Justine didn't exist. It was always about Ava. Mitch would have been jealous if his father had been always about Rhett. At least his father had treated them equally.

Mitch walked to the hub and glanced at the status on the screen when it beeped. "Lydia, please inform Novak about Justine's condition. Perhaps that will buy her some time."

He wondered why he'd said it. Once Novak had made up his mind, there was no room for negotiation.

The monitor displayed a couple of broken ribs and a fractured arm, plus a concussion. Better than he'd hoped for. No internal bleeding. For someone with such a strong, almost indestructible body to have such wounds, she must have hit the cement with great force.

The screen flashed with instructions. Press green to fix and red to do nothing. Mitch pressed green and watched the laser lights beam brightly as they worked magic on her.

"Actually, she'll be transported as soon as she's recovered," Lydia said, stepping beside Mitch and peering down at Justine.

Mitch's heart tugged. Occasionally, agents would get transferred, and at times he had wished Justine would be too, but she had grown on him.

"Lydia, have you heard from Janine yet?" Mitch whispered.

"No." Lydia looked at her TAB.

Russ hiked up his eyebrows, suspicion warranted.

A chime ringing came from Lydia's chip. "I have something to take care of. Talk to you both later." She gave a curt nod and sauntered out.

Russ inclined his head toward the hub and leaned closer to

Mitch. "You think Novak is planning to shut down this site?"

"I don't know," Mitch said, watching the laser lights zigzag up and down Justine's body.

Justine's eyes began to flutter and then opened in terror. When she set them on Russ and Mitch, though, she eased.

"Hey… You're fine." Mitch offered a warm grin. "You're going to be just fine."

"Tessa," she muttered, her voice hoarse.

Mitch shook his head and tried not to allow his own emotions get the best of him. It had been one mind-blowing day.

Two tears streaked down her cheeks when Justine closed her eyes. That emotion coming from someone who he'd always thought was so coldhearted gave him hope they could get her on their side, if she could get rid of her daddy fetish.

Novak's daughter might be his downfall.

"Justine," Mitch said with a stern voice. "You're a good leader. You have proven it to me. A good leader does what is best for the team. A good leader does what is right, even if someone else tells her to do the opposite. Do you understand what I'm saying?"

"Yes. But why are you saying it?"

"Because you're being transferred."

Her eyes rounded, flashing with hurt. "Why?"

"I don't know," he said. "You'll have to talk to Mr. Novak."

Justine craned her neck to see through the hub to the monitors, and more tears streamed down her face. Mitch wished he had more comforting words for her, but his chip chimed.

The message from Lydia read: *We need to get ready for another mission. Something to do with ANS. And another assassination.*

Great. One thing after another. But he paled when he read who they had to terminate.

Mitch sighed with exaggeration. "You've got to be kidding me. Of all the people."

"Who?" Russ asked.

"Councilor Chang."

CHAPTER EIGHTEEN – MAYDAY

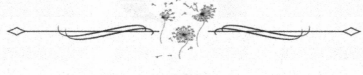

ZEN

Zen tried calling Rhett but there was no response, and he couldn't pull up any messages from his chip or from the glider. Worse, he had no idea where he was. He had followed the given coordinates, but this place was death.

The meteors had completely demolished this city and there had been no attempt to rebuild it. Other cities that had been ruined had some standing buildings—unstable, but still standing. Not here. A giant's fist had crushed it to the dirt.

Even though Zen's gut told him to leave, if Rhett and his team were down there he had to try. They were expecting him.

"What is this place?" Frank's worried voice did nothing to comfort him.

"We'll find out." Zen banked left and guided their transport low enough to survey what was below, not intending to park just yet.

Nothing. Only the skeletons of the crumbled city.

"Are you sure you got the right coordinates?" Frank leaned closer to the dashboard, searching through the thickening fog.

Zen rubbed at his arms, goose bumps forming. He shivered and wasn't sure if it was from the change of weather. Mist formed on the window. Light at first, then heavier.

"Of all the things, does it have to rain?" Zen cursed under his breath.

"It could be a lot worse." Frank clenched his jaw, sounding irate. "Should Rhett be looking out for us? They're nowhere to be found."

"They might already be inside." Zen's tone spiked. "I told them to wait for backup."

"Yeah, well, you know how that group is."

"Sounds a lot like my daughter. I'm going to go back to the original coordinates. We must be missing something."

As Zen spun the glider around, his mind drifted to the past.

Zen was working at the North ISAN laboratory when a hologram of his wife popped over his desk. His wife, Karen, was sitting on their bed, propped up by pillows. Her red hair was tied back and her blue eyes were dark with anger.

"When are you coming home?" Karen frowned.

Zen meant to sound patient, but his voice came out clipped. "I'm not done. I need a couple more hours."

"Couple more hours?" She rubbed her eyes. "It'll be midnight. Cleo has been asking for you."

All the employees had gone home and Zen had decided to stay, but minutes had turned to hours. His obsession had gone for weeks. This job would kill him or ruin his marriage.

Karen only knew the surface of his job description. She didn't know he had been working long hours for Cleo. Zen worried how she might react if she found out their daughter had special powers.

Zen also wanted to get a special serum perfected before Victor Hunt, Ava's father, perfected his. Victor had been working on Helix serum called HelixB76, which gave superpowers to any male or female with a special DNA marker. Zen was experimenting with CHB19—Counter Helix Batch 19—to counteract Helix serum.

Zen took a gulp of his cold, bitter coffee and said the words he would regret. "Don't use our daughter to get me home."

Karen flinched at his spiteful tone, then her shock turned into a scowl. "Don't bother coming home."

The line went dead.

Zen released a tired sigh and rubbed his sleepy eyes. Karen being mad at him didn't faze him. He should call her back to apologize, but he let it go. Nothing was more important than perfecting CHB19.

Cleo had first shown her powers at age four, and Zen had made her promise never to do it again. He'd even told her he would spank her if she did. His poor little girl had been so scared, she'd avoided him the rest of the day. But he had to do what was in her best interest. She was his only child. She was his life.

Desperate, Zen pulled out HelixB76 and CHB19 from his desk top drawer—needleless shots given through volatile compressed gas that passed through the permeable layers of the skin. He inserted HelixB76 on his arm and left CHB19 next to his TAB. And waited.

Dr. Hunt hadn't perfected the Helix serum. It had been too aggressive, but Zen didn't care. For his child, he would risk his life.

A rush of warmth spread through his chest, but was replaced by a cold, tingling sensation. His muscles tightened and somehow his insides were stitching themselves anew. He felt like he could jump off a cliff and fly.

The softest sound of the lab machine's hum resonated louder in his ear. The scent of stale, cold coffee stung his nostrils and he could taste its bitterness as though he had drunk it.

The red, blue, and green from his lab screen were vibrant. When he examined his hands, he saw a faint outline of veins, muscles, and bones. Zen sucked in a breath and pushed back in his chair. He laughed at this phenomenal feeling.

He wanted to see what he could do, so he picked up his heavy chair with one hand, something he wouldn't have been able to do without the serum. He let go of the chair and effortlessly jumped up onto his desk. When he leaped off, he misjudged his strength and collided with the wall. To his surprise, he made a dent, and he felt no pain.

Remarkable. He felt amazing.

Suddenly the room spun. Blood rushed to his head, his heart hammering. The muscles in his arms twitched, his vision unclear. Overwhelming rage came forth too fast, an aggressive madness taking over.

His hands trembled, his body shook. He rammed his head into the wall, over and over, blood coating his forehead and dotting the white polished floor. The need to hurt something or someone controlled him. He stormed to the nearest desk and slammed his fist in the middle, breaking it in half.

This strength—incredible.

Stumbling back, he collided with something. The window. Glass splintered like long spider legs. For the hell of it, he jabbed his elbow into the middle of the original point of the crack, and glass rained down, a few shards cutting him in the fall.

No throbbing. No slicing ache. He felt nothing. Just pure rage to dominate and hurt.

Stop! I shouldn't be doing this. The wrath shouldn't be the source of his power. The walls spun, the earth tilted. Darkness flashed across his eyes, but he clung to the light.

He had to get the counter serum. How could he have done this to himself? What if CHB19 didn't work?

Almost at the brink of losing his mind, he stumbled with pure will to his desk and inserted the CHB19 in his arm. Within seconds, his rage deflated and he slumped on his chair. He was exhausted but in control. But the lab was a mess—the desk broken in half, shattered glass door, the dent in the wall. Zen had to come up with a good explanation

No... ISAN wouldn't care.

ISAN would be proud of the mess and the items he had destroyed. Zen had just perfected CH. CHB19 no more. CHB20 now.

Zen left a message for Dr. Hunt, assuming he was already asleep. Seconds later, his chip chimed and Dr. Hunt's face appeared. His gray eyes gleamed against the backdrop lighting. Walls and monitors like his own came into focus behind him.

"I'm in my lab, Zen. What's this about CH? Tell me what happened."

Zen described the sequence of events from when he'd taken the serum and left out no details.

"This is great news." Dr. Hunt smiled. "Your accomplishment will help me push forward with mine. Good job. We should meet up and celebrate."

Dr. Hunt's approval meant everything to Zen. That man was one of the greatest scientists of their time. Perhaps experimenting on himself hadn't been a misstep after all. Zen had gotten Dr. Hunt's attention. Together they could make history.

"Zen." Frank gripped Zen's arm, snapping him out of the past.

The wind had picked up and a tornado was approaching. Not one big enough to bring them down, but it would take them on a violent ride if they got caught in the center.

Zen guided the aircraft to the side, and saw something—a dome-shape.

"What is that?" Frank said. "Do you see it, Zen?"

Instead of going near it, Zen backed away. He didn't have a good feeling about it.

"Hey, Zen. Something is lifting from the ground. There's another one. It looks like—"

A red laser beam from a hidden arsenal punctured through the dirt and hit their glider smack in the front. The front shield shattered, shards raining all around. Zen tried to focus, but he was in too much shock.

Their aircraft plummeted. Down, down, faster and faster.

Zen reached for the mic to call for help, but he couldn't stretch his arm. Still, he managed to slam the emergency button.

"Mayday. Mayday. This is Zen. Frank and I are at the meeting point. We've been hit. We're going down."

"I'm trying to pull up. It's not working." Frank groaned.

"Hold tight, Frank," Zen hollered over the transporter that screamed with warning beeps.

Their glider whirled like a cyclone as it free fell.

"Eject. Eject!" Frank's desperate command reached Zen's ears, but executing the action became impossible. Everything spun. So dizzy. Zen wanted to vomit.

He had no choice but to succumb to the darkness. Amid the confusion and terror, his last thoughts were of Cleo.

CHAPTER NINETEEN – DISTRESS CALL

RHETT

Reyna escorted Nina and Cora to Jill as soon as Rhett's team landed at the mountain base. After Zeke took off for the black market, Rhett headed to his room to get more supplies. The rest of his team waited at their glider.

Rhett halted. Momo and Coco stood in front of his door.

Momo frowned. "Why are you—"

"Come inside. We'll talk in there." Rhett didn't have time to chat, but he didn't want to brush them off.

"Wow. You have a cool room." Momo glanced about and settled by the table near the back wall with Coco. "Ours is tight. Not that I'm complaining. And what are those?" She pointed at several old monitors and computer screens.

"Never mind those," Rhett said.

He grabbed his backpack from under his cot and shoved medical supplies from the cabinet above him into it. He already had some in the glider, but he wanted more. Since he had to wait for Reyna, he might as well do something.

He opened another cabinet above the cot and pulled out a T-shirt and his cap, the black cap Ava had worn. Her scent still lingered on the fabric. Not long ago, he had kidnapped Ava and brought her to this mountain base. Not too long ago she'd slept in this room. Things had changed so much, too fast.

"Rhett? You okay?" Coco's sweet, concerned voice brought him out of his reverie.

"I think he loves that hat?" Momo giggled.

Rhett had held the cap and his T-shirt like he would cradle a baby. He looked ridiculous.

"Hey, I need to change." Rhett twirled his finger. "Turn around."

"Oh." Momo stiffened, then relaxed with a smirk. "Go right ahead. It's not like you're taking off your pants. I've seen a boy's chest before."

"I'm not a boy. Suit yourself." Rhett gave them his back and changed his old T-shirt for the new one and put on the cap. When he turned back around, the girls' cheeks flushed hot red.

Momo inclined her head. "You're definitely not a boy. You've got lots of muscles."

Rhett rolled his eyes playfully.

Momo leaned into her hip. "You know in six years, I'll be like your age, and the difference in years won't matter. So what I'm saying is, in case things don't work out with Ava, you've got me."

"What's wrong with you?" Coco smacked Momo's arm.

Momo bumped into the table and shrugged. "What?"

Coco rubbed her temple and avoided Rhett's eyes. "Um… what did you need to talk to us about?"

Rhett grabbed a towel from adjacent cabinet and rushed to the sink to wash his hands.

"You have a sink in here?" Momo asked.

Ava had asked the same question. Momo's and Coco's faces appeared behind him in the mirror. When he turned, he almost smacked into the girls.

"Sit over there." He pointed to the cot. "You don't have to be my shadows."

"But you said let's talk." Momo sounded upset and stomped to the cot with Coco.

Rhett shouldn't take his frustration out on the kids. Multitasking and rushing to get going to Ava wasn't working out well.

"Yeah. Sorry." Rhett washed his hands, readjusted his cap, and walked to the long cabinet by the door. "When you were in ISAN, did you hear anything about a secret base? Try to think. Anything that relates to a location or a place."

Coco chewed on her bottom lip and peered up to the ceiling. She opened her mouth like she was going to say something but then shook her head.

A crease formed on Momo's forehead. "You're worried about Ava, aren't you? You couldn't find her."

Coco fluttered her eyelashes, her hands on the mattress. "We're worried about her too. We want to help."

"Thank you, but not now." Rhett withdrew cases of bullets from the cabinet and shoved them inside the backpack. "I might have to count on you soon so get—"

Alarms blared.

"We have incoming." Nick's voice echoed into the loud speaker. "Everyone to your posts."

Timing couldn't have been worse. Rhett prayed someone had accidently tripped the alarm. But from how today was going, he didn't think so.

"Girls, listen carefully." Rhett said. "You need to go to your positions." He holstered his gun and Taser when they didn't move. "Go to your team. Now. I'll be right behind you."

"Okay." Momo gave him a curt nod, her expression serious as

she tugged Coco out the door.

"Rhett." Oz almost ran into him as Rhett stepped out. "Did you hear?"

Footsteps shuffled, his peers running to their posts.

"Yeah," Rhett said. "How many gliders? Are they close? Walk with me to the control room."

"Three. They're circling like they're looking for something, but they haven't landed yet."

Rhett sprinted up two flights of stairs, forgoing the elevator, and pushed through the door. "Is this the best footage?" Rhett leaned closer to look at the aircraft on the old-fashioned monitor.

He wished they had high-tech equipment and drones to detect aerial movement. The gliders looked ordinary—not special, but bigger. Big enough to fit a dozen people at least.

"Yes," one of the men said. "They keep alternating in and out of visibility. Maybe instead of shooting it down, we wait it out. They might leave."

Rhett's fingers moved along the keyboard. "Perhaps. Can you enlarge the footage?"

"What you see is what you get. We don't have sophisticated equipment. I could try to—"

"Anyone there? This is Vince." Vince's voice boomed through the mic. "Zen gave me the coordinates. If you're there and I've got the right place, please let us in. We've come a long way."

Ozzie grabbed Rhett's arm. "What if it's a trap?"

It was Vince's voice. Or at least it sounded like him.

"What's the code word?" Rhett called through the loud speaker.

"The code is CODE. I repeat the code is CODE."

Rhett sighed with relief and unclenched his jaw. He'd thought they had to place their emergency evacuation in action. He worked so hard to keep everyone safe, to keep this sanctuary off the radar, and he'd been successful so far. However, he had wondered if bringing friends from Hope City would attract attention. But he'd had no choice.

"Steady. We're opening the door," Rhett answered and pushed the green button.

"The code is code?" Ozzie gave Rhett an are-you-kidding-me look.

Rhett shrugged. "I didn't make it up. Come on. We need to be down there."

Two dozen of Rhett's men surrounded the gilders, machine guns pointed. Rhett frowned at Momo and her friends. He supposed he needed to give Momo more specific directions. *Go to your team didn't* mean get your team and meet him at the entrance runway.

Vince came out first with hands raised in surrender, then his men.

"Lower your weapons," Rhett ordered his people. "Vince, it's good to see you. Welcome."

"Rhett. Ozzie. Pretty impressive." Vince glanced about, then nodded at his men to confirm all was fine.

"Is Zen with you?" Rhett asked.

Vince's eyes got bigger. "No. He told me he was going to meet you at the rendezvous. You didn't see him?"

"No. I tried to send him a message." Rhett's nostrils flared and he closed the gap between them. "Where is he?"

Rhett didn't mean to take his frustration out on Vince, but Vince had been with Zen last. And how did he know Vince wasn't a double agent like Mitch, only for the other side?

"Whoa, Rhett. We're on the same team."

Vince didn't sound threatening, but his tank size and the way a muscle on his arm twitched had Rhett thinking otherwise. Ozzie stepped forward when Vince reached for his gun and Vince's men pointed their weapons at Rhett. Then Rhett's team raised theirs.

Vince raised a hand. "This is all a misunderstanding. We're on the same side. Zen asked me to swing by Hope City. He told me to bring the rest of your team here to save you a trip. Well, at least the ones that were healed by Marissa." He jerked a chin to the man by the last glider.

When he opened the door, Jo, Marissa, and the wounded soldiers who had stayed behind exited. They looked fine and Jo lifted a hand to Rhett with a small smile.

Vince didn't hold back his agitation. "If Zen isn't with you, where is he? He went with Frank to find you. He never mentioned a different location."

Rhett waved a dismissive hand to his team, a signal to drop their weapons. He had planned to send a team to Hope City and bring back those who were well enough to travel before he left again. Thankfully Zen had taken care of that.

"Come, follow me," Rhett said. "Watch your steps. The ground isn't leveled. Oz, come with us."

On their way, Rhett gave Nick and Katina the floor to welcome their new guests and get them settled.

"How do we find Zen?" Vince jogged to catch up with Rhett and almost plowed into a kid as he looked around in awe at the rocky walls and the high ceiling.

"I have an idea." Rhett took him to his room, straight to the ancient computer system on the back table.

Vince scrunched his eyebrows in confusion. "What is... How

old is this monitor? This isn't a TAB."

"Don't touch anything. Let me." Ozzie pushed between them and tabbed the keyboards. "Um... what are we looking for exactly?"

Rhett raked his hair back. "A distress signal from Zen."

Ozzie's eyes rounded, horrified, his voice softening. "Okay. I'll do what I can."

Rhett placed a hand on Oz's shoulder. "Just do what you do best, Einstein. No stress."

Ozzie's fingers danced away. "I'm checking if any of ours recently called in." After a heartbeat, he said, "None that I can tell so far."

Vince planted his fists on the table and pitched forward. "This place is how old? You're not going to be able to detect—"

"Wait," Rhett said. "Zen took one of the old gliders. Say he flew over an area that had no reception, he could have called it in. He knows we have the older system. Ozzie, check the recording."

Ozzie's eyes gleamed as he pushed play on the recorder. "It's beeping. It's never beeped before."

Vince leaned closer in anticipation.

A fuzzing noise. A crackling sound. Then Zen's voice.

"Mayday. Mayday. This .... Frank and I... meeting point... been hit. We... down."

The words were broken, and the loud beeping from the aircraft made it difficult to hear, but there was no doubt who it was.

"I can't believe it." Vince backed away with his hands behind his neck.

"See." Ozzie jerked his chin. "Don't talk shit about my shit. Can your high-tech machine do that?"

Vince gave a defeated sigh. "Sometimes simple things are

better. Can you pinpoint where he fell?"

Rhett scrubbed his face in exasperation. He wanted to punch the wall. "Yes. Zen is where I was supposed to be. Ava is there. Zen went to the original coordinates Mitch gave Zeke. My team and I were headed the same place but then we got a message from Zen telling us to go to a different location. We ended up at Pearl Valley. Only it wasn't Zen who sent us the message."

Vince pounded on the back of the chair. "We might be too late for the both of them. I'll come with you."

Rage coursed through Rhett at the time wasted and for being sent to Pearl Valley, then at Vince for coming at the wrong time. He needed to get going.

Then inspiration struck. Vince had some cool riders that would come in handy.

"No," Rhett said. "I need you here, but I do know how you can help. I'd like to borrow a few of your Propellers."

Vince hiked an eyebrow. For a second there, Rhett thought he wouldn't hand them over.

"Fine." Vince sighed. "Be careful with them. How many?"

"Perfect. Thanks. I'll take five."

Some things were worth the wait.

CHAPTER TWENTY – CODE

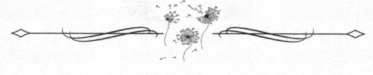

AVA

Another day had passed. A day in which I sat on my bed with my doll and thought of Rhett, my friends, and my mom.

Then Gene had come in. He'd made me angry with all his chatting about how great Novak was.

I'd pounced on him and, of course, he'd electrocuted me with a push of the gadget. I had yet again managed to get to the mattress and recover faster this time. The tingles from the aftershock had worn off and my mind was clear and alert.

The door whooshed open and Novak entered. I scowled and stroked my doll's hair.

"You're looking well," he said as if we were friends. He kept three feet distance from me.

"What do you want? Why are you here?" I said in a flat tone and placed my doll on the pillow.

His facial muscles tightened, like he was biting back anger. I didn't care.

"You will be kind, Ava, or I'll have to—"

"You'll what?" I crossed my arms and narrowed my eyes. "Have me put down like an animal? Is that what you think of me?"

"No. You don't understand," he said calmly, but his cold, cruel eyes pierced mine.

"Oh, I understand. If you truly loved your wife and your

daughter, you'd let them go. Let them live in peace."

He dipped his head and met my gaze. "I can't let you go. This is who I am, and you're all part of the plan. You need to learn how to manifest your gifts. You've only touched the surface."

I slid off the bed. "So it's my fault I'm locked up here? My fault for being born?"

"No. Never your fault," he said. The tenderness in his tone would not fool me. "I'm going to give you a tour. I want to explain what I've been doing. Then maybe you'll change your mind about me. If you behave, I'll even let you visit your friends so you know I'm not the monster you think I am. They have not been harmed."

Friends? Not one, but more?

I decided to play along. I needed to scope out the place. My mental map might not be working, but I could still memorize the outline of this structure.

"Okay," I said with a light tone. "Give me a tour, then."

He smiled. Not a smirk. Not fake. But genuine. It still made me sick to my stomach.

"After you." He gestured to the wall.

"Left or right?" I asked when we stepped out.

"Left."

When Payton escorted me last time, we had made a right. Right was to the bathroom and my mother's garden.

Novak strode beside me, his demeanor casual and light. "While I was trying to perfect HelixB77, I had other plans in line."

We went down the hall, made a right, and then a left.

"This room is where it all began." He pressed his chip and part of the wall opened, revealing a room.

Not a single person inside.

The last time I'd passed here, the room had been filled with people, scientists, and assistants. One woman had been begging to be set free.

"What do you mean?" I asked.

Novak scrubbed at his chin. "It's a place where we took blood samples and gathered necessary data."

I moved closer, examining the space. Eight tables. Each table had two chairs and a metal tray for medical instruments.

"There were people inside when I arrived here," I said. "Men and women alike. Some around Mom's age. Where are they now?"

"I didn't hurt them, Ava, if that's what you're implying." He proceeded forward without me.

I glared, matching his pace. I thought about Rhett's mother and father who had disappeared. Many of my friends who thought their parents were dead might find them here.

Keep asking questions. Find more.

Novak's features tightened. "It's all for the good of science. Our world is dying. People are populating less. Our resources are slim."

"You're wrong. The world is thriving. Yes, we had a major catastrophe, but what almost ruined us gave us more. We have advanced further in technology in a shorter time than scientists thought possible. People are living longer, aging at a slower rate. We need time to rebuild."

"The council makes you see what they want you to see. We lost so many lives during your grandparents' generation, and the number of people is still the same. Every new generation, the number of citizens should double, but people have stopped having children. They are reproducing at replacement levels, if that."

"Why do you care if we don't grow in numbers?"

Novak halted in mid-stride and faced me, looking incredulous.

"You have no concept of war, do you, daughter?"

"I'm not your daughter." *This is not the way to get into his good graces. Try better. You know how to play the game.* "I meant, what do you mean?"

He gave me a cold stare, turned and kept walking. I followed him to the elevator, and he answered when we got inside.

"If we don't have numbers, the chance of being taken over by another country is greater. We won't have the manpower to stop another power from invading. Do you understand now?"

He did make sense, but I would never admit it.

"What does this have to do with ISAN?" I asked. "We have military support."

We zoomed down the next floor and exited.

"Because the number of soldiers we have won't measure up to China, Japan, Korea, Australia, Germany, and many others. We need to act now, and the only way to do that is grow our military forces, especially our soldiers."

"But they had losses too. If we don't have enough volunteer soldiers, then you mean forcing people to become soldiers?"

We went down a short hallway, passing heavily armed security guards. The guards ignored us and allowed Novak to proceed.

He placed his hand on the metal scanner on the wall. When the door opened, he said, "Not exactly what you're thinking. Welcome to my lab."

Had I not despised Novak, I would have given him a compliment. The ceiling was higher than I'd thought possible in the lower level. The high-tech room was filled with sophisticated lab equipment of pods, monitors, large screens set on the walls, and TABs on the tables.

With a wave of his hand, he dismissed workers in lab coats.

They scurried away to another sliding door. The farther down we went, the dimmer the lights became.

"What is that?" I leaned over an egg-like silver pod, half the size of the twin mattress in my holding room. Thick, clear liquid filled the tank.

There were four pods, but only this one hummed.

"Look closer." Novak gestured and touched the pads of his fingers to a small panel attached to it.

A layer of thin material rolled back into its socket to give me a clear view.

"Is that...?" I blinked. Inside some kind of translucent sac was a bundle of... *Oh, my God.* "Is that a baby?"

The infant was curled into a ball with closed eyes.

"She's ready to be born. This pod is my masterpiece. Think of this hub as the embryonic sac. The liquid inside is similar to what we call the amniotic fluid, and the tube connected to the sac mimics the umbilical cord, where the fetus receives all the necessary nutrition, oxygen, and life support. The waste products and carbon dioxide from the fetus are sent back through the same tube."

Novak was a genius. Something I would never tell him. If only he'd used his brain for something good, and not something insane.

Novak weaved around to the other side of the pod, examining the conduits. "I designed it before you were born. There were many failures, but fortunately my diligence and long hours paid off. I called this program CODE. Constructed Ovum Designed Engineering"

"You're crazy," I murmured.

Novak ignored me and stroked the pod like he was stroking the baby. "She's a miracle. This one is a girl and she's ready to be born. This CODE baby had some... complications, the reason she was sent here so I could keep a close eye on her, but she's ready to go back to her brothers and sisters."

Brothers and sisters?

"How many are there?" I trailed behind him to a TAB on the table when he didn't answer me. "Where are they?"

Novak responded to a message on the TAB, then shifted his attention to me. "How many are there? When I feel there are enough, we will stop the program. But we need enough soldiers to first stabilize our nation, and then the world."

My blood ran cold. "How long have you been doing this?"

Novak checked the monitor and headed out the door.

"How many have you created?" I stomped behind him.

Novak spun around, almost bumping into me. "If you were on my side, I would answer all your questions, but you're not, are you? Until then, I don't need to answer. We could be working together. Having my family back is one thing, but having their support is another. Either way, I will finish what I've started and no one is going to stand in my way."

"You can't do this."

I didn't know why I bothered to say anything at all. It was a waste of breath. As if we hadn't just yelled each other, he gestured politely for me to enter another room across from the one we came out from.

"What is this place?" I asked.

Four black leather chairs lined the wall with switch panels. To my left were surgery tables. No special tools, but a machine that looked like an umbrella hovered over them. A glass barrier lined the back wall with four individual prisons.

"This is a small version of my second lab. Again, I've designed all of these tools." Novak stood by one surgery table and pointed to the umbrella-like machine. "I call this machine ROM. Reconstruction of the Mind."

I didn't like the sound of that.

"What are you saying?" My skin crawled as I prepared for the worst.

"Antonio Egas Moniz was a Portuguese neurologist who is credited with inventing the lobotomy in 1935."

"We didn't study him in ISAN history class," I said with mock sarcasm.

Novak ignored my tone and patted the machine. "A lobotomy is an incision into the prefrontal lobe of the brain, formerly used to treat mental illness. Following the operation, responsiveness and self-awareness were reduced, leaving the subject emotionally blunted. When a lobotomy patient is given the Helix serum, it produces an ideal assassin."

I had thought CODE would be the worst, but this...

"The downfall is that they need to be trained," Novak continued. "I have to wait until they're old enough to use weapons. It takes time for CODE children to be ready."

"So, you—you did this to us?"

"No, not to your group anyway. I have a special team that hasn't disappointed me yet. But let me remind you, Ava, if you don't cooperate, you will be next."

Chills ran down to my center. *You will die trying, old man.*

I paused to collect myself. I was in far more danger than I'd thought. A part of me thought I could find a way to escape if I played my cards right, but the threat of a lobotomy made that almost impossible.

I might not get out of here as Ava.

"Anyway ..." He checked his watch and lit a wry smile. He

turned his attention to the black pod-like chairs. "This is where I brought you just before we separated."

I couldn't recall what he had done to me, but he had put me in that chair to erase my memory, and I had seen the proof in the video. That thought slammed me with another wave of chills. I backed away.

Novak lounged on the first chair. "It's actually quite comfortable. You know when you first arrived here, I thought about erasing your memory again, to give you a clean, blank slate. But then it would have been too much work for me and a waste of time. You would have to be basically retrained. So instead, I will use the method that always works."

"You mean you'll threaten me," I said coolly, containing my composure even though I was screaming inside.

"I was going to say coercion, but I suppose it's the same nevertheless."

I gauged closer to the panel. "How do you work that thing?"

If given a chance, I will wipe your memories.

He ducked carefully when he pushed off the chair so as not to hit the apparatus above him. "I've said enough. It's time for you to get ready for dinner and I have a meeting to attend."

CHAPTER TWENTY-ONE – ALARM

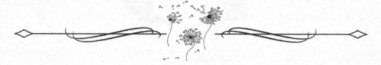

JOSEPHINE CHANG

Josephine was grateful to be out of her high heels and into her dark trousers, a red sweater, and a pair of black flats. She sat on an old wooden office desk, swiping through her messages and trying to be productive, but her eyes kept closing and her head drooping.

Alone in this dilapidated office with nothing but the chipped paint and scent of old socks keeping her company, she wanted to sleep. Or rather soak in a warm bath with a glass of wine.

Extracting Verlot had drained her. She'd been trying to get ahold of Zen, but he wasn't answering her calls. Did she need to worry about him? Zen and Frank had been on their way to meet Rhett, last she heard. Had things gone wrong?

Zen is fine. Everything is fine. No use worrying about something that hadn't happened.

Josephine stretched her arms, and rose to peer out the dusty window. She had a back view of the building, nothing but fallen trees and the bones of half-faced buildings. She spotted a bakery and wished she could walk over and buy a fresh, hot muffin and coffee.

Josephine just needed to get through the day and Verlot would make his speech.

"Dave," she called her captain through her chip.

"Yes, madam."

"Just checking in." She'd heard voices in the background.

"Everything all right?" he asked.

"Yes." Josephine sighed softly, easing the tightness in her chest. "Everything good so far on your end?"

"Not a sound. Are you—"

She waited for him to finish, but he didn't.

"Dave?" She paused and she spoke louder. "Dave?"

"We've been attacked. Councilor Chang, this is Marc. Dave is down. Team one is coming your way." The sound of gunshots rang.

Josephine clicked off and made a distress call to ANS on her chip. She stated her name, the reason for the call, and left the coordinates. She had no idea who she was calling. ANS had never given her a contact name, but Mr. San—who she'd never seen, only spoken with—had told her to call in case of an emergency.

Josephine couldn't get hold of Zen, so this was an emergency. After she hung up, she patted her gun holstered on her waist and rushed down the halls to Verlot's room.

Verlot had said his men were coming for him, but no one knew where they were.

Was one of her men a traitor? She had no reason to believe so. She'd known all her soldiers for the past three years. Still, one of them could have been paid off.

"Something wrong, Councilor Chang?" Verlot said in a cool, relaxed tone.

Josephine despised him. He would not escape. She had sacrificed so much. She was not going down.

"Why would you think that?" Josephine flashed a fake smile and tapped at his hub.

No use trying to lie to him. He knew.

He offered a smug grin, his arms to his side from the metal cuffs, preventing him from raising his arms higher. "I told you my men would find me."

"They won't find you in here." She gave him the same smug grin and pushed the red button by the door.

The sound of metal clanking ricocheted. Steel bars shot out from the floor all around the room, joining together to form a barricade. The whole room, even the ceiling, had been encased.

"What's going on?" Verlot's gaze darted around frantically as the room sealed itself into a metal square box. "What are you doing?" When she didn't answer, he said, "You're crazy, bitch."

Josephine released the top lid of his hub and pointed a gun at his forehead. "I'm crazy as you make me be. I'm not a violent person, but I will be for you. Now, no more talking. I'm really tired of your voice."

His nostrils flared. "You don't have the guts to kill me. I bet you hired that redhead to do your dirty job, didn't you?"

"I'm warning you, I've been trained. I know where to shoot to cause you a lot of pain. I could have Dr. Machine fix you up, and only to shoot you again and again. Your choice."

Verlot growled.

"How did your people know to come here?" Josephine asked.

He didn't answer, just kept his sharp, cold eyes on her.

Josephine paced around Verlot's hub, considering her next move. Either way, there would be too many deaths. It was too late to think about what she had done. There was no going back. It had all started when Mr. San had reached out to her and revealed who he was.

"Getting nervous, are you?" Verlot offered a victorious smirk.

"You should be. You haven't met my CODE soldiers."

She stopped in front of him, pointing her gun downward. "You should be ashamed of yourself." She'd lost her patience mulling over all the things he'd gotten away with. All the lives he'd taken. "How can you experiment on our children? They are our future."

"Exactly. Children are resilient. They do what they're told, especially these groups of kids. Release me and I'll be lenient. With *you*, not Martinez and Jones. They're idiots. But you, you've got balls. You can change your mind and join me."

"Shut up," she ground out.

"It's not too late."

Josephine turned her back on him to get an update. "Marc, come in. Marc?"

She shouldn't be talking in front of Verlot, but she wasn't going to release these bars just to talk to Marc face-to-face.

Marc didn't answer, but outside the room, bullets were fired and soldiers shouted.

"It's over, Chang. I told you what would happen. They're coming for me."

The contempt in his tone made her want to pull the trigger. It would be so easy to get rid of him, but she was no murderer. That would make her no better than him.

Josephine smacked a button to mute Verlot's voice. She'd had enough.

CHAPTER TWENTY-TWO – RESCUE

MITCH

It was getting difficult to go on missions for Novak, especially when Mitch was assigned to assassinate one of the rebel teams—not just any member but Councilor Chang, for crying out loud.

How did Novak even know where Chang was? Shouldn't she be in the city with the other councilors?

The coordinates weren't familiar. Where was Novak sending him?

"We're almost there, but there's nothing here except for abandoned, crumbled buildings," Russ said. "Why would Chang be there?"

Sitting on the passenger seat, Mitch rubbed a hand on his thigh, the ISAN suit material smooth and thin. "I don't know. For the first time, I don't know what to do. How are we going to get away with this one? We have to bring Chang in. We can't screw up another mission."

Russ glanced to the team assembled behind him and back to Mitch. He rubbed at his temples, and then looked at Mitch.

"What?" Mitch furrowed his brow.

Russ checked the hologram map. "Well, I can't believe I'm about to say this but… we could blame it on the team?"

Mitch's mouth fell open. "Russ? I'll be damned. You're

155

kidding, right?"

"I'm tired." Russ's chest rose and fell dramatically. "I don't know how long I can do this. Every rebel soldier I kill eats away at me. One day, there'll be just the ribcage holding an empty space. I tell myself I have no choice, but when does this end? I thought we were taking out criminals. Never thought I would be a murderer, and especially never thought I would be on my way to assassinate Councilor Chang."

"I hear you."

"We assassinated a lot of women and men. Do you ever think about them? Most of them were probably innocent."

The self-loathing in his voice awakened something inside Mitch he didn't want to revisit.

"We didn't know," Mitch said softly and looked out the window. The view of the oppressive destruction made his mood worse. "I'm not trying to justify what we did, but we were given misinformation. I won't think about the people I've killed. I thought I was doing the right thing. And you should do the same. After I found out the truth about ISAN, I regretted ever being part of it. The only reason I kept going was to find my father. I convinced Rhett to do the same."

Mitch had to see his plan through. Only he hadn't expected to care for even more people, like this good guy next to him. He wanted to bring all his friends with him when he escaped ISAN.

"Looks like we're here." Russ swiped across the hologram screen, getting ready to land. "I suggest you think of a plan because I've got nothing."

"Why me?" Mitch frowned.

Russ offered a sly grin. "You're good at scheming and deceiving. That's what you do well."

Mitch chuckled. "Did you just give me a compliment? Are we getting along?"

Russ cackled and tapped the screen to close. "I think it's a start of a beautiful friendship. But seriously, we're here so think fast."

Mitch guided the teams out when they landed and fanned out behind the closest crumbled building. Two ISAN-East teams and guards were in his hands. He pointed at the ruined building across the street—their destination.

"Ready?" Mitch said, and gave Russ a hard look, and then to Bethany and Stella, who used to be on Justine's team.

Mitch held up a fist, a sign to get moving. Stealthily, they sped down the street with Tasers aimed, weaving around potholes, fallen rusted street signs, and abandoned cars. They hid behind the side of the designated structure.

"Team B, Stella's team, follow Russ," Mitch said through his chip and pointed at Russ. "Team A, follow me."

Mitch took Bethany's team to the left front of the building, while Russ took Stella's team around the back to the right front. Chang's guards were deployed at the entrance, casual in their stance. They looked half asleep. Most were sitting on the ground chatting like it was more of a hangout.

"On my mark, everyone," Mitch said through his chip.

The plan was to tase Chang's guards, then Russ and Mitch would tase their team members. Mitch had no idea if the ridiculous plan would work, but he had nothing else.

After Mitch found Chang, he would have to explain why he was there. Obviously, he wouldn't kidnap her, but he had to come up with details to make it seem like Chang had left before they arrived.

Just as Mitch was about to give the order, several aircraft

landed. He recognized the ISAN aircraft to his right, but not the ones on the left. They certainly weren't the rebels. Rhett wouldn't have parked so close.

Chang's guards startled and engaged closer, treading carefully toward both gliders. When ISAN's glider door opened, all hell broke loose. Bullets rained over the entire area. Mitch signed his team to back away. The transporters to his left opened fire at ISAN.

"Go around to Russ's team," Mitch said to Bethany. "I'll meet you there."

Mitch dashed to a flipped-over car, and then ran to a beat-up wooden desk for protection.

"This is ANS. Stand down. You're surrounded." Their speaker boomed through the dusty clouds.

One ISAN assassin came closer. The soldier was clad in the newest ISAN suit, thicker and more formfitting. When the soldier revealed the face under the hooded mask, Mitch swore.

A kid. About thirteen. They were the army from the south. Perhaps the same group he'd seen at Pearl Valley. What were they doing here? Had they been told to get rid of Chang, too? It was the only explanation.

Why would Novak send both teams? And somehow ANS knew and they were here to stop them.

Mitch ran to Russ.

"We can't go through with our plan," Russ said, taking a peek by the beat-up billboard. "I just checked my messages. Team South got the message we would be their backup."

Mitch's pride deflated. "Why are we their backups? They're just kids."

"I don't know, but what are we going to do?" Russ said over the exchange of bullets resonating. "Make the call or I am."

Mitch gave his team directions and guided them to Team South. A girl with long, braided dark hair came forward.

"My name is Davina. What took you so long?" she snapped.

Mitch didn't like taking orders from a little girl, but he bit his tongue from saying something he would regret. "What's the status?"

"I'm going in with my Team B," Davina said. "There are twelve in each team. Team A will stay behind. I have no idea how many guards are inside."

Mitch told Russ to stay behind with Stella's and Bethany's teams and went around the side of the building with Davin's team, while heavy artillery fire was exchanged. Davina gestured at one of her soldiers, and the girl punched through wood and cement with her fist.

She was like Justine, but stronger.

Davina led them down a long, dank hallway, their boots pounding along the dusty tile floor. Lights from the hallway flickered as they weaved around uplifted tiles and concrete. They passed a couple of office rooms but no sign of Chang. Mitch had a bad feeling about this.

Davina halted at a dead end. "She's not in here," Davina spoke through her chip. "I repeat. Chang is not here. Do we abort?"

"Who are you speaking to?" Mitch tried not to inhale the scent of old socks.

She looked at Mitch as if he'd grown a second head. "Mr. Novak. Who else?"

Novak had never been available during their missions, nor had he ever supervised one. Why now? These must be his special soldiers. Novak was taking a personal interest in them. He trusted this group to fight but perhaps he thought they still needed backup.

Some with more experience. The reason Novak had sent him and Russ.

Davina shifted her attention back to her chip, but one of the girls who had been sniffing around like a hound dog pointed to a wall.

"She's in there," she said.

"That's a wall," Mitch snapped.

Davina shoved Mitch with a finger. A finger. Just one. Mitch slammed against the opposite wall. She had pushed Mitch aside like he was some kind of a pest. Her strength was remarkable. Mitch stood back and decided it was best not to argue.

Davina narrowed her cold, dark eyes. "Bring it down."

Five girls effortlessly socked their fists over and over into the wall, making dozens of dents, but not punching through.

One of the girls stopped, her eyes wide in terror, and yelled, "Put up your shields."

In ISAN, "Put up your shield" meant a bomb would detonate. Mitch threw himself behind Davina and ducked low as the walls exploded outward. Closing his eyes, he prayed to stay alive.

Scorching heat rolled over Mitch. He clenched his teeth as he trembled, bearing the pain and hot air searing over his combat suit so that it burned against his skin. Without a warning, he was violently tossed in the air.

He should have landed hard, hard enough to break a few bones, but instead thumped on the wreckage. It happened so fast he needed a moment to register where he was when he snapped out of his daze.

Not wreckage. About half a dozen ISAN soldiers lay face down and Mitch was on top of them. The wall they tried to break through, untouched. Someone was surely on the other side and had caused the explosion.

Mitch rolled over and thudded on the debris, coughing. Smoke clouded around him. He throbbed with pain, his muscles weak. Fire lingered in pockets on the tile. A pair of black boots appeared in his downward position. He peered up to see Davina.

"Next time, stand behind someone your own height. Look what happened to me when I had to save your ass. We failed the mission to assassinate Councilor Chang. Novak is going to be pissed." Davina patted at flames on her arms and walked to the other half of her team with a swagger that reminded him of Ava.

Mitch rose, stumbling. *My God.* The surrounding walls had blown up. Patches of fire still lingered, but the room with steel walls remained intact. Even more surprising, the six assassins standing beside Davina had scorch marks on their faces and elsewhere, but didn't appear fazed by their wounds.

Helix could suppress the pain of a bullet wound, but not burns to this degree. Still, they had survived the blast and Mitch along with them, thanks to Davina. But the other girls on the ground didn't get up.

Dead, Mitch supposed.

"Hey!" Mitch ran after Davina.

They had taken off without him. When he caught up, he squinted from the sunlight, and ran toward the ISAN glider.

Russ's eyes were wide when he spotted Mitch in the sunlight. "Mitch! You're okay. Thank God. What happened in there?"

"I'll explain it later. What happened out here?"

Flames danced in pockets all around them. ANS's ship was gone. ISAN gliders were the only ones left.

Russ dusted some white powder off Mitch's shoulder. "Just before the blast, ANS took off. I didn't see Chang come out. Is she—"

"No," Mitch whispered so only Russ could hear. "I think they either took her out or… there's a room inside the kids couldn't get to. This place must be built by ANS."

Russ eased his furrowed brow when footsteps approached and placed a light hand on his weapon.

"Mitch. Russ. We're told to head back," Davina said.

"Where are you going?" Mitch asked. "And thanks for saving my ass back there."

She crossed her arms and leaned into a hip. "I wasn't trying to. You got lucky. You picked the right person to hide behind."

Mitch arched an eyebrow. Her heartless choice of words blew his mind. "What happened to teamwork? I'll watch your back and you'll watch mine."

"Teamwork only applies to my team."

"I see," Mitch said and hiked a thumb to the crumbled building. "Are you going back for your injured? They could still be alive."

"They're dead. If you don't have any questions for me, I'll be on my way."

Unbelievable. Mitch used to be like her—cold and uncaring. But on a soft-faced child, her bluntness was unnerving.

"Where are you going again?" Mitch asked.

Davina rolled her eyes. "If you don't know then you weren't meant to know." She sized him up. "You're cute, but not as cute as the other girls say."

She swaggered away. Her loud whistle to get her team's attention would have scared the birds had any remained in the pathetic-looking trees nearby their gliders.

Mitch groaned.

"I know. I know," Russ said. "They're heartless. Novak's dream assassins. I wonder what lies he feeds them."

Russ's sympathetic tone calmed Mitch's nerves.

"Or rather what kind of serum he poisoned them with." Mitch clenched his jaw. "Of the assassins we trained, Roxy came close to being like Davina, only caring about getting the mission accomplished, but she at least cared about her team. This batch of kids, they aren't human. After I find my father, I'm out of there with Lydia. You can come with me or stay. It's up to you."

Russ peered up at the dark clouds, watching the ISAN glider soar away. "I'll help you find your father. I'm with you all the way, until the very end."

Something in Mitch's core softened. He hadn't liked Russ until recently. Mitch had thought Russ too uptight and too fond of Novak. Now he realized he'd had a friend all this time.

"Until the end," Mitch said, his gaze meeting Russ's with a newfound respect.

CHAPTER TWENTY-THREE – PRISONERS

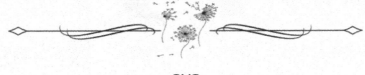

AVA

After dinner, Novak came to my room and told me to follow him. He took me to a chamber opposite from the lab—the layout was the same except there was no fancy equipment, only a TAB on a table in the center of the room. Nothing tangible. Nothing I could use as weapon.

An unbreakable see-through barrier kept the prisoners in. I went to the first cell. A girl sat on the cot with her face down.

"Naomi. Is that you?" I lightly rapped on the glass.

The girl turned. When recognition kicked in, she rushed toward me.

Naomi still had on the jeans and sweater she had worn coming here. Though her eyes were red from crying and her dark hair a mess, she looked unharmed. No bloodstains on her clothes or her face.

"Ava. You're alive. I thought you were…" Though tears were pooling, she smiled. "It's so good to see you."

With Novak in the same room, I kept my emotions at bay. "What happened?"

"You didn't come back."

My heart sank to my stomach. This was all my fault. I took a quick glance at Novak, who was scanning something on the TAB. Novak concentrating on a task gave me an opportunity to speak a little freely.

164

"I'm sorry." I tried to whisper but the quiet room projected my voice. "I'm going to get you out. I promise. Tell me what happened?"

Naomi looked past me to Novak then back to me. "Janine came to me. She told me what you told her to tell me, and then she went back to her post. A while later, a few guards came out." She pointed at Novak. "That crazy man told me you were dead. He put me on this machine. Some contraption went on my head. And…" She froze.

The clicking of Novak's heels made me turn as I imagined him pointing a Taser at me. But after a few steps, he stopped, and he held no weapon.

"Allow me finish," Novak said. "Naomi's mind is a bit fuzzy from all that tampering I did."

"What did you do to her?" I snarled.

Please, not the lobotomy. But she seemed fine. Alert. Emotion seemed intact.

"I asked her if she knew where the rebels were hiding, but she refused to tell me. So I tried to pry it out of her memory."

"She doesn't know and neither do I." I had to lie or he would do the same to me. "We came here together. I don't know if anyone survived. So you're getting nothing. Where's Janine?"

Novak released a sharp, humorless laugh. "You're truly remarkable, Ava. I'm very impressed with your boldness, your demands."

My pulse raced. *Calm down. Don't give him ammunition.* "You lied to me, didn't you? You told me Janine betrayed me."

Novak's gray eyes gleamed, like he had some secret to reveal. "Did I say that? You must have heard me wrong. If what I said were true, then Janine wouldn't be in here."

I went to the next cell.

Janine came rushing, trembling, her voice frantic. "Ava. I'm so sorry. I was careful. I swear it. I—"

"It's okay." I patted the barrier as if somehow that would calm her down. "It's not your fault."

She wiped her tears, then her eyes homed in on Novak. Her glare alone could have killed him.

"You have to get out," she said. "You have to warn your friends. He knows things I didn't tell him. He did things to my brain, my memory. He's going to do it to you. He'll find out everything."

"Don't talk, Janine."

I needed to calm her down. Novak didn't like to be provoked. He didn't tolerate any kind of rebellion, especially when he looked bad in front of an audience, even if it was just me. It was enough for him.

"He's not only experimenting on children, but adults too. Our parents. Many have died. Their bodies can't handle the serum. They were here, but they're gone now."

"I know, Janine. Please, stop talking. Look at me."

No matter how hard I pounded the glass and tried to get her attention, I had lost her. Her attention was fixed on Novak.

Her fists rounded by her side, trembling. "He's already killed many. He's building an army."

"Janine. Stop. I know."

I hit the barrier again and looked over my shoulder. Novak stood in the same position. His wicked smirk told me he planned to do something.

"You have to get out," she said. "You have to tell the world. There are ISAN soldiers in different countries. My time expired the day I chickened out. I should have killed as many guards as I could, but I ran away. I'm not running anymore."

A door cranked open inside Janine's cell, and a metal rod poked out from the back wall. Janine looked over her shoulder and then back to me with a small, defeated smile.

"Go to hell, Novak," she said. "Always having other people do the dirty work for you."

Another sound cranked.

Janine's eyes widened with desperation. "Ava, I have something to tell you. Save the ba—"

Bang!

My heart jumped to my throat as I jerked back. Janine's blood smeared on the glass. Fast as a snap of fingers, she had been hit by a bullet.

I tried to process what had happened, and endlessly asking what I could have done to stop her from talking. But save who? I didn't know anyone whose name started with the letter B.

"Well, that was inconvenient." Novak closed the hologram monitor. "I really didn't want to kill her. So ungrateful for pardoning her the first time. Disregard her rambling. I suggest you listen or Naomi will be next. Now, let me take you to my next guest."

Shaken to my core, I couldn't wipe away the image of Janine's brain splattered on the glass in front of me. Not wanting the same fate for Naomi, I behaved and kept my mouth shut.

Novak took me to the last cell. Nothing could have prepared me for who I saw next.

"Zen?" I covered my mouth with a hand, suppressing a scream, standing inches away from the barrier.

Calm down, Ava. Calm down. It doesn't mean everyone else is here.

Zen's usual sleek hair looked disheveled and he had bags

underneath his eyes. He wore a similar gray, loose outfit like mine. He looked happy to see me and terrified at the same time as he rushed to meet me at the glass.

"Rhett is on his way," he whispered. "You have to do something. He's determined to find you. We were shot down. Frank is… dead."

I nodded. "Shhh. He can hear you." I mouthed the words and tugged on my ear.

Zen seemed to understand what I was trying to convey. He closed his eyes briefly, and when he opened them, he released a long sigh.

"Ava. I'm sorry. I didn't know Novak was Dr. Hunt. Novak is your father."

"It's okay." I began to back away. "He told me. Don't say anything, okay. I know everything."

"Ava…"

How was I supposed to escape now? How was I going to save everyone? I needed to change my plan.

"Don't say another word." I retreated even more to where Novak stood, who was scrolling through his messages on his chip. "You have me, Novak. Let my friends go. You won, okay? Release them. I'll do what you want."

Novak regarded me but didn't respond. That was a no.

I gave Zen my back and walked toward the exit. Surprisingly, Novak didn't try to stop me.

CHAPTER TWENTY-FOUR – AMBUSH

RHETT

After Vince gave Rhett permission to take five Propellers, he gathered his team and left to find Ava. Ozzie, Brooke, Reyna, Tamara, Mia, and Nina squeezed in the back of the glider and Cleo sat in front on the passage side.

Rhett checked the hologram map and clicked on the autopilot button. He couldn't see as the fog had become thick and mist clouded the windows.

He glanced over to Cleo and adjusted his cap. "We're going to find your father. He's a smart man."

Before Rhett left, he had told her what had happened to her father. He'd thought about not telling her, but if he were in her shoes, he would want to know.

Cleo didn't look at him. She idly polished her gun on her lap with the hem of her shirt. "You better be right, Rhett. If something happens to my... He's all I have left." She blinked and paused to gather herself. "I'm sorry. You lost so much too. We all have. When does this end? I'm so tired."

Rhett cupped her hand. "Hey. Your dad and Frank are fine. Ava and Naomi are fine. We're going to find them." Because he didn't know what he would do either.

Zen had been like a father to him, to all of them. Sure, they didn't agree on a lot of things, but Zen had always done right by

169

all of them. He gave the resistance a home and a feeling of unity, a family, a purpose.

"Looks like we're almost there," Reyna said softly, gazing out the window.

"It looks like hell," Brooke said.

"I hope we don't run into those creatures." Tamara flipped her pocketknives while keeping her eyes on the view.

Rhett wished he had something—anything—that could keep his pulse level. He looked over his shoulder at Mia and Nina. Mia pushed back her red hair, taking in slow deep breaths. Nina twirled her nose ring and shocked herself from her electrical spark. The girls had assimilated quickly.

Rhett had instructed Ella and Cora to stay behind to help protect their home base. He didn't like separating Mia and Ella, but he didn't see the point of bringing them both when they had similar powers.

Alarm suddenly shrilled. Their glider shook hard enough to dislodge anyone not strapped in.

"What's going on?" Reyna said.

"We've been hit." Rhett checked the monitors to see where the missile had come from, but the window had misted with condensation.

The glider lurched again.

Ozzie looked out the window. "Visibility is near zero. Just land."

Ozzie slammed against the side of the cabin. The transporter had been hit again. Rhett strapped the Propeller onto his wrist. It looked like a watch but with a square-shaped thin metal face, where he controlled the unit. He tugged Cleo out of her seat and guided her toward the back.

"Get your Propellers ready," Rhett hollered down the aisle, over the warning beeping. "We have to evacuate." He grabbed his backpack from a cabinet, shoved his cap inside, and hiked the pack over his shoulder. "Everyone get your weapons. Ozzie, get the emergency pack. Reyna, get ready to open the—"

Metal clanking sounded rapidly. Bullets tore through down the aisle. Had Rhett's team been in their seats, they would have been sitting ducks.

Reyna opened the side door. With the wind gushing in and the glider freefalling in an incline, everyone teetered, losing their balance.

"Jump. I'm right behind you," Rhett ordered, his hands anchored on the door handle, the mist dampening his face. His pack swung to the side and thumped on his back.

Ozzie and Brooke leaped together. Next, Reyna and Tamara. Then Mia and Nina were given their own. Before the team had left the base, Rhett explained how the Propellers worked. He was glad he'd listened to his instincts and asked Vince for them.

When everyone was out, he clicked the button on the square, wrapped his arms around Cleo, and jumped. He felt high with a rush of euphoria. He loved the speed and the danger, always reveled in the freedom of body and gravity joining as one.

Cleo screamed, her voice lost to the beating gale.

A bubble-like shield engulfed them in an instant as they plummeted, gliding with the wind. It would have been an enjoyable ride under different circumstances.

The misty rain usually didn't bother Rhett, but he didn't know where he was headed. And being in enemy territory didn't ease his mind.

Please let us land safe. That is all I ask.

They had been fifteen minutes from their destination when the first shot had hit. That they had been shot down might mean they were closer than he had calculated.

When Rhett pressed the oval-shaped button on the hologram monitor connected to the control on his wrist, it showed him a clear image of the ground below, crisscrossed with red laser lights.

"They're shooting at us, Rhett. Can we shoot back?" Cleo leaned to her side of the window.

"Everyone, watch out. We have incoming." Mia's voice resonated through Rhett's Propeller.

Rhett weaved the transporter to the left to dodge the laser beams. Too many. There were too many. He had to do something.

"Get the one to your left, I'll get this guy," Cleo said. "Yes. Target down." She gave Rhett a light sock on his arm. She sounded proud of herself.

To Rhett's right, Mia's Propeller lurched forward.

"I've been hit, but I'm okay," Mia said. "The machine has this line—like a lifeline. It was full when we got on, but now it's only half. What does that mean?"

Means you're screwed if you get hit one more time.

"Mia, stay in front of me." Bad advice, but Rhett didn't know what to tell her. Then an idea came to his mind. "Nina. Can you extend your power outside of the shield?"

"I can try."

"Work on that and get ready when I count to three."

"Where you going?"

Rhett ignored her and switched over. "Hey, Ozzie. If we don't do something, we're all dead."

"Wow, thanks for that tip, Rhett," Brooke said. "Got anything else to enlighten us with?" Rhett almost laughed. He would have, but they were in a hurry and desperate.

"Yes, I do, Brooke. Oz, remember that mission when I surprised the driver and—"

"Oh, hell no, Rhett. There's no freakin' way I'm—"

"Oz, are you with me?" Rhett looked over his shoulder when laser beams barely missed him. "Don't make me do this by myself. Lives depend on us." He switched over. "On the count of three. Nina, get ready. Don't fail me."

"No pressure there," she murmured.

"One. Two. Now. Cleo, hold on tight." Rhett's voice boomed through everyone's Propellers before he banked hard to his left, while Ozzie went right. They flipped upside down, then continued heading straight for their targets, firing away from their Propeller.

Nina, on the other hand made a U-turn, coming toward Rhett, like a lightning diva, she poured her power straight down the middle. Tentacles of her lightning extended, sizzled, and wrapped around six of their enemies' gliders, electrocuting them.

"Rhett," Mia shouted. "The light is flickering. Something's wrong."

"Don't panic, Mia," Rhett said. "Try to keep…" She was going down too fast. "Nina, I need you again. Try to slow Mia's Propeller. Whatever you can do."

"On it." Nina's glider zoomed, her electrical lights pulling on Mia's hub, but the speed of the falling aircraft seemed too heavy and powerful.

"I'll try to clear her path," Tamara said.

"I'm right beside you," Rhett said, flying over a deserted golf course and a half-faced hotel.

Mia was falling toward an office building and the Propeller couldn't keep her safe from the impact. So Tamara fired at the walls, which crumbled into chunks, dust and smoke powdering the vicinity. Nina's lightning rod continued to encase and anchor Mia's hub.

"Nina," Rhett said. "Can you grab hold of Mia if I tell her to release the hub?"

"I don't know. She's too far. She's almost down."

"I can't eject, Rhett," Mia said, her breath heavy. "It's damaged. I'll have to fall. Just in case I don't make it, please tell Ella I love her. And thank you, all of you, for accepting us with open arms. It's been an honor."

"You're not dying today, Mia," Rhett shouted. "This is an order. Get hold of her, Nina." Damn it, he didn't want to lose any more friends.

"I'm trying, Rhett," Nina hollered, her voice strained.

Nina dove faster, her powers growing. Even the clouds seemed to mimic her desperation as they darkened and rumbled. No matter the effort, Nina was too late.

Mia crashed at the place where Tamara had fired. Her half-exposed Propeller bounced off the ground and skidded along the debris while Nina's lightning rods grabbed Mia just as she was tossed upward. Nina brought her down safely around the crushed cement and landed her Propeller. The rest followed.

Rhett's knees dug into the dirt as he hovered over Mia. He unzipped his pack and shot her with a dosage of painkiller from his medical bag.

Brooke knelt by Mia's head. "She's bleeding on her left shoulder. She's been hit by a bullet."

"Hey…" Mia groaned, fluttering her eyes open. "I'm still… alive? I don't feel so good."

Rhett held her hand. "Mia, everything is going to be fine."

Ozzie squeezed between Brooke and Tamara, withdrew a small box of medical supplies from his backpack and handed it to Rhett.

Rhett took a pair of scissors from the box and cut around the bloody sweater at her shoulder. The blood had stopped somewhat, but the hole looked nasty.

Reyna's forehead creased and she took a deep breath. "If I take out her bullet, we need to stitch her back up. Do we have—"

"I can do it," Nina said, on her knees beside Rhett. "It'll hurt like hell, but I can close it up by zapping it." She wiggled her fingers. "Don't worry. I'm not making this up. I've done it before."

"Well, we can either talk about it or actually save her life." Brooke shrugged. "Just saying. What are we waiting for? Reyna, do your magic. Do I need to look away? Are you going to like stick your finger inside her wound? Cause that would be really freaky."

"Mia. Hold on." Rhett squeezed her hand and gave Reyna a nod.

"I haven't done this in so long." Reyna bent lower, hovering her mouth over Mia's wound. She inhaled slowly at first. When nothing happened, she sucked in air deeper. The bullet's face peeked through. Mia moaned and shifted.

Reyna's face turned red the harder she pulled. The bullet moved upward. Half of its metal body showed. Then Reyna caught it in midair before it had a chance to go into her mouth.

Nina swooped in and released small amount of power over Mia's wound. The lights were beautiful, sizzling and sparkling, and mended the wound with a livid, puckered seal. Mia squirmed again. This time she belted out a scream, her back arching.

"Give her another shot of painkiller," Rhett barked, as Mia squeezed his hand harder.

Ozzie reached inside his bag and handed it to Tamara, who

administered the dose. Immediately, Mia relaxed and lowered her body. Her breathing steadied.

"Done. That should do it." Nina slumped down on her butt and rubbed at her pierced nose. "Don't ask me to do anything today, Rhett. I'm out. I'm exhausted. I used all of my energy slowing Mia's propeller."

"We need to hide." Rhett surveyed the area.

Nothing but fallen telephone poles, a few rundown homes, and then he spotted a perfect cave-like hideout in one of the warehouses. Half of the building had collapsed, but the other half seemed stable. Good enough.

"There." Rhett pointed behind them to the far left, about sixty yards. "ISAN knows we've crashed. They're going to come back. It'll get dark soon and who knows what's out there? Besides, we all need to rest."

Another delay in getting to Ava.

A part of Rhett wondered if he should go on alone, but no. Having a strong team gave them a better chance of rescuing Ava and Naomi, and now Zen and Frank might need rescuing too.

"Cleo, where do you think you're going?" Rhett said when he spotted her sneaking away. "You won't make it far going alone. I know you want to find your father like yesterday, but I can't lose you too. Going by yourself is crazy. You know I'm right."

Her back still to Rhett, she sighed. "Fine. I'm going to scout the perimeter while it's still light."

"Tamara goes with you." Rhett looked at Tamara to confirm.

Tamara gave him a curt nod and rushed to Cleo, walking in the middle of the empty road.

CHAPTER TWENTY-FIVE – ANS

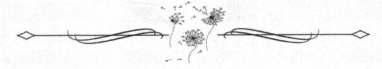

JOSEPHINE CHANG

Josephine waited for ANS to come to her rescue as she paced about the room.

Without warning, the floor groaned and vibrated and a section of the ground near the file cabinet slid open. She halted by the door and pulled out her gun.

A handsome young Asian man with dark hair and kind brown eyes came up an underground staircase. Six men appeared after him, holding weapons that were triple the size of a Taser and bulkier.

Josephine shouldn't have been surprised. ANS had renovated this building in the middle of a meteor-ruined town. Few instructions had been given to her. One—keep Verlot in this room. Two—release the steel walls in the event of an attack, and call ANS on a special line.

"I'm Mr. San, Josephine," Mr. San said in a smooth deep voice, his gaze shifting to Verlot inside the hub.

Josephine shoved her gun back into the holster. "Mr. San, I wasn't expecting you." His guards, yes, but not him. And she certainly hadn't expected him to look like a rock star in jeans and a leather jacket.

He offered a tight grin. "I apologize for not telling you we'd come from underground instead of the front door. I wanted to take care of this matter personally. I'm escorting you and Verlot to safety. You did make the call, didn't you?"

"I did." She eyed the darkness. "ISAN guards are trying to get in. They want him." She gestured to Verlot and unmuted the sound from the hub. She wanted Verlot to hear that his team was not coming to his rescue.

"My people are out there too." Mr. San offered his hand. "Please, come with me. My men will handle Verlot."

Verlot shifted, his forehead creasing. "You can't kidnap me. I'm on the Remnant Council of the former United States. This is treason."

"Hold on." Josephine pressed a button on the monitor and shut Verlot's sound off, then returned to San. "I can go down the stairs myself. Just lead the way."

"Please watch your step." He waved a hand. "I'll be right behind you."

Josephine descended one step at a time, the cool air caressed her face like a gentle kiss. When she reached the last step, she turned left. The dim tunnel seemed sturdy, the space spotless, and a hint of soil scent permeated in the air.

"When did ANS build this place?" she asked San, who walked beside her.

"Not too long ago. ANS was organized first as SAN, then one faction of SAN was reformed into ISAN by Verlot. He thought ANS had disbanded, but we were recuperating and building to a stronger unified group. We're not as big as ISAN, but we will get there. I'm hoping to recruit some of the rebels to our unit."

After Josephine rounded the corner, she looked behind her. The two men wheeled the hub, the other four flanked in protective position. When Verlot's glare met hers, it warned of revenge.

178

"Where are you taking us?" Josephine asked.

Their steps echoed along the tunnel in every direction. One could get lost in here.

San pulled up his hologram monitor, then closed it. "To my glider. From there, I'll take you back to your office. And I'll take care of Verlot."

"I can't get a hold of Zen," Josephine said, worried.

"If we can get a lead on his whereabouts, my men can help."

Josephine halted. "Mr. San. I kept your secret as you asked, but now that the rebels know about ANS, I will have to inform them about my association. We need to work together if we are to stop ISAN, or we will end up destroying each other. Do we have an agreement?"

"Yes, of course." He dipped his head and met her gaze. "After you."

San dropped Josephine off at her office and told her he would be in touch. Josephine didn't ask what they would do with Verlot.

Josephine held a press conference later that evening, stating Verlot had suffered a stroke and was in critical condition. Further details were forthcoming.

Josephine didn't feel what they were doing to Verlot was heartless. Verlot had destroyed families, taken children, molded them into weapons. As a result, she felt no guilt regarding his fate.

She had to get things done, even if it meant manipulating the system to her advantage.

CHAPTER TWENTY-SIX – SAVE THE BABY

AVA

Rhett had been on his way here with Zen, but Novak had said he would send them on a wild-goose chase. Maybe they'd been separated. Had Novak broken his word? Not that he had ever been trustworthy, but he had seemed genuine. Plus he wanted my cooperation.

The door whooshed and Payton entered. Having witnessed Janine's execution, and knowing Naomi and Zen were in a holding cell, Payton's warm smile ticked me off.

"What do you want?" I snapped.

Payton lowered his eyelashes as if I'd hurt his feelings. "I'm here to take you to see your mother."

His tender tone made me feel horrible, but instead of answering, I waited by the door. When Payton neared, the wall opened. I didn't wait for him to usher me. I knew the way.

Payton brushed his shoulder against mine. I'd thought he had accidentally bumped me, but he meant to get my attention. "Justine is on her way here."

I trained my eyes ahead and kept my surprise to myself. "Why?"

Payton put his hands behind his back and kept pace with me. "Perhaps your father wants her to know she has a half sister and a half brother?"

I scoffed. "That's going to make her day."

When Payton chuckled, I did the same. A short reprieve, but reprieve nevertheless.

"Well, here we are." Payton gestured for me to enter first.

When the door slid opened, Mother was standing there as if she'd known we were coming. She wore a similar outfit, but blue this time, with the same beige sunhat. She didn't greet me or Payton, instead dashed along the walkway. I quickened my pace and followed her to the far back corner where she lowered herself to the rose bushes.

With bare hands, she scooped up dirt from a hole she had dug earlier. It was deep enough for her to plant the small bed of purple lantana flowers at her feet. I stepped lightly so as not to spook her, but she heard me.

"Are you back again, visitor?" She put the lantana inside the soil and used her hands as a shovel.

When she didn't call me by my name, my heart twisted, and I inhaled to keep my emotions at bay. Having lived these past years thinking she was dead had been difficult enough, but seeing her like this was torture.

I had to shut down that part of me that wanted to hold her and sob over the years I had missed her. My mother was alive and well, and that should be enough.

"Yes," I said and flashed a glance at the fake sun, wondering if Novak was listening or watching us. "How are you?"

She didn't answer. Mother patted the soil, then rose. She dusted her hands, dirt showering down, her nails caked with soil.

"Come. Come." She scurried to the opposite end passing the sunflowers and the small gurgling fountain. "See my vegetables." She beamed. "Carrots, squash, and tomatoes. I need more." She turned to Payton. "I want more seeds, to make more."

181

Payton's eyes widened. He looked surprised Mother had spoken to him. "Sure. Of course. Whatever you need. But I don't have any right now. I'll get them for you later."

I should know better, but I couldn't let this opportunity to slip by. Who knew when Novak would allow me to see my mother again?

"Who is Ava?" I whispered to Mom.

Since she mentioned that name the last time, I thought it was safe to bring it up. I hoped she would give me more insight into what she'd meant by "help." There had to be more to this.

Payton looked at me with concern and shook his head.

Mother bent lower and cupped one of the tomatoes on a tower-style cage, vines snaking up. "This is Ava. This tomato was once a baby. She grew fast and strong." She plucked it out with a hard yank. "If you force it out too soon, then she will taste sour."

I scooted closer to her and whispered. "Who is Ava?"

"No." Payton gently gripped my elbow and spun me around. "This isn't a good idea."

"Let go of me." I pulled my arm back, then I squeezed my mother's shoulders so she would face me. My mother's situation was beyond frustrating and I was running out of time. "Do you remember me? I'm Ava. I'm your daughter."

The crinkles in the corner of her eyes softened and I thought… I thought for a second she remembered, but her features twisted into a scowl.

"Ava is a tomato, not a girl." She snarled and turned away, her back to me.

The words were a punch to the gut. The sliver of hope I'd held on to unraveled as I stood there, unable to move.

You have to keep trying. Draw out her memory.

"Ava?" Payton's sympathy drew me out of my reverie.

I steadied my quickening breath. Dismissing Payton, I stood in front of Mom. "Are you proud of Ava?" I asked.

Mother stroked the tomato still in her hand like she would my hair. "She was a tiny seed at first, but she grew to be beautiful. Look at her." She held it up to my face. "Ava was so small. The vines did not grow well around her." She waved at the tower-style cage. "When she saw the other tomatoes growing, she decided to do the same. She found a home, a family. Ava finally thrived and blossomed. She is the biggest. She is resilient like the dandelion."

I dabbed at my tears when I realized she was talking about me. *I'm here, Mother. I'm Ava, your little girl.*

"But she's scared," I said.

Mother gently placed her palm under the other tomato and studied it. "Everyone is scared. There would be no such thing as courage if there was no fear. You see, all these tomatoes know they will be plucked and eaten, but they flourish anyway. Nobody knows when it's their turn to be picked, so they do their best. They do not need to worry about things that haven't happened. Such a waste of time and energy when it could be used for other thinking."

A ping came Payton's chip.

"I need to take you back," Payton said warily.

"No! No! No!" Mom threw the tomato against the wall.

I blinked and wiped a smudge of juice that had splattered on my face.

"Mom. Stop." I wrapped my arms around her, her chest rising and falling in the same rhythm as mine. "Shhh… It's okay."

When I pulled back, I saw something on her lower arm. I snatched her wrist and examined her skin. There were words there. *Letter. Baby.* What did they mean to her?

It didn't matter what I did or said, she grabbed me and kept screaming, twirling us again and again. Payton tried to stop us, but Mother dragged us farther away, stomping over the squash and carrots.

"Save the baby," she whispered over and over again.

"What do you mean?" I said, perturbed by our lack of communication.

"Save the baby," she said frantically before she was pried off me.

Two guards had entered and grabbed her, using force to keep her steady. Payton clamped his hand on Mother's head. When her muscles eased and her shoulders slumped, the guards released her.

Novak raced toward us when the door swished open, and shot a dagger-filled look at Payton. "What did she say?" When he didn't respond. Novak looked at me. "Your mother isn't well. Forget whatever she told you."

Save the baby? What baby? The baby in the POD? Why?

Novak hadn't mentioned anything about killing the baby. He had brought the CODE baby to this site to keep a closer eye on her, he had said. So why would Mother be concerned?

"I don't take anything she says to heart," I said and rammed my fist to his chest. "You did this to her."

Novak raised a hand to his guards when they raised weapons at me. "Stand down. She won't hurt me if she knows what's good for her mother." He confirmed with a steely gaze on me.

"Of course. I won't hurt you," I said with a mocking bow.

Novak regarded me. His eyes seemed to soften and then became cold as ever. "Payton, take Ava back to her room. It will be a reminder she won't get to spend time with her mother if she puts a hand on me again."

CHAPTER TWENTY-SEVEN – LONG NIGHT

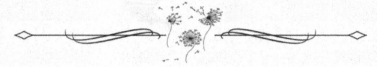

RHETT

After a quick survey of the abandoned warehouse, Rhett's team settled for the night in a far corner where the wooden crates were stacked and part of the wall had crumbled. It made a good hiding place.

With his head resting on his lumpy backpack, his spine against the cold hard concrete, Rhett couldn't sleep. He couldn't stop thinking about his girl. After endless restless shifting on the ground, he shook Tamara, who was nestled against the wall.

"Is it time?" Tamara rubbed her sleepy eyes.

"Not, but I can't sleep." Rhett stared at the wooden crates they'd moved to create a barrier.

"Me either." She sat up and stretched her arms to the high ceiling and peered down at Cleo, Mia, and Nina, who were laying on the ground under a solar blanket from Ozzie's emergency pack.

Rhett jerked a chin toward the exit. Tamara followed. He shivered at the cool air and glanced at the full moon fading. They walked to the side of the building and climbed up a ladder to the roof.

Ozzie and Brooke were sitting by the edge of the roof, kissing. Rhett wasn't surprised but he cleared his throat. They flinched and stared at Rhett and Tamara with shocked expressions.

"Is it time already?" Ozzie asked, his face coloring. He got up and gave Brooke a hand.

Brooke pushed off the ground and dusted her pants as if nothing had happened. "So, we'll be down there." She flashed all her teeth and walked hand in hand with Ozzie.

Rhett and Tamara went to the edge of the building, set themselves down, surveying the grounds, particularly where Mia had crashed. From up there, they had a clear view of the ruined city. He surveyed along the crumbled buildings to the parked cars, the gas station, and surrounding trees, but he didn't see any threats from ISAN.

Rhett had seen so much devastation this scenery didn't faze him, but he couldn't escape the memory of Mia falling to her death.

A mixture of yellow, orange, and red peeked like a small dome in the darkness.

"It's so beautiful. It's been so long since I've seen a sunrise." Tamara gawked at the east, soaking up the view as she dangled her legs over the edge.

Rhett, too, was mesmerized by the yellow and red bursting through the clouds. It reminded him of the day he'd taken Ava to the top of a building outside the city. She had always wanted to see the city lights. Rhett had given her the view on her birthday; although he had kidnapped her to do it. That seemed ages ago.

Rhett shifted his attention back to the empty road. "Do you have any goals? Let's say ISAN is destroyed and there's nothing to fight for—or against. What would you want to do?"

Tamara crinkled her brow as if Rhett had asked her something weird. "Ava asked Brooke and me a similar question. I have no family. Zen took me in. In a way, he's my guardian. If it wasn't for him, I would be stuck in juvie. Or ISAN would have found me eventually, but I don't know if I would be the person I am now. It's a scary thought. What if I was like Roxy? Do you know her?"

"I've heard of her."

"Not only did she want her team to be the best, she cheated, and she was cold. When her team died, she changed, but then we never knew what had happened to her. Novak told us she was sent back to her foster parents, but we all knew that was a lie."

Rhett swung his legs over the edge like Tamara.

Tamara crossed her ankles and ran her fingers along the pebbled edge. "To answer your question, I think I'll be wherever Zen is. It's strange. I know Zen doesn't think of me as his daughter, but I also know he has a special place for me in his heart, like he has for you."

Rhett smiled half-heartedly. "He told me if he had it his way, he would have a dozen children, but his life turned out differently. Like how ours did. I'm sure none of us ever imagined being in the position we are now."

"Nope." Tamara stretched her legs and raised her arms to the cloudy sky, which had gotten a bit brighter.

"Tell me the truth, okay? I promise not to get mad."

Tamara stiffened and slowly peeled her eyes from the road. "What do you want to know?"

"Did you suspect Gene was Ava's twin before Mitch told us?"

Tamara flicked a pebble off the edge and watched it disappear. "I wasn't hundred percent sure, but I did feel a connection between them. I didn't know why I felt that way, but you also have to understand that I'm trying to figure out how my power works. I didn't want to say anything to Ava because I had no evidence. Going on feelings wasn't enough for something that important."

"Good point," Rhett said and planted his arms behind him.

"How about you? Where do you see yourselves?"

Rhett peered up the sky, where the sun glowed brighter than it had seconds ago. "Behind the mountain base is a small community, untouched by the meteor. My father has a five thousand square foot, two-story cabin with five bedrooms, that overlooks the mountain and the lake. It's the most peaceful place I've ever seen. Ava and I will live there after we bring down ISAN. We'll raise our adopted kids. There are surrounding cabins that have been abandoned. I was hoping our friends would want to join us. When I say friends, that includes you."

Tamara kept quiet, her eyes rooted to the mountains. Rhett thought he had offended her or had hurt her feelings, but then Tamara beamed a smile, her eyes glistening in the dawning light.

"Thank you, Rhett. You have no idea how much that means to me. As much as I wouldn't mind being with Zen, it's different when I'm with Ava and Brooke. We're like a family."

Rhett draped his arm around her in a hug. "Yes, we are. Thank you for watching after Ava. You have no idea what that meant to me. When we fight for the same cause, we are joined by a common bond. We have to be a family and work as a team, or we have no chance."

Tamara and Rhett chatted until it was time to head back. No sign of ISAN so far. ISAN had not sent any new reinforcements to find them. Rhett had a few theories. Either a team would attack when they came out of hiding or would be waiting at their secret base.

Rhett got up and offered his hand. "We should get going."

Tamara took it and pushed up. "Thanks," she said and headed toward the ladder.

Back at their hideout, everyone sat in a circle on a wooden

crate. Ozzie unzipped his emergency backpack. They needed to get going, but they had to eat first.

Ozzie handed everyone a peanut butter cracker bar. "This should fill you up all day. I only have few days of rations left for all of us." He passed around pearl-shaped jelly-looking pills he'd taken out from a bottle. "I've never had to take one before, but this pill is supposed to be enough for one day's worth so you won't be dehydrated."

Rhett tore the seal and took a crunchy bite. The peanut cream melted on his tongue like butter. It tasted better than he'd expected. After he finished the bar, he took his water pill.

Mia and Nina already had finished their rations and began folding their solar blankets.

"Should we get going?" Cleo asked, tapping her feet like a drummer.

Rhett understood Cleo wanted to get to her father, but if she didn't calm down, she was going to make irrational decisions.

"What about Mia?" Tamara popped the pill in her mouth and swallowed. "Is she okay to leave?"

Mia shuffled her feet and rubbed her arms. "I'm a bit sore, but other than that, I feel fine."

"Okay, then. Let's go." Rhett dusted the crumbs off his shirt and swung his pack over his back.

"Stop." Brooke shot her head up, craning her neck. "Do you hear that?"

Ozzie pulled the Taser from his holster. Rhett held up a fist and waved for his team to scatter and hide behind the chunk of cement that had once been part of a wall.

Feet shuffled faintly behind Rhett. The only evidence someone had been here was their dusty footprints.

"We were all keeping watch," Tamara whispered, crouched beside Rhett.

"Tamara, I'm going to get a closer look," Rhett said. "On a count of three, I want you to get our team out to the front."

Tamara hiked an eyebrow as if to say *you've got to be kidding me.* "No offense, but I'm faster than you. So, you get the team out, and I'll be right back."

Before Rhett could stop her, a rush of wind brushed his face. She had zoomed out of there. Rhett raised his fist again and waved toward the exit.

"Where did Tamara go?" Brooke grabbed Rhett's shirt, concern on her face.

"She'll be back." *I hope. She'd better.* "Go. I'm going to wait for her here."

A thump. *Thwack. Whoomph.* More thumps. A pounding of footfalls. Rhett released a lungful of air when Tamara came sprinting back to him.

"What happened?" Rhett figured it was okay to raise his voice.

Tamara slowed and sauntered toward him. "They were drifters. I was going to leave them alone but then they came after me."

"How many?"

"About six."

"Six?" Rhett twisted his lips, narrowing his eyes.

She shrugged sheepishly. "Okay, about eight?"

"Not okay." Rhett's voice rose in pitch along with his irritation. "First of all, you shouldn't have taken off like that. Second, you should have requested backup."

"Rhett, don't be like a big brother." She walked on ahead with that assassin swagger. "You know I can take down a lot more than eight. The drifters are lucky I only knocked them out. Come on, slow poke. We've got people to save."

Rhett shook his head with a grin, trailing behind her. He knew she could take on a lot more on her own, but still, it wasn't worth her life.

He trudged on foot across the dry, cracked land, keeping a triangle formation. Nothing but unfertile ground. No life. No birds in the sky. Not a single squirmy insect. Even the tree branches were splintered and barren.

They entered a deserted, destroyed city, one worse than others Rhett had seen. Roads were covered with wood, plaster, and broken pieces of what had once been a freeway.

Ozzie stepped over a piece of metal and deflated tires. "Wow. Is that an airplane?"

"There are dozens more over there," Mia said, weaving around a broken chair.

"I think we're standing on what used to be an airport." Rhett climbed on top of a yellow car with the word "taxi" written on the side to get a better look. "Careful. Watch out for potholes."

Billboards, large freeway destination signs, and collapsed trees littered the ground. Rhett spotted drifters, but moved on ahead with his hand on his Taser.

"Hey, there's a motel sign." Brooke cackled. "We can check in and take a rest."

Laughter rang softly in the thick, dusty air. Brooke had a great sense of humor and often lightened the oppressive mood.

The wrecked city and trash continued to pave their path. Brooke ran ahead and halted at fifty feet. She grabbed a handful of dried dirt and tossed it outward toward empty space.

"She's gone mental." Nina snorted.

"No." Mia pointed. "Look."

Rhett's heart slammed up his throat. "Behind me!"

Brooke had revealed a section of a cloaked glider that belonged to ISAN. Although there was much to fear, Rhett felt relieved they were finally at the destination.

Ava was here. He could feel her in his marrow. It had only taken him a half a day, but he would have walked forever to find her.

"The entrance is on the other side," Tamara said.

Rhett raised a fist, opened it, and swept the hand forward to let his team know they were on the move. Stealthily, he guided them around several aircraft, then behind an entrance shaped like an igloo.

Nobody was there. Not a single guard. His instincts screamed this was a trap. Novak would not be so careless to leave the entrance unguarded, and he bet on his own life the door was unlocked.

With his Taser ready, Rhett stormed through the door. Unlocked, as he suspected.

CHAPTER TWENTY-EIGHT – A MESSAGE

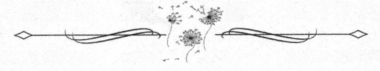

MITCH

Mitch marched into Russ's office the next morning and found him at his desk, his head in his arms. He lifted his head, revealing baggy eyes and messy hair, looking like he'd just woken up.

"That bad? What's going on?" Mitch plopped on the chair across from him.

"I couldn't sleep. I reached out to a few agents and they had no idea what I was talking about regarding a secret base or Ava being captured."

"I couldn't find anything either. So you came here instead. Why didn't you come get me? We could have gone out to get a drink."

"You would've come?"

Mitch shrugged. "Depends on the time."

"Around two."

"Then no," Mitch said tightly.

"Figures." Russ stretched his arms to the ceiling and yawned. "What time is it?"

"Six. I woke up and then I couldn't go back to sleep." Mitched leaned his elbows on Russ's desk. "I was going to go work out, but then I got a message from Novak. He wants me to go to his lab tomorrow. He sent me the coordinates and it's the same place I gave Rhett. Do you think something is up?"

Russ's eyes flashed wider and he straightened his spine. "Gene isn't at his home base so he must be there as well. You think Novak suspects our involvement?"

Mitch pressed his head on the cold table. "Do me a favor. If something happens to me, keep an eye on Lydia, will ya?"

A long pause.

Mitch peered up.

Russ glared at him. "You better not do anything stupid."

"It's too late for that, don't you think?"

Russ leaned back. "Yup. For all of us. Whatever happens to me, I don't care. Novak is wrong. I'd rather die trying to stop him than live with guilt. Guilt is worse than death."

Mitch pushed up his long-sleeve black training shirt. "Nothing is going to happen to you. Novak has nothing on you. Rhett is my half brother. If he has Rhett too, I'm thinking Novak might use me to get to him. I have no idea. This is so messed up." He lowered his forehead on the table again and banged it lightly. "Wait. What am I thinking? This is good. This will give me a perfect opportunity to snoop around the facility."

"Just be careful. Maybe I should go with you."

Mitch appreciated the offer, but Novak hadn't requested him.

"And say what?" Mitch leaned back in his chair. "That you wanted to come with me? 'Cause we're best buddies?"

Russ's face reddened. "Now I know why Ava thought you were a prick."

"Well, she's not the only one. There's a line of people. I just tell how it is. I don't paint a pretty picture."

"No, you don't. You're kind of famous for that."

Mitch snorted. "I wish I was famous for far better things. Are you hungry? Let's grab breakfast."

After Mitch and Russ finished their meal, they went their separate ways. The teams worked on mental missions with Russ, then they went to Mitch in the afternoon. Mitch grilled them through physical training.

With Justine gone, Mitch's days had been less draining and frustrating. He had to admit, though, he missed her. She had been tolerable and unexpectedly pleasant the last week. Something had changed in her—or perhaps something had changed in him.

Mitch wiped the sweat from his forehead with the small towel that had been draped over his shoulder, He had just sent the last team back to its rooms when Russ and Lydia walked in briskly, looking alarmed.

Mitch snaked the towel around his neck and prepared for the worst. "What happened?"

Russ glanced around to make sure no one else was in the room. "Have you checked your messages?"

"No. I haven't had time," Mitch said. Lydia's grave expression gave him chills. "Want to tell me or are you both going to continue to stare?"

"Novak requested that the three of us join him at the secret facility." The fear in Lydia's voice was palpable.

Mitch hadn't told Lydia that Novak had ordered him to go already. He made no comment and drew up his message from his chip. Not that he didn't believe Lydia, but he wanted to see how Novak's message was worded.

As usual, it was straight and to the point with hardly any explanation.

Mitch swiped his message off and faced his friends. "Let's not worry without cause. I'm sure it's nothing. He probably wants to include us in his new plan as senior members of the training staff. This is good. We could snoop around and find more dirt on Novak. Maybe we can finally get some answers. Did you reply yet?"

"No. I wanted to tell you first," Russ said.

"I didn't either," was Lydia's response.

Mitch pulled his towel and wiped the sweat off his temples. "Well, let's not be weird about this. Don't give Novak any reason for suspicion, if he even has any. Let's all respond, but not all at once. We'll leave together. Everything will be fine."

He said it more for himself. He wanted to believe.

CHAPTER TWENTY-NINE– ROOM 128

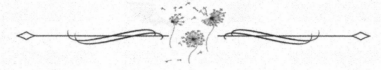

RHETT

R hett's boots padded softly on the smooth floor. Holding his Taser in front, he stealthily led his team down the hall with gray walls. Too many doors on either side of him. Rhett assumed Novak wouldn't throw Ava into a tiny cell—she might even have a whole room to herself—but he'd rather check, just in case.

Rhett raised a fist to halt his team and pointed to a metal door emblazoned with the number 124. Ozzie tried to open it, but it wouldn't budge. Ozzie tried the next one with the same result.

When footsteps approached, Rhett raised a hand again and guided his team to the closest hallway. It was the ISAN corridors all over again. The similarities gave him the creeps. Rhett's pulse thundered in his ears when footfalls came closer… closer. The closer they came, the faster his heart pounded. He backed against the wall and waited.

Entering the facility had been too easy. Knowing he was leading his team into a trap put him on edge and tugged on his conscience. Rhett had to take every precaution and ensure they made it out. So even when he heard Gene's voice in the hallway, he let it go.

Rhett could force Gene to take him to Ava, but there was no way to be sure he'd tell the truth. Rhett didn't know the blueprint of this place, so he made a judgment call.

Ozzie patted Rhett's back and lifted an eyebrow. He was probably thinking the same thing— capture Gene. Brooke, on the other hand, went rigid. Rhett didn't blame her. The sound of Gene's voice turned Rhett's blood to ice. But for Brooke, it must be a thousand times worse. Ozzie also had another motive to kidnap Gene—revenge for what had been done to Brooke. Rhett wished he could give Ozzie that chance, but it was not the time.

"Make sure to give Ava an extra dose," Gene said.

He must be talking to Ava's caretaker. It confirmed Ava was here, and more importantly, she was alive.

"I hear voices toward the end of the hall. Should we go?" Brooke whispered.

Rhett didn't hear anything, just quiet now that Gene had left. But Brooke could hear what others couldn't, so he trusted her. He held up a fist and tiptoed onward. Brooke stopped Rhett when they reached the last door.

"Do you think it's wise to go in?" Mia asked, taking in slow breaths.

Rhett felt as anxious as Mia, but before he had a chance to answer, Cleo opened the door, reckless with the need to find her father.

Whoever had been in here had left. But where? There was only one door.

Several sets of dark leather reclining chairs lined the walls on both sides. Syringes, scalpels, surgery tools, and medical supplies were arranged on metal trays.

Ozzie dashed for the TAB at the center table and did his magic while the others surveyed the space.

"Look at this." Ozzie's fingers flew over the hologram

keyboard.

"What is that?" Brooke looked over Ozzie's shoulder.

Numbers appeared on the hologram screen to the left of the chart. Then more grids appeared, revealing information about the assigned number.

Data: Number. Gender. Age. Birthdate. Sector. Occupation. Children.

"What are you looking at?" Tamara squeezed between Brooke and Rhett.

Cleo pointed. "Some of these messages were sent to Korea, Japan, China, Italy, France, and so many others. ISAN is spread out that wide?"

"It's possible," Rhett said. "But let's focus on the data. Number: X412. Gender: Female. Age: 47. Sector: North. Occupation: Programmer. Children: two females ages thirteen and fourteen."

"This is crazy." Nina's voice shook. "It's a long list. There are mostly females, but some males. Ages range from forty to sixty. Various occupations and different sectors. And even the children category has something in common. The ages range from thirteen to twenty."

Rhett was sure his father was on that list. "Ozzie, can you narrow the results to males over fifty years?"

"Ava didn't call me Einstein for no reason." Ozzie focused on the task, his fingers swiping away on the screen.

Brooke closed her eyes like she was concentrating, then opened them. "Hurry. I hear footsteps. Many of them."

Ozzie scrolled down the list, which shrank to males only. One of the contenders was exactly what Rhett had been looking for. XYM76. Age 55. West sector. Occupation: Council guard.

Children: Mitch and Rhett.

Rhett stared at the screen. He didn't know whether to feel angry, happy, or terrified. His father was here, had been all this time. What did they want from him?

"Rhett." Ozzie placed a hand on Rhett's shoulder.

Rhett followed the line to the last section column. "120. 122. 124. 126… These are the numbers to the rooms we passed earlier with no doorknobs. It has to be their holding space. That's just a guess, but what else would they use that many rooms for?"

"Come, on. We have to go." Reyna tugged on Rhett's arm.

Rhett clutched Ozzie's shirt, pulling him out of his seat. "Room 128," Rhett said. "Remember that room. My father is in there."

"We're too late. Hide." Brooke positioned herself flat against the wall and aimed her Taser at the entrance.

Reyna and Tamara overturned a gurney and hid behind it. Rhett flipped a table tray, all the contents clanking on the ground, and grabbed Cleo to get down with him.

The door slid open and a metal ball rolled to the middle of the room as it slid closed again. Smoke hissed out of the gadget. Tamara, who was closest, rubbed her eyes, and Rhett knew it was a sleeping bomb.

"Mia," Rhett shouted over the fog fizzing faster.

"I'm on it." She peeked out of the first leather chair and sucked in her breath to seize the smoke into her mouth and tunneled it straight up out to the vents.

Behind the second chair, Nina extended her arms toward the metal ball. Tendrils of blue and silver from her fingertips shoved the gadget back where it came from. Then something metal was thrown in the room, about the size of Rhett's fist. As it spun, it fired bullets in machine gun-like fashion.

"Watch out!" Ozzie hollered, protecting Brooke with his body.

Bullets pelted them, pinging every which way.

Mia blew air and produced a shield with her breath.

Reyna crouched low and wrapped her power around the spinner, creating an invisible barrier. The bullets bounced within the tight small bubble, ricocheting like mad.

"I can't hold it much longer. Do something," Reyna hollered.

"I can help." Mia somersaulted and tucked herself behind the gurney with Reyna. "On the count of three, let go. One. Two. Three."

When Reyna dropped her shield, Mia blew the bullets back toward the door. Metal pinged against metal as the bullets created crater-like dents along the wall.

"Stop. I'm coming in," said a voice. Not just any voice—Ava's.

Ava walked in, her hands up in surrender. Rhett rose halfway, only to be yanked down by Cleo.

"That's not her," Cleo said. "Can't you tell it's a hologram?"

Cleo was right. Rhett wanted her to be Ava so much that he'd just stood without caution.

"Ava." Tamara ran toward the hologram, not seeing the lie.

"No, Tamara." Brooke dove for her and brought her down to just before the smoke exploded in Tamara's face.

No, not smoke. The detonator spat out acid, sizzling the tile. Mia had blown air out of her lungs to protect the girls and to keep the mist from reaching them.

Ava's hologram vanished, and it crushed Rhett. To his horror, the doors slid open and Zen walked in bound and gagged with Novak at his side.

"What a lovely reunion." Novak gave a fake grin.

Rhett stepped in front and fired his gun, aiming straight at the center of Novak's forehead. He never missed. They didn't call him Sniper for no reason. But this one... went through.

"Dad," Cleo said.

Cleo had recognized her father wasn't a hologram, but Rhett shoved her back to her crouched position. Something wasn't right. Rhett had spotted a figure in the shadows from his vantage point.

"Look." Rhett shook Cleo a bit to get her attention.

The true Novak materialized behind Zen with a gun pressed to his skull. Novak's appearance, always in a suit and tie, had not changed; however, his hair was lighter and his eyes... gray. Was he wearing contact lenses now? Or was that the true color? And he looked different somehow.

Zen's eyes grew wide when they halted on his daughter. His muffled words held no meaning, but his terrified expression said it all.

"Like I said, what a lovely reunion," Novak said. "If you don't want any harm done to Zen, I suggest you cooperate. First, place all your weapons down and raise your arms high. That includes Tamara's daggers, even the tiny ones she has inside her back pockets."

How did he know that? Rhett didn't want to surrender, but he had no choice. Perhaps getting caught was a good thing. Novak might lead them to Ava faster.

"Do as he said," Rhett gritted through his teeth.

Weapons clanked and hands raised.

"Come in and get them," Novak ordered.

Soldiers rushed in, clad in dark, high-tech uniforms. Where had they been when Rhett and his team had come in? Waiting to spring the trap, of course. Luring them in without exchanging gunfire was the safest and fastest way.

Ava was alive.

Rhett's father was here. Room 128.

But what fate awaited them… he didn't know.

CHAPTER THIRTY – A NEW ALLY

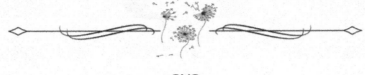

AVA

I hadn't felt sick after dinner last night or the breakfast this morning—no tingles down my arms or my palms. My body had gotten used to the suppressant, I supposed. Either that, or it was doing its job and then I would be ultimately at Novak's mercy. Terrifying thought.

Save the baby. Why would mother take interest in a baby? How did she even know about it? Novak wouldn't have taken her to visit the lab. What reason would he have to do so?

Had Janine been trying to tell me the same? And if so—why?

As I lay on my bed, I thought of Rhett, my friends, and especially Brooke. Though Gene told me the rebel base had been destroyed and everyone was dead, I refused to believe it. Gene could be lying to get me riled up. I didn't trust anything that came out of his mouth.

When the door slid open, I didn't bother looking up and kept my gaze on the ceiling. I already knew who it was.

"What do you want?" I didn't hold back my annoyance.

"I'm here to take you to the washroom," Payton said, always the same neutral tone.

I pushed off the bed and advanced toward the exit. Payton dismissed my glower and ushered me forward. My footpads resonated down the empty gray hallway, the only sound until he spoke.

"Keep your head straight but tilt your chin down when you speak to me. Justine is on her way here."

I reminded myself to focus on the polished white floor. "Justine is coming already? Do you know if she's coming alone or with a team?"

"She's not coming with a team unless you count Mitch, Russ, and Lydia as a team."

"What? Why?"

"I don't know."

Something in Payton's voice told me he was afraid. This was my chance to get a feel if he would help me. I was taking a risk in trusting him.

After we rounded to the hallway, I said, "Payton, I need to get my friends out. Can you help me?"

A few heartbeats passed. He stopped in front of the washroom. "When?"

That one word gave me hope. I even lit a small smile. "When is Justine coming?"

"Tonight. But they're not coming together. Justine has her own escort." Payton glanced down the hall, then back at me. "Scoot back a little. Tilt your head down and speak to my chest. How do I help you?"

I stared at his sweater, which reminded me of the blue sweater Rhett had worn when we had separated at the Black Market, and my heart stirred uncomfortably. *Focus, Ava.*

"I need access to the prisoners' cell, to my mom, and then to a glider. Can you arrange that?"

"It's going to be difficult, but I think I can with Mitch's help."

I scrunched my nose. "Why would you ask Mitch?" I tried to play dumb, but Payton could read me like a street sign thanks to

205

his gift.

"Follow me," Payton said, stepping farther in. He pressed on the control panel and the shower rained down, then he scooted closer to me. "Mitch and I have talked. I know enough."

I wanted to trust Payton, but this could be a trap, and Mitch wasn't here to confirm. My nostrils flared when I recalled he was my father's lackey. I had to make a judgment call.

"How much do you really tell Novak?" I said over the pouring water.

"Enough for him to be satisfied." Payton cupped my shoulders. "I think a part of you always knew I was on your side, but you could never be sure. I had to play the part, like we all do, have been doing. I'm his pet—that's the way people from all factions describe me, but they don't know that I had no choice. I follow Novak like his shadow and gather intel. There are things I know that no one knows."

"Like?" I drawled.

"Like how I don't have parents." He lowered his hands to his side.

I gave him a puzzled look and leaned against the wall close to the shower. "Most of ISAN's assassins are orphans."

"You don't understand," he whispered sharply, and his change from gentle demeanor to cold made me recoil. "I never had parents. I'm a CODE baby."

My mouth split open. "You're kidding me, right?"

When he lowered his head, I got my answer. My mind mulled with questions. Most important one: Had he been lobotomized? He was always docile and obedient. I didn't want to ask him, in case he didn't know.

"There are others like me," he said. "Brooke, Ozzie, and Reyna, too."

"What?" I blinked and blinked at this new revelation.

Brooke and Ozzie had said their past memories felt hazy, but Ozzie remembered Brooke from a facility. Reyna had never shared much about her past, either. Perhaps she too couldn't recall and didn't want to admit it. Now it all made sense. But how would I tell them?

"We were the first batch," Payton added. "Then there was a gap. I don't know the details. I speculate there were hiccups. Now, there are many of these CODE children. They're based somewhere in the south. I also found out that there are international CODE babies. There's a base in Sokcho in South Korea. Rumor has it, there's a rebel team out there, too."

South Korea? My next destination. "What do you know of that one infant in the hub?" I asked.

"What do you mean?"

"Novak showed me an infant in an incubation chamber. He told me the baby was special."

"I don't know anything about that baby. Sorry."

I crossed my arms. "Why are you telling me all this? What's in it for you?"

Payton looked offended and whispered sharply, "Nothing. I have nothing, Ava. No parents. No family. I'm a living machine, created for one purpose. What kind of life is that?"

"I'm sorry. There's nothing wrong with you. Born from a real womb or not, you deserve better."

The strain in his forehead eased. "This is why I'm risking my life. You've been nothing but kind to me. You made me see there are good people in the world and some things are worth fighting for."

I snatched the collar of his shirt. "Help me escape and come with me. You'll know the meaning of freedom and what it means

207

to have a family."

He flushed, either from the steam behind us rising like drifting clouds or he felt embarrassed.

"Do you think your friends would accept me? I've been helping Novak. Everyone has pegged me as his lackey, I'm sure of that."

"Yes, they would accept you because they all escaped from ISAN. They would understand because they were once in your shoes."

He dipped his head and shrugged. "Well, I meant... I'm not normal. I wasn't... I was made."

I cupped his cheeks, forcing him to look at me. "You just told me you're not the only one. But I will never tell unless you want me to. Your secret is safe with me. To be honest, we're all fighting our own battles to forget our past. We won't be safe until ISAN is down and out of our lives. But first things first. We need to get out of here."

He nodded. "Before I turn off the shower, you should wet your hair and change. Gene should be here soon."

I rolled my eyes. "Great. What a way to make my day."

Payton chuckled. "Your favorite person thinks the world of you."

"Like hell he does." I snorted.

"Ready to go?"

Reality and gloom replaced our tense camaraderie. Time to get serious and strategize.

CHAPTER THIRTY-ONE – NEW FACILITY

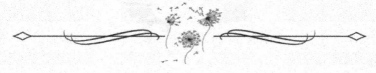

JUSTINE

Justine couldn't get the image of Tessa being impaled by that creature out of her mind. No time to say goodbye to her teammates, but that was how ISAN operated. Nobody cared.

During the ride, the driver sealed her window and she couldn't see out. Pleading with him was useless. She thought about playing the Novak-is-my-daddy card, but decided otherwise. Father would lecture her, or worse—punish her.

After they landed, Justine's escort covered her head with a black cloth. She felt like she was being kidnapped. So she did what any ISAN trained assassin would do—counted the steps and listened with her powerful hearing. And she did it without Helix. An advantage for her.

Rushing wind slapped her hair. A pungent stench stung her nose—heaps and heaps of trash, she guessed. Her boots crunched on dried earth.

A crank. Metal grinding on metal.

Cool air caressed her face, and dim light appeared when her mask was removed. She blinked to adjust to her vision and was floored to see a wholly unfamiliar underground base.

"Justine. Welcome."

She spun. Her father smiled with his arms extended. He always looked like he was going to a business meeting wearing a suit and a tie. But he had lightened his hair. He looked like a different man.

Justine glanced over her shoulder. There was no one behind her. The guards who had escorted her in were gone too. Novak was actually smiling… at her. She swelled with bliss, but at the same time she was terrified.

He wants something. Or this is a test.

"Mr. Novak." Justine plastered a fake smile.

"Come. Let me show you around."

With every step toward him, her knees wobbled. He clasped an arm around her and guided her down the dim hallway. Unless her eyes were deceiving her, his dark eyes were now gray. Contacts? Why on earth would he change his appearance?

Her instincts told her to get out, but then what? She had no transportation. Worse, she had no idea where she was or where to go. Justine certainly couldn't return to ISAN if she was on the run.

Justine had no family. No friends. No 4Qs. She would be a fugitive, a *traitor*. Oh, for the love of God, she would be in Ava's shoes but with no help. She shoved back the unwelcome thoughts.

Novak brought her out of her mental frenzy when he spoke. His gentle voice sounded strange, even made her nauseous. Someone had flipped the rules and forgotten to tell her.

"There are a couple of people I would like for you to meet," he said.

"Why? Who are they?" Apprehension seized her. Her pulse jumped and she broke into a panicky sweat. What he said next spun her world inside out.

"Your family."

"Family? You mean you found Mom?" Justine shoved her trembling hands inside her training suit pockets.

"Not exactly. I'll explain about your mom very soon, and then you'll meet your brother and sister."

Justine halted, refusing to take another step. Her temper skyrocketed. "Why didn't I know before?"

Novak's gentle expression faltered as his lips thinned. His true self coming forth. "Everything has its time. You shall see. Now, are you going to come with me or do I have to make you?"

Justine knew he couldn't keep up that phony, loving father act for long. She was surprised he'd held up the facade the length of the hallway.

"Seems I have no choice." She mimicked his tone, surprised she was bold enough to do it.

An excited little butterfly fluttered inside her. All this time Justine had thought she was alone. But indignation ate away the little happiness. Novak had kept them from her all these years.

They entered a sophisticated lab.

"This is pretty impressive." Justine gave a wolf whistle, admiring the hubs and monitors. "What are all these used for?"

"Come. I want to show you a miracle."

Too busy admiring the high-tech equipment, Justine hadn't realized Novak had walked away. She strolled leisurely to him, elated he wanted to show her something. She leaned over an egg-like silver pod, humming. Thick, clear liquid filled the tank.

"What is that?" Justine's voice left her in a squeal.

She knew what it was. In shock, she blurted the words, and she needed to know that her father saw the same thing, that this was his great secret.

"She's a CODE baby. CODE stands for Constructed Ovum Designed Engineering

"But how does it… I mean… You can't make babies… That machine… It's impossible."

211

"Yes, I can, Justine. I created this machine, and this infant."
He patted the hub.

Justine's father was brilliant, perhaps too much for his own
good. She believed he was capable of building anything, but this...
Oh dear God, what was he planning?

Justine stared at the sleeping infant. So innocent. A chill
prickled along her arms. Little did this baby know she would be
ISAN's assassin. Little did she know her life was not her own. For
now she was safe in a bubble home, but after birth, she would
become a weapon.

"How many?" Justine asked, terrified of the answer.

"Enough. And there will be more."

"Why do you need them?" Justine continued to stare at the
little girl. The little girl curled up as if tucked in a mother's womb.

Novak droned on about how there weren't enough soldiers and
how they needed the numbers in case of World War III. She only
half-listened, still mesmerized by the infant, and she disliked
history and never paid attention in class.

"So, what's your answer?" He shifted one foot to another as if
running out of patience.

Justine caught the last sentence and bristled. An answer? For
what? When had he ever *asked* her for anything? He only ordered.

"Sorry." She recoiled sheepishly. She had to think of something
to say. "I—I was too mesmerized by how the infant's fingers are
curled toward its mouth."

Novak grinned, his eyes set on the hub. "Some infants suck
their fingers. This proves the infant is sustainable and would never
know the difference between a real and designed uterus."

"That's amazing," she said only to say something, but felt sick
to her stomach.

"So, what's your answer?" He crossed his arms. "Would you like to be the captain of my CODE soldiers?"

"A captain?"

Justine about fell on her knees. How many times had she wished to be a team leader? How many times had she put in a request only to be shut down? Justine had lost her hope when her father had placed Payton as their lead. Had Mitch put in a good word for her?

She'd known it. Her father believed in her. He loved her. Novak didn't want to show favoritism—that had to be the reason why he'd never made her the leader. But away from the others, he showed her his love. Justine could hug him. She longed to do it, but he began to speak again.

"Well, don't look so surprised, Justine. I understand your reservations. You have to know that I have a plan for everything. You were meant for better. If you don't want this position, I could assign another."

"No," she said in a rush. "I would love to. I will make you proud, Father."

You were meant for better. She couldn't stop smiling.

"I know you will. It's one of the reasons why I wanted you to come here before you were sent to one of the South bases. There are two. The second one was designed for CODE soldiers, hidden from the other quadrants. After we are finished here, you'll come with me."

She beamed.

Novak paused briefly to look at a message from his chip, then met her gaze again. "Do you have any questions?"

Justine had many, but decided to ask the most pressing ones first. "How was the infant created? There had to be an egg and sperm?" She blushed at her comment.

Novak frowned, then eased. "After we rebuilt from the devastation, many families were still separated. ISAN created a system to bring lost families together through DNA matching. In the process, I discovered a special marker. I asked for donations, eggs and sperm, to research the effects of radiation. People were so concerned about saving our people and rebuilding our world that they never asked questions. They weren't aware of my motives to build an army. And that is how I met my wife."

Justine's mouth slackened. "That's how you met my mother?"

"You're special, Justine. It's the very reason why I asked you to lead these soldiers. You can relate to them. I know you will make me proud."

Not an answer.

You can relate to them. Her veins chilled. She planted her hand on the hub to keep her grounded.

"What do you mean I can relate to them?"

"Know that I care for you just the same as my own children."

His own children? She was not the only one. He had two others. He had mentioned a brother and a sister. None of this made sense.

"What do you mean?" Justine balled her fists, bracing for the answer. Novak was full of surprises. "Am I... Was I..." Her attention went to the infant and something in her middle ripped open.

Novak's eyes were stone cold, his voice harsh and commanding. "You are one of the CODE babies, and you are my daughter. Half of you is my genetic material, and half came from your mother."

Justine's eyes stung and she shook with rage. She never cried because Novak didn't approve, but she felt tears pooling. Novak had tossed a bomb at her. Now he watched, waiting for her to die at this unfathomable truth.

"My mother was just a donor?" Her voice cracked and she clutched her fingers tighter on the hub.

"Yes," he said.

Justine retreated a step, her soul crushed. A part of her felt repulsed. "The picture of you and the blonde woman. You told me she was my mother. She isn't, is she?"

"She is your mother, but she never wanted children. She had the special marker, so I asked for her eggs. I never loved her. The picture was part of my cover."

He said it like it was inconsequential, as if none of it should affect her in any way.

"Why are you telling me this? You should have let me believe—"

"A lie, Justine? You need to know the truth. Knowing you are a CODE child, the others will follow you without question. You will be easy for them to relate to."

Justine grappled for words, but none came. Everything made sense now. Why she couldn't recall her mother's face. Why she couldn't recall a childhood or any part of her past. She only recalled Novak visiting her in a facility, something that looked like... this one.

When Ava, Brooke, and Tamara had talked about their past, she'd wanted to share hers too, but she hadn't, but not because she wanted to be standoffish. If she had told them she couldn't remember any of it, they wouldn't have believed her. She was sure of that.

Acid rose up to her throat and nausea undulated through her.

At least he'd told her the truth. Better late than never, she supposed.

Novak was giving her a chance to lead his CODE soldiers. It was more responsibility than Ava had ever had. Justine bet the CODE soldiers were more capable than any of the girls in her compound. She'd bet those soldiers weren't wild and crazy like Ava and the others.

Perhaps Justine could handle this team well. Her father believed in her. The thought gave her confidence. Regardless of how she had been born, created or designed, she was still a human being in every way.

"Fine, I'll do it," she said with a stern voice, straightening her spine.

Novak smiled. "You made the right decision."

Justine glanced at the infant and said, "What if I said no?"

He simply replied, "You never say no to the person who has your life in the palm of their hand." A short pause gave her time to digest his words and his mocking smile. "Justine, it's time to meet your siblings."

CHAPTER THIRTY-TWO – SIBLING REUNION

AVA

I had been anxious about a lot of things in my life. Going off on a mission and having to kill was one thing, but seeing Justine face-to-face and knowing she was my half sister... my heart pattered out of control.

A sick part of me couldn't wait to see the look on her face, but the other part didn't want her to know. Another sibling who didn't care about me, or I them. What was the point of having a family if we hated each other?

"Are you ready?" Payton asked, not the usual soft tone, but harsher.

I hadn't heard him come into my room. What was his problem? I soon found out when I slid off the bed and turned to him by the door. I snarled at the sight of Gene. Of *course* he would be there. Novak would want to tell Justine about the both of us.

Justine was going to get the shock of her life, just as I had when I'd found out Gene was my psycho brother.

"You don't seem happy to see me, sister," Gene said.

"Well, that shouldn't be anything new to you." I passed him and exited behind Payton.

Payton, who usually strode beside me, walked briskly ahead.

"What's wrong, Payton? Are you upset?" Gene would get a punch for his tone if he didn't stop pestering.

Payton banked left and continued to ignore him.

I rushed to Payton. "Is Justine here?"

Payton met my eyes with sympathy and lowered his voice. "Yes. I hope it goes well for your sake. You know how Justine is."

"Honestly, I don't care what she thinks. I don't like it any more than she does. It is what it is." The last sentence was Rhett's phrase. My heart swelled. I missed him so much. "Can you do me a favor? Can you check the system and see if Rhett or any of my friends have been captured?"

"I'll do my best."

"What are you two whispering about?" Gene said.

I imagined Gene grinning with sardonic pleasure. He was trying to rile us up. Well, it worked, but I wasn't going to allow him to get the best of me.

Payton and I turned our heads to say, "Shut up."

I rolled my eyes when Gene snarled behind us.

The door slid open to the lab with the CODE baby. Justine and Novak came into view, standing a few yards from the hub.

Justine blanched at the sight of me, then her gaze bounced from Payton to Gene. She reached for a weapon, but she carried none.

"Ava? Why is she here?" Justine bit out.

Novak walked toward me and stood in the middle, a solid divider between Justine and me. More for my sake than hers.

"Meet your siblings, Justine," Novak said. "They already know about you."

"All of them?" Justine ground out, sounding like a spoiled child who had just been told she had to share her toys.

"No, not Payton," Novak said. "Ava is your half sister and Gene is your half brother."

Justine gave me once over, then she did the same to Gene. "This is a joke, right?" She glared at Novak, a vein on her neck twitching. "Why are you doing this? And Gene? He's a psychotic nerd. You've got to be kidding. What does Ava have over you, *Father?*"

"Justine, calm down." Surprisingly, Novak's tone was passive. "Ava and Gene are twins. I'm their father."

"Are they CODE children too?"

CODE children too?

Gene cocked his head, squaring his eyes at Justine with contempt. "I don't like it any more than you do. How do you think I felt? You're just a CODE child. I will never think of you as a real sister. You're a freak."

Justine bristled, her face the same color as Gene's red sweater. "Nobody calls me freak, you freak."

I gaped. Had Gene known Justine was a CODE child before? I should be used to Gene knowing more than I did. The fact that Justine didn't deny it or ask questions meant it must be true.

"Stop this instant," Novak barked. "You're both acting like children. I brought Justine here to make amends with Ava, and also to tell her about her family. I've appointed Justine to lead the CODE soldiers. And soon, Ava and Gene will lead all of ISAN as we prepare for war."

"What?" Justine growled. "Then that means Ava will be head of all units?"

Gene gave a satisfied smirk. "Oh, thank God I'm with Ava."

Justine's nostrils flared, her jaw clenching. "I wasn't talking to you, idiot."

Gene walked past Novak and stood closer to Justine. "The only idiot in this room is you."

Payton, standing on the other side of me, flinched when Justine slapped Gene. She tried to do it again, but Gene caught her hand and locked her in his arm with a twist.

"Let go of me." Justine struggled in his grasp. Then she flipped him over and backed away, rubbing at her arm. "Don't touch me, freak."

Novak waved a hand. "Enough, before I send you both to solitary."

Seriously? A time out? Let them kill each other and save me the trouble.

Justine unflexed and flexed her fingers. "Send me back. I don't want to be here."

Gene got up, slicked his hair back, and straightened his sweater. "Justine is not ISAN material. Just kill her and be done with her. She knows too much."

Justine's eyes grew wild and focused on Novak like a scared little mouse. When he didn't answer, she said hurriedly, "I take it back. I'll stay. I'll do whatever you want me to do."

A sly, secretive grin spread on Novak's face.

Justine craned her neck to focus on the CODE baby near her, and cradled her arms to her center. Gene continued to glare at Justine. Payton kept quiet, stiff as a log. As for me, I'd had enough.

Novak could plan and pretend I would be the perfect daughter he wanted. Never would I side with him. Never would I think of him as my father, or Gene as my brother, or Justine as my half sister.

Never!

NEVER.

"Where do you think you're going?" Novak asked when I strolled toward the door.

"Back to my room. You're all are crazy."

"But then you'll never get to see my surprise, Ava."

Something about his tone raked a chill up my middle. I halted just before the sensor.

"Gene, would you like to do the honors?" Novak asked.

Gene's lips curved upward, the sly grin said he was going to enjoy what lay ahead. Something terrible was about to happen. I felt it in my gut.

When Gene reached the table in the center, he tabbed on the monitor, and a light flickered. Then people in separate cells appeared on a hologram screen.

I had prepared for the worst, but this... I never would have guessed. Novak told me he was going to send them off on a wild-goose chase. And I, foolishly, had hoped he would do something he promised for once.

Rhett, Ozzie, Reyna, Tamara, Cleo, Mia, and a new girl were locked in individual cells. Even Naomi was there. Rhett sat on a cot with his head down, cupping his face. He must regret coming here.

The camera moved to the last cell, showing a figure I knew too well. I almost shouted with joy, but managed to swallow it. I didn't want to give Gene any reason to ask Novak to turn the monitor back on. Gene had been too busy snarling at Justine and hadn't seen it.

Brooke was alive.

Seeing her gave me new hope and inspiration. We girls should lift each other up, support each other. We should ignite each other's beautiful souls and not douse them in darkness. And that was the kind of friendship I had with some of the girls at the rebel base.

Novak watched me closely. "All I have to do is send a signal, and then well, you know what will happen."

I hate you. I hate you with every fiber of my being.

"There's no need for that." I had to think fast. One way or another, I needed time with Justine alone, to get her on my side. Novak hadn't said anything about me hurting Gene, so I pounced on him.

Gene pressed the coin-sized gadget as I expected. My body sizzled in midair and dropped. I curled up in the fetal position as pain seized my body. I quaked like a fish out of water, a knife slicing through me again and again.

As the effect dwindled, unlike the first time, I drew the power and absorbed it into my system to save for my day of glory. I must have looked like I had gone to hell and back. I sure felt like it. When I managed to peer up, I met Justine's horrified eyes, her jaw slackened.

I'd thought she might smile, or perhaps even laugh. Instead, she lacked for words, her expression haunted.

Novak shook his head, standing inches from me. Still on the floor, I didn't attempt to move as I rode out the pain.

I'm so sorry, Rhett. You fell in love with someone like me. Now you and my friends will pay the price.

"This did not go as I had planned." Novak narrowed his eyes on me as if I had disappointed him. "Gene, come with me. Justine, stay with your sister. When she's ready, bring her to the dining room. We're having a family dinner."

Good. What I'd hope he would say.

Justine's face sharpened with aggression. "Why do I have to stay behind? And she's not my sister. She'll never be my sister."

Novak must have given her a death glare. Something shut her up.

"Fine." Her voice softened and she nudged me with the toe of her boot. "Get up. I don't want to wait here longer than I have to. This place gives me the creeps."

Just you wait until I'm fully recovered. You'll have a thing or two coming from me.

I waited until Novak and Gene were out before prying myself up. I didn't want them to see how fast I recovered now, compared to the previous times I'd been electrocuted. My muscles had learned to tolerate the stimulant, but the agony was still the same.

No matter. I could endure the suffering as long as I had my mobility.

"Hurry up. Get up. What's wrong with you?" Justine spat, but there was a hint of concern in her voice.

"Did you seriously forget what they did to me?" I wanted to match her callous tone, but I had no energy.

Justine crossed her arms and bit her finger, regarding me jadedly.

"Have you known all along?" I asked as I flipped over and lay on my back.

Her eyelashes fluttered. "Known what?"

"That you're a CODE baby?"

"No. I just found out," she murmured.

I was shocked by her honesty—more so that she answered at all.

"It doesn't make you any less of a human being, you know." I pushed up on my knees and brushed fingers through my hair.

"I never told you I thought of myself as less."

Her jealousy always got the better of her. It was always about her trying to best me in everything.

The tingling sensation along my fingertips began to wear off, and I moved with more fluidity. I didn't know what I had done to deserve this animosity, but I had to fix it. If I could get her on my side, she would be one more person to help me escape.

"I never thought you were less than me," I said and rose. "In fact, I always thought Novak had made a mistake assigning me as a lead. He should have given that position to you."

She scrunched her features, then a hint of a reserved smile showed. "Well, I'm glad we agree on something."

I straightened my shirt. "Not just one thing. I don't like Gene. He *is* such a nerd and completely psychotic. So that makes two things we have in common." I flashed a grand smile.

Justine lowered her hands to her side, her rigid stance relaxing. "He's a prick. Novak kiss-ass."

And you're not? I almost laughed, but I agreed with her with a straight face.

I rubbed at my temples and released a sigh. "I can't believe we're half sisters."

"Well, it came as a surprise to me too." She grimaced. "We don't even look alike. People might not… Let's not tell anyone about this. I don't want anyone to know I'm related to Gene."

I raised my hand halfway. "I won't, but those who know you are Novak's daughter might put two and two together if they find out Gene and I are twins and Novak is our father."

Justine shot out a disgusted noise. Then she asked, "You're not here of your own free will, are you?"

"No, I'm not." I looked where the hologram screen had been. "If I don't find a way to release my friends, he's going to kill them."

She scoffed. "You're still with the rebels."

She needed to know about her father and all the horrible things he'd done. I didn't know how she would perceive the things I was going to tell her but I had to try.

I told her how Novak took the assassins' memories to ensure their compliance. I told her how he not only grew infants in the pod, but had them lobotomized to mold them to be perfect soldiers. And still more, about the protein drink and how we didn't need Helix to access our abilities.

When I finished, Justine's stoic expression turned sour. I'd thought I had gotten through to her, but instead she lashed out.

"You're lying. You... you want... He... Novak is...." She paused between words as if unable to make up her mind.

I huffed in frustration and shoved my hands inside my pockets to keep from strangling her. "Just to be clear. I hate Novak. If I ever get the chance, I'm going to kill him and your half brother, Gene. He hurt Brooke. If he had his way, he would kill you without any hesitation. If you want to leave ISAN, you can come with me. Think about what kind of life you want. The choice is yours. It always has to be yours."

She blinked and blinked, soaking in my declaration, or rather astounded by it.

"Well... I don't... I think... this is too much. You don't know what you're talking about." She sounded defensive and afraid.

Perhaps that was a good sign.

"No one has the right to direct your life." I walked away.

"Where're you going?" Justine's footsteps padded behind me when I took off. "Wait. I'm supposed to take you. You can't walk yourself. That will make me seem incompetent. Please."

I halted by the door with a roll of my eyes and waved her forward. I couldn't believe I was going to let her have her way, but she'd said please.

This could be a start of a beautiful sisterhood... nope. Who was I kidding?

225

CHAPTER THIRTY-THREE – FAMILY DINNER

AVA

Justine kept close enough for me to follow her, but she made an effort not to walk beside me. I didn't mind. Probably better that way. She might say something to trigger my temper and I might do something I'd regret. We had made some sort of progress and I didn't want to hamper it.

Back there, in that room, was the most we'd ever said to each other about something that wasn't related to a mission. Our conversation about her joining the resistance might backfire, and I was risking the chance she would squeal to Novak, but I took a gamble that there was more to her than just an ISAN assassin. She must want more.

Justine strolled in first at dinner, her demeanor guarded. With her back tall, she held up her chin. As for me, I focused my attention on Gene, who appeared in my line of vision next to Novak, drinking wine, and then my mother across from them.

My mother never lifted her eyes from the assortment of food on her plate. Either she didn't hear us or she simply refused to look up.

Unlike her attire at the garden, she wore a long spring dress with a flower pattern. Her hair was nicely combed and her light makeup brought out her features, making her look more alive. Regardless, I knew her true self was in slumber, locked up in the dark recesses of the hell Novak had created for her.

"Welcome. Have a seat." Novak waved at the empty seats. "We were waiting for you."

I pulled up a chair next to Mother, and Justine sat on the opposite of Gene. I ran a finger along the ridges of the fine oak table. A bouquet of red roses in a vase sent a pleasant scent in the air. Mother's flowers from her garden.

The elegant white dishes with gold trim angered me. While the rebels at Hope City ate from old cracked dishes, Novak ate from fine china. But there was no Hope City. I had no idea who had survived besides my imprisoned friends.

"Sweetheart," he said to my mother, "I want you to meet Justine. You remember me talking about her, don't you?"

Novak's tender voice made my skin crawl. Mother hummed instead of giving Novak her attention. She glanced about the simple room that held only a dining table, chairs, a couple of paintings of sunflowers, and nothing else.

Novak propped his elbows on the table, his fingers entwined. "Justine, this is Avary. I don't expect you to call her Mom, but she is your stepmother."

Gene twisted to fully face Novak. "You've got to be joking, Father. She's a pod prodigy. She's not..." He grimaced at Justine, searching for words.

Justine gripped her spoon, her hand trembling. "You say that one more time, and I'll—"

"Justine is more human than you'll ever be," I said. "Don't understate her intelligence, her beauty, or her ability."

Justine gawked at me.

Gene fluttered his eyelashes, looking hurt. "What does it mean to be human, sister? I would like to know."

Mother flinched. I placed a hand on her thigh to calm her. She still wouldn't look at me.

I squared my gaze on Gene's. "Being human means to be better than you think you are. To test the boundaries. Sometimes it means giving more of yourself. Even if it's hard."

"Enough, Ava," Father said.

"It means doing the right thing even when others are against you."

"I said *enough*."

Novak's loud scolding didn't stop me.

"Being human means to live. Living means loving someone, and them loving you back. To know what it's like to have friends. All these things you know nothing of."

Novak pounded his fist on the table, the crimson liquid in the wine glass undulating like the ocean. "Eat your dinner." Novak scooped up rice pilaf with his spoon and shoved it in his mouth as if he hadn't just had a temper tantrum.

I'd said more than I meant to, but sometimes… sometimes words were stronger than action.

Justine's perky lips tugged a bit at the corner. She tried to hide it, but I had seen it. Mission accomplished.

After escaping ISAN, I'd learned what it truly meant to live. I learned that I should surround myself with good people, people who lift your spirit, people who forgive you when you make mistakes, people who love and support you for who you are and all that you can be.

If Justine could feel and experience what I had been through, I was sure she'd change, too. You don't know what you could have if it's never offered.

I at least had a mother who loved me unconditionally. She had been the first person to show me there was love and good in this word. But Justine… she only had Novak. What kind of role model was he? It was no wonder she'd turned out the way she had.

Gene ate Mother's home-grown vegetables. He didn't deserve to enjoy her fresh food. He took a sip of red wine and wiped his mouth with the cloth napkin at the same time Novak did. Like father like son.

How had I missed the resemblance? They even looked the same. Their thick, perfect angled eyebrows, their sharp masculine noses, their square jawlines—so similar, so uncanny. I saw so much of Novak in Gene. I'd thought they should have been father and son once, before I knew they were. I laughed inwardly.

Mother's stoic expression had not changed during dinner. She moved robotically, unlike the graceful woman she had been. It saddened me to see her this way. Novak had made her into a docile being and someone who couldn't think for herself. She had lost herself in this pathetic excuse for a man.

I'm going to get you out of here, Mother, and then you can begin to heal.

CHAPTER THIRTY-FOUR – A VISIT

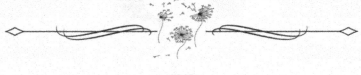

AVA

That night when lights were out, Payton came to my room. He had promised to give me some time with Rhett and my friends. We didn't have a glider, so busting out of this compound was futile. Regardless, I needed to see them. They needed to know I was alive. That alone would give them hope.

"Do you remember what I'd said?" Payton asked as we stood close to my bedroom door.

"Yes. And you remember what *I* said?" I whispered.

"Yes. I lie here until you get back. If Gene or one of the guards come by, I tell them you knocked me out and escaped."

I took a step, stopped, and turned back to him. "Thank you, Payton. When we leave here, you come with me, okay?"

His eyes rounded. "You want me to go with you?"

"Yes, of course. Unless you don't want to. It will be your choice."

His small smile grew bigger. "I don't want to be here. Novak thinks of me as a CODE child who belongs to him, but I have a mind—a soul. This is no way to live for the rest of my life."

My heart hurt for him. I knew that feeling all too well. "You deserve so much more. I will remember what you did for me. I owe you."

"You owe me nothing. I only care about your friendship.

And… that I have your protection. If I go with you, your friends might want to—"

I placed a hand on his shoulder. "They won't. I promise, but if it makes you feel better, I promise you have my protection."

He nodded. "Thank you, Ava. You should hurry. Twenty minutes until the guards shift again. Go."

Quiet as a mouse, my footsteps swift and light, I turned left, and then went all the way until I hit a dead end, then turned right. No sign of guards. No sign of Novak's lab workers. Just me and the empty hallway.

Cautiously, I entered the only door—a lab with a tall ceiling. A cool draft greeted me and then the stale smell filtered through my nostrils.

This room looked similar to the one in which Novak had housed the memory-erasing machine and the CODE baby in the pod. It even had a table in the center with TABs and monitors.

The farther I walked, the brighter the span, extending through the darkness. With my heart pounding, I ran to the first square. Only a cot and nothing else.

Empty.

I went to the second.

No one.

I rushed to the third, fourth, fifth… all vacant. Payton wouldn't lie to me. I was missing something.

A secret room? No.

The cells looked exactly the same—a cot and toilet. No body. A hologram mirage? Maybe not, but I had to try. I rapped on the first.

No sound.

I banged on the second.

I was about to move on to the third when the response came, the same but faint. A breath escaped me. I knocked again, and received the same answer. But this time, I heard a voice. A voice that shook me to my core.

"Ava. Is that you?"

"Rhett," I said, even though he couldn't hear me.

Think. What can I do?

I went to the monitor set on a long table with TABs and panels. I had no idea what kind of danger I would place them in if I had pushed one. One of the buttons said *lights*.

Too simple? Maybe not.

I took a chance. At worst, the lights would become brighter, right?

Oh, God. Please. Let this be the one.

When I pressed it, the ceiling light dimmed, but the lights inside the cell flickered. As if a layer of fog had been lifted, the fake image cleared from cell number two and a few others, revealing my team.

Rhett had been the one pounding the barrier. He had his palms pressed to the glass while the others sat on the cots. Rhett's bright amber eyes were trained on me, as if he couldn't believe he was seeing me.

I ran to him, my pulse racing. He looked fine. No bruises. No blood. No signs of torture.

"Ava." His voice sounded muffled—barely audible. "Can you hear me?" he asked.

"Yes." I nodded frantically, so happy to see him. *Don't cry. Not now.* "Are you okay? Are you hurt? What happened at the rebel base?"

I hated seeing him here, but at the same time it was *so good* to see him. I had missed him so much. My heart exploded with joy and pain.

Rhett lowered his eyelashes and his eyes lost their sparkle. "Our home is gone. Many died. Many soldiers and kids… they didn't make it."

I clutched at my chest, agony cleaving through the seams as hot teardrops escaped. Hearing it from Rhett was so much worse than from Gene. Gene had told me out of anger, but Rhett told me from anguish and loss.

I closed my eyes in respect for those who had passed away. It was a horrible death, one that could have been prevented. I should have never taken refuge at Hope City.

"I'm so sorry, Rhett." My palms met his, the coldness of the barrier assaulted the warmth on my arm.

"Oh, Ava," he said, caressing the glass as if he was stroking my cheek. "Remember what I've told you. You can't save everyone. Find a way to get out of here. Live your life to the fullest."

"What are you talking about? I'm not going to leave you or any of my friends."

He had experienced devastation at Hope City. Seen too many deaths. Sometimes when one person couldn't see the light, another had to carry the torch. I would carry that torch and make it brighter for the both of us.

"Yes, you are," he said. "If you get a chance, you take it and run. Do you hear me?"

Rhett's stubbornness would not penetrate the glass and it carried no weight on this side.

A soft pounding broke my attention. I dashed over to the next cell without telling Rhett what I was doing.

When Brooke met my gaze, no words were needed. I pressed

my hands to match hers as tears streamed down my face. I had thought she was dead, but to find her alive, I got emotional. Just like Rhett, I could see no sign that she'd been physically tortured.

Her lips curled, her voice soft, but there was sadness in her eyes. "I'm kind of in a bind, want to get me out?"

I loved her playfulness even in the most terrifying times.

"You know I'm already working on it." It was a promise I intended to keep. "Just hold on, okay?"

"If you do, I promise to give you lots of juicy details. Not that I've experienced firsthand, but I'll make them up." She winked.

"I can't wait. I'll be back, okay?" I retreated step by step, not wanting to leave her, but I was running out of time.

I quickly went to each cell, letting the rest of my friends know I was alive and that I had someone who would help us escape, though I didn't address Payton by name. Then I went back to the monitor, studying the layout. I had to know which button to press with certainty.

I ran back to Rhett. "I have to go, but I promise to be back."

He pressed his forehead and palms on the barrier. "I love you. Be safe."

I placed my hands to match his. "I love you, too."

I broke away from Rhett, and a whoosh from the sliding door had my heart thundering.

"I thought I would find you here, sister." Gene's tone was friendly but his expression was anything but as he swaggered toward me. "You've been very naughty."

"How did you find me?" I held my ground and readied my curled fingers.

"The ever-so-loyal Payton. You knocked him out. I actually didn't mind that part. In fact, I'm glad you did, but then you went out of your room. You have a curfew, little sister. Did you forget?"

"I was looking for Mother, but guess who I found? My friends. So either let them out, or I'll have to hurt you." I mimicked his sarcastic tone.

"You would go against your own flesh and blood?" His voice dipped lower.

I walked backward toward the center table. "If you care for your life, you'll do as I say."

He let out a dry laugh, making his way to me. "Do I need to remind you of this?" He took out his little coin-size gadget.

I tensed, recalling the razor-sharp pain slashing through my bones. "Do it. What are you waiting for?"

"Are you sure about that?"

"Go ahead. Do your worst." I advanced on him. Perhaps if I held him tight enough when my body convulsed, he would feel the electric current too.

"You asked for it, little sister." A sharp mischievous edge to his tone.

I stopped when nothing happened to me, but Rhett convulsed before he dropped to his knees.

"What are you doing? Stop it," I hollered, overrun with guilt. Gene was punishing him to get to me. "Stop it. Stop it. Stop it."

"I'm returning the same love Rhett gave to me. Now, if you don't want me to do it again, go back to your room."

His tone disgusted me. I wanted to tell Rhett that I was sorry, but I needed Gene away from my friends before he decided to hurt them, too. So I complied and walked out wordlessly, even more determined to get my revenge.

I had to save them all and find a way out. Payton was my only hope.

CHAPTER THIRTY-FIVE– MEETING WITH NOVAK

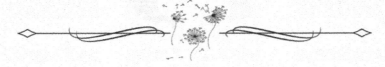

MITCH

Goosebumps trickled along Mitch's arms when the destruction surrounding ISAN's secret base came into view.

He had imagined a beautiful tall building, not a bunker under an uninhabitable city. A place to hide secrets. Or dump bodies.

A young guard dressed in an ISAN suit, armed with a Taser, greeted them at the entrance. "Welcome. I've been assigned to take you to Novak upon arrival."

"Thank you," Lydia said and meandered ahead without the guard.

"Ma'am. You don't know the way." He went after her.

"Then you'd best hurry," she said over her shoulder.

My strong girl. She was going to show everyone who was boss.

They wound through long gray hallways and many numbered doors, and were finally escorted into a room with only two sofas, a single sofa, and a tea table.

Where were the rest of Novak's guards? Yes, there were many rooms and hallways, and one could easily get lost, but it seemed like Mitch and his team were the only ones there. They were just about to settle on the leather sofa when the door whooshed open and Novak entered.

"Welcome," Novak said in an uncharacteristically cheerful

tone.

Posed with grace, Lydia showed no fear or disdain. She gave her best smile, her dimples indenting.

Novak flashed a quick grin. "Please. Have a seat." He eased into a single sofa and leaned back with a note of casualness.

Mitch sat between Russ and Lydia. When Lydia crossed her long legs, Novak's eyes wandered along her beautiful, smooth skin, starting at her heels and moving up. Mitch wanted to punch him.

Mitch cleared his throat and accidentally bumped his elbow with Lydia. "So, what's the reason for taking us away from our duties?"

While he tried to speak lightly, his voice might have cracked. Novak could have the three of them executed and no one would know.

Novak slung his arms on the armrest. "I'm going to move East and West to this facility. It can house all of us. What do you think?"

A long breath escaped from Russ and he relaxed. "If you think this is a good idea, I'm all in."

"I don't see why not," Mitch said. "Having two teams train together would be beneficial, and having more agents would be a bonus. Sabrina and her crew are amazing. We can work together."

"Lydia, how about you?" Novak asked. "What are your thoughts?"

"Have you asked Sabrina as well?" She gave him a tightlipped smile.

"I did, though I haven't invited her staff to visit as of yet. I wanted my most loyal team to have the first visit."

Why emphasize loyalty? Something smelled fishy.

"What an honor. Thank you," Mitch said as he placed his

hands on his lap. "How is Justine, by the way?"

Novak sleeked back a strand that had loosened. "I brought her here to meet her family."

"Family?" Russ's green eyes glistened, his voice rising. "You found her mom?"

"No. Not her mother. She has a half sister and half brother. And... Justine is my daughter. But you already knew that."

It was no use denying it, so Mitch kept quiet. Russ and Lydia didn't say a word.

Novak flicked some lint off his sleeve and cleared his throat. "Gene and Ava are twins, and I'm their father. Their mother has been living here for a while. I didn't feel comfortable announcing that Ava is my daughter, being that she's a traitor. She's here now, and we're working things out."

But not of her own free will.

Russ paled. He looked like he could vomit any second. "What about Gene?"

"Gene is here," Novak said. "The three of them are learning to get along. Isn't this fantastic? I have two of the most powerful assassins on our team."

He called his own flesh and blood assassins.

"Is Gene feeling... well?" Lydia uncrossed her legs, bumping her knee into Mitch's. "I mean, he's been through a lot."

Novak adjusted his blue and black checkered tie and leaned forward. "Gene needs therapy. Not for being locked up by the rebels, but for his temper. Gene ripped out the first therapist's heart and snapped the second therapist's neck. Would anyone like to volunteer to be the third?" He let out a laugh.

Mitch swore under his breath, curling his fingers on the fabric of his training outfit pants. There was no humor in his statement or his laugh. Mitch didn't know how to react.

Novak continued. "I supposed I shouldn't have lobotomized him like the other assassins, especially since he already had such complex DNA. The only people he seemed to be tamed around were Ava and his mother. He wants their approval for reasons I cannot comprehend."

Mitch's blood ran cold. Novak had gone psychotic.

Russ blanched. Mitch was sure he wasn't breathing.

"Anything else we should know?" Mitch asked with stability he mustered from somewhere.

How badly he wanted to take this man down. Three against one, they could contain him. But if they captured him, then what? Not a wise move.

Novak tapped his polished dressed shoes and stood, peering down at the three of them, gloating. "Wait here and I'll have an escort take you to your rooms. I want you to get comfortable first, before dinner. I wouldn't advise wandering around. It's like a labyrinth in here and we wouldn't want Gene to find you. He's had a bad day and he might take it out on anyone he sees."

Mitch clenched his jaw, inhaling to steady his nerves. "What about the trainees at our site? We didn't inform them we would be gone this long."

Novak halted a couple of feet before the sensor and kept his back to them. "Don't worry about that. I sent a substitute. You know, just in case you didn't make it back."

Mitch didn't like the way he'd said that. Perhaps he was being paranoid. Novak was always short and to the point.

"Fine. I'll message them as well." Russ swiped at his arm to open his chip.

"Don't bother, Russ," Novak said, his back still to them.

"There's no personal reception here. Only at the main control room."

Novak had everything covered.

Novak turned the slightest. "Oh, by the way, I have a group of rebels detained and one of our own who was supposedly kidnapped or killed at the battle in Pearl Valley—Nina. And also Rhett. I captured them all by myself by using Ava as the bait. You see how easy that was? Now, excuse me while I go back to my office so I can decide what to do with them. Maybe during dinner we can discuss it as a team, if I can't make up my mind. How does that sound?"

His accusatory tone already had Mitch on pins and needles, so he had to force out the words. "Sure. Whatever you think is best."

"Good. I'm glad you three are on my side. It would pain me to treat you like enemies." He shoved his hands inside his pockets and strolled out without looking back.

Russ, Lydia, and Mitch exchanged no words. Most likely this room was monitored anyway. They needed a miracle.

CHAPTER THIRTY-SIX – SAN'S COMPOUND

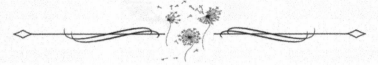

JOSEPHINE CHANG

The guards who had escorted Josephine to the ANS compound took off the fabric hood covering her head. Bright light became dimmer until her view came to focus on an attractive Asian man seated across from her in a simple, clean office with white walls.

"My apologies for the hood, Councilor Chang." Mr. San placed his folded hands on the metal table, next to a small handheld TAB. "This is for your protection as much as for ours."

"I understand." Josephine ran a hand to smooth out her hair, admiring an oil painting of the ocean behind him. She wished she was there instead.

"I hope you had a comfortable flight."

"I did." She shifted on the black vinyl chair to get comfortable. "Your men have been accommodating."

"Good. Would you like anything to drink?" He waved to his left, to the table with water and sodas.

Josephine unhooked the top button of her black cloak and draped it behind her. "No, thank you. I had a glass of wine on the way. And a delicious sandwich. I hadn't had one in a long while. We're always eating fine meals during our meetings. I actually favor simple food."

"I have to admit, I'm the same way," San said. "Have you tried

Crazy Burgers?"

"No. I've never heard of it."

Mr. San's eyes rounded. "They're the best. They not only serve burgers, but the best pastrami sandwiches."

She practically drooled over the imagined fast food. "I'll have to try it."

"I'll take you. It'll be a date." His cheeks colored and he tried again. "I meant—"

"I know what you meant." Josephine crossed her legs and relaxed her muscles. The light conversation eased her tension. "Besides, I owe you a meal. You saved my life."

He flashed a quick grin. "I have kept my word. You do what I ask and I keep you safe."

"So, let's get back to Verlot, shall we? Has he given you any new information?"

"No, but he asked for you." San flashed a glance at his TAB that beeped to indicate a message, but he ignored it.

Josephine furrowed her brow. "Why?" She supposed she shouldn't be surprised. He probably wanted to assault her with his words.

He rose from his seat and grabbed his TAB. "Shall we?"

Josephine followed him out the door and gaped at the glass wall. His people were monitoring streets and highways in different regions.

"They're searching for any unusual activity," San said. "Our goal is to intercept the special beings before ISAN does."

"How many?"

"So far, about twenty."

"May I see them?"

"Come, this way."

Mr. San had assured Josephine ANS was different than ISAN, but confining them and testing their abilities seemed no different to her. However, he claimed their testing was voluntary, and San would help them utilize and contain their abilities. She supposed it was a good thing. Transparency went a long way toward trust.

After going down a long hallway, San entered a grand chamber. A group of female teens were strapped in chairs with metal bands over their foreheads.

"They're getting their brainwaves and pulse measured," San explained. "We're studying the relationship to high activities, stress, temperature, and how these variables affect their gifts."

They moved on to the next group. The girls ran faster than possible on the treadmill.

"This scene needs no explanation." His lips twisted. "Unless you would like me to explain what they are doing?"

"No. I think I get the picture." She smiled.

His soft eyes lingered on her mouth, then turned. "Here, tucked in a special corner, our specialist works one-on-one with them. We learn the extent of their power. When we discover their abilities, we teach them how to control and manipulate, so they may return to society, knowing they are safe to themselves and to the citizens."

"I like that plan," Josephine said, gazing at the first window.

Inside the square room was a woman with a white lab coat and a girl about sixteen years of age, talking. The girl wore a comfortable sweat outfit with her long hair tied back.

She seemed focused, and most important, content as she listened to the instructor's instruction. San tabbed a metal panel against the wall, allowing their conversation to be heard.

"Charlotte. You ready? If you feel uncomfortable or if you're not ready, let me know. We can try another day."

Charlotte nodded.

"They can't see you." San answered Josephine's unspoken question.

Charlotte's unblinking eyes focused on the stack of bricks, five layers. Silence filled the space as Josephine anticipated what she would do. When Charlotte placed her hand on top, a spider line crack formed. The splinter spread and split the first brick in half. Then she did the same to the second brick.

The girl panted, wiping beads of sweat off her forehead. "I can't. It's all I can do."

The instructor set her hand on Charlotte's shoulder. "You did great. Don't worry about the other bricks. With practice, it will come easier."

If the interaction between them was any indication of what this facility was about, then Josephine felt assured these girls were in good hands.

San took her to the next stall. A male instructor flipped a girl onto a mat. She was blindfolded, and she landed hard.

"What is he doing?" Josephine's voice was razor-sharp. She didn't like how the girl had been tossed about.

San disregarded her panic and said, "Just watch. When Paula is on cue, she's quite impressive."

"I can do this." Paula rose with determination. She extended her arms like an antenna, still blindfolded.

The instructor moved swiftly to her left and right. Paula shifted toward the sound, but if the instructor were to tackle her, she would fall.

Josephine folded her arms, anticipating the worst. The instructor edged toward the girl's back. Paula had missed the movement, and was facing the wrong way. She was done for.

But Paula whirled and blocked a punch from her instructor. She clutched his arm and flipped him over, blindfolded all the while.

The instructor took off her cloth, gleaming with pride. "That was brilliant. I knew you could do it."

"I homed in on my ability," she said. "I heard your arm move and I felt the direction. It's unbelievable."

"Their senses are heightened beyond imagining," San said and directed Josephine out of the room.

They rounded to another hallway and went down the stairs. Cool air and the dim lighting gave Josephine goosebumps. They passed through the first metal door into Verlot's cell.

Verlot placed the book he was reading on the mattress and met her at the glass barrier. His room was spacious enough—a cot, toilet, and sink. He had plenty of room to move about. And for a prison, the place didn't stink of urine.

San pressed a button on the panel next to the cell door. Voices could be heard both ways.

"How kind of you to visit me, Councilor Chang," Verlot spat, his face contorting.

Josephine glared. "I assure you, the pleasure is not mine. Why have you requested to see me?"

"I've missed you." His malicious smile did nothing to ease Josephine's anxiousness, even behind bars.

"Say what you have to say or I'm leaving. You're wasting my time. Next time you ask for me, I won't come."

Verlot strolled back to his cot and sat. "I have nothing to say. Like I said, I've missed your pretty face. Oh, wait. Have you heard the news lately? Anything regarding my absence?"

"No one cares," Josephine said flatly.

"Well, don't worry. My people are working behind the scenes. You know I'm not the only one running ISAN, don't you? Why don't you tell her, San? Or are you trying to hide information from her? We worked well together until you betrayed me. Do you plan to do the same to her?"

San stiffened, then met Josephine's gaze. "I was going to tell you. Novak is Dr. Hunt."

"What?" It took a second for her to register his words, and another second to ask him to repeat it.

"Dr. Hunt created a new identity for himself: Novak. He dyed his hair black and wore brown contact lenses. He's also had his voice deepened."

"Who told you this?" Josephine couldn't believe it.

San opened up his TAB and pulled up hologram images of Novak and Dr. Hunt. "My team figured it out and Verlot confirmed it. Apparently, Verlot was the only person who knew. They planned it together. If you add the changed elements on Dr. Hunt, you can see the resemblance is uncanny."

"Then that means Ava's father is Novak?" Josephine's voice came out in a whisper as she stared through the barrier, looking at the clean sink.

"Ava is missing." San closed the TAB. "She might be with Novak as we speak. Do you think she would side with her father?"

Josephine crossed her arms, holding herself centered. She couldn't believe what she was hearing. All this time, Novak and Dr. Hunt were one person.

"No." She laced her fingers though her hair and let out air. "I met Ava at the rebel base. She's committed."

"Not if she's lobotomized." Verlot picked up the book and

pretended to read.

Josephine pounded once on the glass. "What do you mean?"

She knew what he meant, but she needed to hear it from the devil's mouth.

"You should relearn your history, Councilor," Verlot said. "And you might want to ask San why he hasn't told you Zen's whereabouts."

San scowled at him.

"What's he talking about?" Josephine said with an even tone.

San clicked the button on the panel. "Verlot can't hear our conversation." He pressed something on his TAB and faced her, his back to the prisoner. "I was going to tell you, but he beat me to it."

She frowned. "It's the first thing you should have said to me when I got here."

"Relax, Councilor. My men are on their way. They were instructed to park their glider at a distance and march on foot. We want Novak surrounded and surprised."

Josephine felt a little better. "I can contact Vince. He could have a team there as well."

"There's no need. I've got it covered." His astute tone indicated his decision was final.

Josephine shifted in her stance, her feet aching from standing all day. "What do you mean by 'I've got it covered?'"

"Councilor. You can trust me. We're on the same team."

His genuine tone suggested she could, but she was not used to taking orders. Josephine wanted details.

"I'm sending my team," she said with conviction. "My team knows Zen and the rebel crew. It's best to send a squad that knows how to work together."

San rubbed his chin, contemplating. "Fine. Your team has twenty-four hours to retrieve them."

She gripped his arm when he turned to walk away. "What happens if they need more time?"

San grabbed the hand still clutching his sleeve and slowly peeled it off. "Then my team intervenes."

Josephine narrowed her eyes. "I don't understand. Why can't they—" As she spoke, she finally realized his intentions. "Your team isn't planning to go inside, are they? You're going to destroy the facility. There are citizens in there. My people. You can't just blow up the place."

"Novak will be in there with his best assassins and assets. I think it's about time we take down a key player."

"And what about my crew?" Her eyebrows pinched at the center. "You're not allowed to strike until every one of them is out, do you hear me? As one of the Remnant Councilors, I'm commanding you."

For the first time, they weren't seeing eye to eye. Perhaps they never had.

San's eyes were glacier cold. It seemed he didn't like to be ordered. "Councilor, you are a novice to the world of ISAN. Do keep in mind I've been at this longer than you. Finding any of their bases is like finding a needle in a haystack. When a once-in-a-lifetime chance comes by, we do not let it go. This is a battle. If we don't win these battles, a war will be inevitable. Because you are a Remnant Councilor, I will back down for twenty-four hours. Come nightfall, regardless of who is in or out of the facility, I'm going to blow it up."

Josephine stared hard at this unfathomable man. He'd been good to her. He'd even saved her life. How could this be the same man? She had to take into account that he'd been fighting a war with ISAN long before she'd known both networks existed.

Josephine would give him the benefit of the doubt that he was not a cold-hearted being. But he was tired and wanted the battle to end. Still, how could he mean to blow up the facility with her people inside?

Never.

She would never let that happen.

CHAPTER THIRTY-SEVEN – NEW HOPE

MOMO

Some of Momo's friends had to share a room with four or more people. Others had to share with people they didn't know. The rooms were shoebox-sized with two bunk beds, a single dresser, and a small desk and a chair.

Momo considered herself lucky to bunk with Coco, Jo, and Marissa. Momo didn't know how that happened, but she wasn't going to complain. She had washed and changed into spare clothes—a mismatch of sweatshirts and pants—a size too big, but at least they were clean.

Coco was already in bed on the bottom bunk. Instead of climbing to the second level, she tucked under the blanket with her friend. Not the first time, and she knew Coco wouldn't mind. Sometimes, Momo slept better next to her friend.

Momo felt fortunate to have a place to go, a place to call a home. She missed Hope City, their hideout they had built, but she missed Bobo more. Momo thought about him every day. Sometimes, she'd forget he was gone, but she would never forget *him*. She shifted on her side, trying to find a comfortable position on the flat pillow, careful not to wake her friend.

Why did bad things happen to good people? Like Debbie, their leader, and the rest of their crew who died in that blast. Momo said a silent prayer for them and ended with, "You will always be remembered. Renegades forever."

Momo knew it wasn't their fault, wasn't *her* fault, but the truth was, they hadn't gotten to Debbie in time. Time had been crucial, especially for Rhett and his team. They'd also needed a lot of luck to find Ava and Naomi.

Momo wanted to go with Rhett, but he wouldn't let her. She understood his reasoning, but he also had to understand that she was capable. Momo had grown up the second she'd held a weapon. She had seen gore, death, and destruction.

Momo was an assassin and one of the leads for her team. She could handle more than he believed, and she wished he would stop treating her like a child.

Momo flashed her eyes opened when Jo entered the room, Marissa shadowing behind her. Jo's jeans, though faded, fit her well, and so did her blue sweater.

"What's going on?" Momo sat up and studied Marissa's concerned gaze, and then Jo digging into her backpack on the desk by the door, her movements frantic.

Coco sat up, rubbing her eyes. She smiled at Momo and then shifted her gaze. "Jo. Are you going somewhere?"

"No. I was…" Jo paused for a good measure, staring at nothing in particular. "Vince told me…"

Momo hated when adults paused to think and didn't finish their sentences. It was like reading the last chapter in a novel that had a cliffhanger.

Jo opened the door when a soft knock echoed in their small space. So strange for it not to open on its own. Momo wasn't used to places that had been built with no advanced technology.

A man wearing dark jeans and a black T-shirt with big muscles, maybe bigger than Rhett's, stood over the threshold.

"Vince?" Jo sounded surprised. "How can I help you?"

Speak of the devil.

Vince eyed the younger girls but didn't bother to address them. "Can I talk to you privately?"

What Jo said next made Momo's jaw drop.

"Momo and Coco are in charge of our group when I'm not around, so whatever you have to say, you can tell them too. So why don't you come inside and talk to us? No sweeping details under the rug. We need to know exactly what's going on. They may look like kids to you, but I assure you when you get to the battlefront you'll want them beside you, not behind you. The more they know, the better."

Vince's twisted lips hinted at a frown. "Fine. My men spotted a group of young ones, kids around Momo's age, in the south territory. They're all wearing caps that said Renegades."

Coco's eyes beamed, but Momo dared not hope.

"Where?" Jo's hand shot up to her chest as if to hold in her heart.

Vince peered in farther into the room. "They've been moving around the same neighborhood. The coordinates indicate they're near the structure ISAN blew up."

Jo anchored her hand on the back of the chair. "Do you have a close-up frame?"

"No. My men didn't want to scare them so they kept their distance. If we were able to spot them, then the chances are ISAN might have too."

"I should go," Jo said.

Vince leaned against the door. "You can't go alone. I can assign you a group, but I can't ask Rhett's people since he's not here."

"I don't need your men." Jo glanced between the girls. "This should be dealt with a small squad. I'm going to take Coco and Momo with me. I just need to borrow a glider."

"Very well. You can go tomorrow."

"Thank you." Jo tipped her head forehead. "Why was your team there?"

"Councilor Chang had asked me to check it out. So you can thank her. I also stopped by to let you know I'm on my way to meet Councilor Chang. If you need anything, you can talk to Nick, Jill, or Katina. Sleep well." He gave a curt nod to all of them and left.

Momo couldn't believe what she'd heard, but she hoped with all her heart that Debbie and the other half of her team was alive. Tomorrow. She couldn't wait to scout.

Marissa tugged on Jo's sweater. "You said you were taking Momo and Coco. Can I come too?"

Marissa was the smallest and the shyest one in their group. She looked even smaller, wearing a sweatshirt double her size.

Jo regarded her for a second, and then stroked her blonde hair. "I think it's best if you stay."

Marissa shifted sharply, moving away from Jo as her features contorted with hurt. "Is it because you think I'll get in the way?"

Momo had wondered what ISAN saw in Marissa. Besides having the ability to heal, she was no soldier. She had a difficult time in training and kids made fun of her. Momo had never been on the same team with Marissa, so she decided not to judge her.

"No, of course not," Jo said. "I'd rather not risk too many lives if I can help it."

Marissa stomped her foot once, her face coloring. Momo had never seen her like this.

"I might not be able to fight like Coco and Momo, but I'm as smart and useful. I wish everyone would stop looking at my size. Sometimes being small has its advantages. Also, I can heal them if they're injured. That's pretty powerful." She crossed her arms with a huff, a dramatic way to close her statement.

Jo exchanged questioning glances with Momo and Coco, but when she turned back to Marissa, she said, "Okay. You've made your case. And you're right. Sometimes being small does have its advantages."

Marissa beamed. "Debra and you have told us, even the small among us can make a difference. We just have to believe. It's about time us small people helped the big people."

Momo raised her hand. "I second that. It's what I've been trying to tell Rhett."

Jo slumped on the bottom cot, tired and worn. Marissa joined her.

"I know, Momo." Jo sighed and raked a hand through her hair. "It's really difficult for us grown-ups. We should be protecting you, not using you as weapons."

Coco squeezed her blanket like a teddy bear. "But times are different. If we don't get out there, there might not be a future left for us."

Jo twisted her lips. "You're right. Debra and I took you away from ISAN to give you a hopeful future, but as long as ISAN exists, you'll never be safe."

"No matter how far we run, ISAN will be after us," Momo added.

"So we might as well work together." Marissa raised her hand. "Every ability matters."

Jo looked between the three of them. "From here on out, I promise to treat you all like grown-ups, but you can't do everything like an adult."

"Oh, darn." Momo snapped her fingers. "There goes drinking and swearing. What I love to do most."

They shared a giggle.

"Let's take a vote as grown-ups do," Jo said when laughter died. "Since Momo is the captain when I'm gone, and Coco is second-in-command, the three of us need to vote if Marissa can join us."

Marissa frowned, but held up her chin.

"I say, yes." Momo gave her a thumbs-up.

"I say, yes, too," Coco said.

Jo smiled. "I say, yes, so that makes it unanimous. Marissa, you're in."

Marissa's eyes gleamed as she clasped her hands together.

This wasn't how grown-ups operated, from what Momo had witnessed. They demanded and ordered people around with one leader in charge, but this way was fun and fair.

Jo got off the bed and shuffled the blanket to the side for Marissa. "It's time for bed. We're leaving after breakfast." She smiled at the girls and said, "Goodnight."

"Goodnight," they all said in accord.

Momo liked making Marissa smile and having her on their team, but at the same time, she missed Bobo. The three of them had done everything together. It felt like Marissa had replaced him.

Bobo wasn't physically here, but she felt his love.

You will always be remembered... in our hearts and in our memories. Renegades forever.

CHAPTER THIRTY-EIGHT – ALL TOGETHER

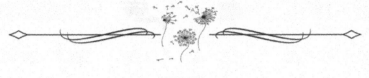

AVA

I paced in my room. Anxious. Worried. Payton had told me Mitch, Lydia, and Russ were coming last night. Had they spent the night at the compound or had they left? I had asked him to monitor my mother's whereabouts so when the time came to escape, he would know where she was. He had a glider on standby. We just needed an escape plan.

Payton entered my room and I didn't know whether to be happy or panic. "What's happening?" I asked.

"I don't know, Ava, but Mr. Novak told me to bring you to the meeting."

Payton's voice was soothing like always, but it held a slight edge. He worried too.

I expected to be escorted into a room with a table and chairs, but Payton took me to an empty room. Mitch, Lydia, and Russ were twelve feet from Novak, Gene, and Justine. Seven guards stood behind the agents, and another eight guards were behind Rhett and Cleo to the right of Gene. None were bound with cuffs. Where were the rest of my friends?

My heart rate kicked up, fear pounding against my ribcage. What was Novak up to?

"Ava is here," Novak said. "Our group is back together."

Mitch, Russ, and Lydia only looked at me with stoic

expressions as I stood next to Novak, Payton beside me. I tried not to look at Rhett and Cleo.

Six young assassins sauntered in with Zen. Not just any assassins, but...

"Roxy." Justine raised her voice. "What's she doing here?"

Whatever Roxy was thinking behind that scowl of hers, it wasn't friendly. The other assassins' expressions hadn't changed since I entered, as if they only had the one. I recognized a few as those that had supposedly defected. I had forgotten their names, but not their faces.

Then horror reeled through my mind. Instead of killing Roxy, Novak had made her, and the others, compliant by erasing their memories and lobotomizing them. I felt sick. More than that, we were outnumbered.

My pulse raced. Palms sweaty. Something bad was going to happen.

"Let me tell you why we're all here." Novak stood between Rhett and Zen. "We're going to finally put an end to this ridiculous rebel group. But first, we need to get rid of a traitor. It has come to my attention that Councilor Chang sent a spy to my network. I've known for a while but I waited for the perfect time. And this is it."

Novak walked toward Russ, stopping several feet from him. I couldn't breathe as I screamed inside my head. Novak shifted to Mitch. Mitch stiffened, but held up his chin.

Novak raised his gun to Mitch's skull.

"He's no traitor." Rhett's word pushed through gritted teeth. "Your source is an idiot."

"You're right, Rhett," Novak said. "He's not the one. Here you go, Mitch. Don't look so worried." Novak handed Mitch the gun and took his position next to me.

"What do you want me to do with this?" Mitch seized it with a trembling hand.

"I want you to shoot the traitor." Novak's lips spread into a wicked grin.

"Who's the traitor?" Mitch lowered his weapon.

"You know who it is. Shoot her, or I'll shoot Rhett."

One of guards jabbed his gun on Rhett's back.

"No." I growled. "Don't do this. Please, I'll do anything."

Lydia paled and took a stumbling step back.

Mitch gave pleading eyes to Novak. "She's innocent. She's—"

Russ took a step forward. "You've got it wrong again, Novak. I'm the traitor."

No, Russ. What are you doing?

Novak scrubbed his face in annoyance. "You shouldn't have said that, Russ. Now I'll have to kill you too. Mitch, prove to me you're no traitor. I'll let everyone free if you shoot Lydia in the head."

Mitch clenched his jaw and raised a shaking hand, aiming the weapon at Lydia's head. "I'm so sorry," he murmured.

Would he? My heart squeezed. He wasn't a fool to believe Novak would let us go, right?

"It's okay, Mitch." Tears streamed down her lovely cheeks. "You would expect me to do the same. Thank you for being so good to me. Perhaps in another life, we could have more time together." She fixed her eyes on Novak with hatred enough for all of us. "You're a monster. I don't regret anything I did for Councilor Chang or for myself. You might have won this battle, but you won't win the war."

Good for Lydia. She tipped her head like a true leader, staring death in the eye. Such bravery. But she killed me with her declaration for Mitch. She was in love with him, and he loved her. When had this happened?

My heart thundered.

"On the count of three, okay?" Mitch's voice cracked, his hand steadier, eyes fixed with resolve. "Close your eyes, babe. One... Two... Now."

Lydia headbutted the guard beside her and stole his weapon. She shot at the person on the other side of her, crouched low and took out another guard, while Russ jabbed the soldier holding him hostage in the chest and knocked him out.

Mitch turned to Novak and fired. A click went from Mitch's gun, but Novak didn't fall. The gun wasn't loaded.

"Stop or he's dead," Novak commanded.

Lydia and Russ halted as two guards jabbed guns against Mitch's skull, one on each temple. Mitch's effort was a good attempt, but it would go nowhere while Novak was still standing. He had too many soldiers.

"Oh, Mitch." Novak clucked his tongue and pulled out a gun from behind his waistband. "This is how you do it." He pulled the trigger.

Novak shot Lydia in the chest.

Justine screamed. I covered my mouth to keep from doing the same.

Oh, God. Lydia. I'd never known she was on our side. She was always nice and gentle, keeping an eye out for us.

Mitch got on his knees, cradling her, burying his face in hers. "*No!* Lydia."

"Don't worry. You can join her." Novak shot Mitch in the

back.

Mitch thumped sideways beside her, blood pooling around him. He looked in utter shock as I was. Mitch couldn't move, but he was alive.

Rhett tried to break free from the guards, cursing. Zen and Cleo looked horrified. I jabbed my elbow at the nearest guard's throat and flipped over the next one, but Roxy pressed a Taser on my skull.

Justine gripped her father's arm, shaking him, and raised her voice in disgust. "Why did you shoot Mitch?"

Novak pushed her off. "Too many have deceived me. They thought they would get away with it. I have eyes and ears in and out of ISAN." Novak sauntered over to Russ, who was held by guards on both sides, and whacked his head with the butt of the gun. Russ dropped next to Mitch.

"No!" I screamed from the top of my lungs. I'd thought Novak was going to shoot him.

Everything happened so fast, I couldn't process it. I couldn't breathe. We would all die if I didn't do something. Mitch and Lydia were still breathing. But I was helpless without my power. Even if I brought down some of the guards, Novak had a gun, and six assassins trained like Roxy, not to mention Justine and Gene.

Novak shifted and raised his weapon toward Zen. *No. Not Zen, too.* Rhett and Cleo could be next.

"No. please." Cleo stood in front of her father. "Don't hurt my dad. I'll do anything."

"Does your daughter know, Zen?" Novak said.

"Know what?" Cleo said.

Zen shook his head, pleading for understanding with his eyes. "I did it to keep you safe, Cleo. If I hadn't done what I did, ISAN would have taken you from your mother and me."

"Is that why your wife ran?" Novak placed his gun to his side. "You should have told your wife about Cleo's power. You killed your wife. Not ISAN."

Zen crinkled his facial muscles, rage in his tone. "I will take blame for my wife's death, but I will never feel guilty for what I did for my daughter."

"What power?" Cleo shouted, gripping her father's arm.

"You were born special like your friends," Zen said, his voice low. "I created a serum, CHB20, to suppress your ability. The protein drink."

"What's my power?" Cleo asked, her blue eyes darkening. "You should have told me." Tears pooled in her eyes, her lips quivering. "I can't believe you did this to me. All these years. You had plenty of time to tell me. You had no right."

"Please, Cleo." Zen gripped her shoulders. "You were so small. ISAN would have ruined you."

"You know now, Cleo," Novak said. "When you find out what your gifts are, do tell. I'll welcome you with open arms. I would never be ashamed of who you are."

"Go to hell," Cleo spat. "I would never side with you."

"Very well, then. Now that Zen has confessed, say goodbye to your father." Novak aimed and fired.

"Nooo!" Cleo screamed, an ear-piercing sound that shook my bones.

Her scream got louder and louder, shaking the walls and everything around us. I had to cover my ears. Everyone else did the same, crouching. I felt a stab to my chest from her scream, some kind of vibration shooting through me. Had she gone any longer, she might have killed us.

Zen should have been dead on the ground, but the bullet had veered a sharp turn, hitting a guard behind him. Cleo's scream, like a magical force, blocked the bullet from hitting its mark.

Her gift. She moved objects with her voice.

When Cleo stopped, she went pale, and her eyes rounded. For a second, the room went silent.

"Well, that was awesome timing, Cleo," I said.

One of the guards thumped Cleo's head, knocking her unconscious, Novak fired at Zen. Zen collapsed to the floor. Everything happened so fast. It felt like a dream. I couldn't process it all.

Novak frantically glanced about and checked something on his chip.

Was that fear I sensed?

"Roxy, have your team take Rhett and Ava to the main lab," Novak barked. "Put them on the ROM machine. The rest of the prisoners can stay here and die in the explosion. Our facility has been found. The timer has been activated. This place is going down. Gene and Justine, get your mother and meet me at the escape pod."

ROM machine. *No!* Novak planned to erase our memories.

Roxy and the assassins grabbed Rhett and me and dragged us out of the room.

My fingers tingled and the blueprint of the facility flickered in and out. I felt a soft wave of heat rising to the surface, starting from my toes and up my spine.

Something had happened when Cleo screamed. I believed she'd brought down the sonic barrier.

CHAPTER THIRTY-NINE – NOVAK'S MACHINE

AVA

"**Y**ou don't have to do this. Come with me," I said as Roxy and two other assassins dragged me to the next room.

Roxy slammed me to a chair. Across the room were four empty cells with see-through glass barriers.

I could have fought her, but with a gun pointed at Rhett's head, and without the ability to draw on Helix fully, I had no chance against six assassins.

"Ava. Why aren't you stopping her?" Rhett asked as the three other girls held him on the hub twelve feet from me. He tugged and pulled with no success. "What's going on?"

"Because she can't," Roxy said through clenched teeth, clasping the metal chains secure around my wrists.

When she slapped a button on the panel beside me, metal straps tightened around my ankles, then something anchored around my head. I yanked at the straps, but it was useless.

"Listen, Roxy," I said. "Novak did horrible things to you and to your team. You remember them, don't you? They're all dead. Novak took away your memory to make you less human."

"I told you to keep your mouth shut." She raised her gun to strike me.

When I craned my neck to the side, my hair falling over half my face, she pulled back with a blink as if recalling something.

Novak entered and broke the spell.

"Girls, step aside." His steps were swift as his eyes were focused on me. "We need to hurry. When I'm finished, I'm going to need your help carrying them to my pod."

"If you let Rhett go, I won't fight you, I promise," I said.

Novak inputted commands on the control panel on my chair and said, "You should have made that offer days ago, Ava. It's too late."

"What are you going to do to us?" Rhett had lost the will to fight. I heard it in his weary tone.

Novak glanced at Rhett, then back to me. "I'm going erase your memories and lobotomize you both. I'm tired of your betrayal. It's time to fix this problem."

"You hear what Novak is going to do, Roxy?" I said. "He did that to you. I know you can hear me. Help me. I can free you."

"She doesn't need your help," Novak said coolly, no ounce of anger from my threat. "She's happy to serve me. As you will be. In a few minutes, you both will become mine."

Roxy's stoic expression and lack of argument told me I couldn't count on her. She was far too gone. She belonged to Novak.

This couldn't be the end.

I had been coaxing Helix as I tried to buy time. Under normal circumstances, Helix came to me fast, but it had been slumbering too long, and it was taking time to charge to full capacity.

Novak didn't know my powers were coming back. He had no idea Cleo's scream had broken the sonic vibration. Or did he? He *had* frantically checked his chip.

"Would you like to say any last words to each other? Make it quick," Novak said. "After the procedure, you won't remember one another."

"Rhett. I'm sorry. Novak created some kind of sonic wave to inhibit my power and there's nothing I can do about it." I needed Rhett to know that my lack of effort wasn't from being scared or loss of hope. And I wanted Novak to think that I believed he still controlled me. "I'm so sorry. I failed us."

"It's okay, babe. Remember what I said to you, you can forget memories, but you can never forget emotions. I will always love you. And Novak is wrong. I will never forget you. Even if he takes out half my brain, my heart won't let it. You're the best thing in my life. You are worth every gamble I took to find you."

"Rhett should have stayed away from you," Novak said, his face hovering near mine. "He is the reason you became weak. He made you wander off from the course I had set for you. You let the useless emotion get in the way. This is your fault, Ava. You should have been stronger."

I growled and spat in his face. Spittle dripped down from his cheek. He took out a handkerchief from his pocket and wiped it away.

"I'm going to forgive you for that because you're my daughter. You and your brother are everything to me."

His profession of love repulsed me. "You're a hypocrite."

Novak cringed, the lines on his forehead deepening. "You don't understand." He stormed to Rhett's control board.

"How can you live with yourself after all you have done?" I said.

His eyes held no mercy as the veins on his neck twitched, and said with a lethal calm, "It doesn't matter what you think of me. After this is over, you will obey."

"No. Please. You can't." I yanked, tugged, pulled with

everything I had.

It can't end like this. He can't win. I've not come all this way to make no difference.

"Stop fidgeting." Novak walked toward me. "It's no use. You'll love your new life. Goodnight, pumpkin."

The lights flickered in the lab and something hot zapped on my skull, searing from my head and down to my toes as fast as lighting. Blazing pain, the same that Gene had inflicted on me with his gadget, seized me and I couldn't move or scream.

Silver and blue electrical lights danced and sparked. Thin tendrils coiled around my body like a python. I couldn't understand how I saw these lightning bolt lights.

Memories flashed through in a timeline that started when I'd been an infant. My mother and father. They adored me. They were so happy. I was just a toddler, but I felt their joy and love.

More memories, good and bad, rippled faster and faster. My foster father, Naomi, ISAN, Mitch, Brooke, Tamara, Ozzie, Reyna, Justine, and then Rhett.

Oh, God. Rhett.

Rhett leaped down the trash chute, and I ran the opposite way to give my team a chance to escape. If I had to do it all again, I promised myself I would never have left Rhett's side. But I had. The reason why we were here.

This machine was taking my memories, or was trying to. I wouldn't let it. I yanked and fought, shoving at whatever held me in place. I managed to escape the hold, as my body continued to convulse from the power of the machine. I shook out of the trance, indignation replacing my fear. I struggled to turn my head.

"Rhett. Look at me." I found my voice through the rippling pain.

Blue and silver lights snaked around Rhett's head and down his body. With his teeth clenched and back arched, sweat damping his forehead, he slowly craned his neck to me and said, "I. Love. You. Will. Never. Forget. You."

The machine had not affected him yet. *Good.*

I felt his pain, his fear, and most of all, I felt his love.

Not today, Novak. You do not win today.

It was time to release myself. Helix rose from being buried deep within, and I called it to come out from a deep sleep. Helix that didn't belong to ISAN or Novak. Helix belonged to me. And no one would claim me without my permission.

Heat rose into my veins. Helix came flooding through the broken dam. Instead of resisting the machine's power, I soaked it like a sponge. Every last drop. Spark by spark, layer by layer. Pain by pain. I took it all in, the energy rippled through my bones and muscles.

All the colors of the rainbow streaked across space, then the electric rods undulated through me. The power fed me, building me into someone stronger. Someone unbreakable.

When I had enough of the fuel, I released myself and gave the machine back what it had given me. The cuffs on my head, wrists, and ankles released with a pop. Electrical lights exploded. Parts from the machine snapped apart.

Novak ran toward me, his features contorted in shock, but still determined to detain me.

"You asked for it, Father," I seethed. "You want me. Come get me." I extended my hand, tendrils of lightning energy shot toward him.

With wild eyes, he halted, but too late. The force of my power enclosed him with violent tremors and tossed him across the room.

He slammed into the fourth cell's glass barrier and dropped.

Roxy and her team were firing at me. I raised my hands and stopped the bullets in midair, then twirled my finger and directed my electric bolts to them. The tendrils took hold of three of them and shook them until their limbs flopped.

A couple of the assassins closest to me and Roxy went flying across the room and broke through the third cell's barrier. Shards of glass exploded outward and dropped along with the girls.

Rhett. I have to get to him.

When I turned to Rhett, I saw myself in the reflection bouncing off the first cell's glass barrier. I was beautiful. A lightning storm incarnate. Silver, blue, and purple wisps weaved through me, and coiled around my body.

My eyes—fantastical—flashing like electric bolts. Mesmerizing. Wondrous. Deadly. At my fingertips, power surged. If given a chance, I could bring down the entire facility by releasing the amount of energy I had stored within my being.

I snapped out of my own spellbinding gaze, picked up the Taser Roxy had dropped, and shoved it inside my front pocket. Then I ran to Rhett.

"Rhett. Rhett." I unhooked the metal strap on his forehead, then those on his wrists and ankles.

"Ava." Rhett groaned and his head slumped to the side, his eyes unfocused.

Relief washed through me. Rhett gasped suddenly, going rigid. Lights from my fingertips tangled around him and shocked him without my control.

I shook my hands as if that would release my pent-up energy and grabbed him again. "I'm so sorry. I didn't mean to. We have to get out of here. This place is going to explode."

Rhett chuckled, but I didn't know if he understood. He could barely move.

Booms thundered somewhere inside the vicinity. The ground rocked. I stumbled sideways and righted myself by holding on to the strap.

I pulled Rhett out of his chair, draped his arm around my shoulder, and took him toward the exit.

CHAPTER FORTY – TEAM WORK

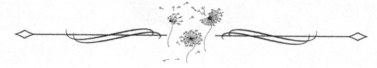

JUSTINE

Justine's crazy father had shot Lydia and Mitch. She wanted to scream. No, she *had* screamed. Screamed with ear-splitting agony she didn't know she could feel.

These agents were her role models. They were the only family she had known. Justine wanted to help them, but she was so scared her father would shoot her too. The thought that he would kill his daughter should be the driving force to get out and yet she couldn't.

Not loyalty, but out of fear.

How could her father shoot them?

You know why, a little voice inside her said. The voice that knew her father was insane, but she didn't want to believe it.

People thought she was this bitch with an attitude. Okay, so she did act all prissy at times, but that was because she was insecure. She'd put up a front because she'd thought she wasn't good enough to be on their team. They all had great abilities. If she could be honest with herself, she didn't know how to talk to people. No brainer. Look who her father was.

None of her teammates knew she had a therapist who had diagnosed her with social anxiety. She tried to do better, but that had been when her team left her. Justine was furious. She'd blamed her team for her behavior, but in truth, she had only herself to blame. No one could make anyone do anything.

When Roxy and the guards took Ava and Rhett, Justine followed Gene down the hall, rounded the corner, and entered a room. Ava's mom looked so scared, rocking in the corner. She wore a long summer dress. When she peered up, her eyes were red and puffy. She had been crying.

Justine felt sorry for her. She had no idea what the woman had been through, but from last night's dinner, she knew there had been rough times. Mentally and emotionally, it seemed.

What had her father done to his wife? Had he experimented on her as well? Had he lobotomized her to make her compliant?

"Mother, we have to go." Gene gripped her arm, but she yanked away.

"Baby. Ava. Baby. Ava." She kept repeating, alternating those two words.

"Why does she keep saying that?" Justine asked.

Gene ignored her.

"Mother, we have to go. This place is going to go boom." Gene seized her harder this time, dragging her out.

Ava's mother acquiesced but continued to repeat her diatribe.

"Stop saying that." Gene shouted at her. "The baby is gone."

Ava's mother made an animalistic growl and elbowed her son in the stomach. She bolted fast for someone her age, propelled by determination. Justine followed her into the lab where she had seen the CODE infant, but there was no sign of her.

Gene pointed. "You search over there and I'll look here."

Scowling, Justine went through the double doors. She had entered the opposite side from where the rebels were locked up. Ava's mother wasn't there, but what Justine saw had her immobile and speechless.

Brooke was inside a cell, her palm flat against the see-through barrier. Spider lines began to form on the glass. When she pushed her way through with her shoulder, shards of glass splintered on the ground.

Brooke ran to the next cell Tamara was in and placed a hand on the glass. A tiny crack formed with a pop. Brooke halted and craned her neck and gave Justine the hint of a smile, the kind that seemed to say "you're my friend."

Justine should stop her, but something inside her couldn't, especially when she saw Tamara in her prison. Even though she couldn't hear Tamara, she could read her lips. Tamara said Justine's name and asked her to help Brooke.

I have a chance to do something right. Take it.

Too late. Gene came through the other door.

"Well, well, well." Gene clapped. "Someone came back from the dead. Someone in your team has healing power."

Brooke put her trembling hands to her side. Gene had told Justine what he had done to Brooke. No, he had gloated.

Justine had thought she would be happy about a traitor's death, but she had been surprisingly saddened by the news. Even grieved Brooke until now, when her emotions had become confused.

Brooke inhaled a deep breath and held up her chin. "You talk too much."

Gene's nostrils flared. "Justine, what are you doing just standing there like an idiot? Go find my mother. I'm going to enjoy killing Brooke. Again."

Justine flinched at Gene spitting orders. He wasn't the boss of her. How dare he call her an idiot?

"Not if I kill you first." Brooke flexed her fingers.

"Do as I say, Justine," Gene barked and ran toward Brooke.

Brooke blocked a punch from Gene with her bent arm, but Gene being faster, jabbed her face with his other fist.

Ouch. That had to hurt.

Brooke came out of her daze and jumped on top of a table in the center of the room with TABs and monitors. When Gene attempted to do the same, Brooke kicked him in the face.

Gene growled, crimson dripping to the white tile from his cut lips. After he wiped his blood, his movements became faster. Blow after blow, Brooke tried to keep up, but Gene punched her ribcage. She went flying across space, smacking into Tamara's cell.

Tamara banged on the glass, shouting at Brooke to get up. Even muffled by the enclosure, her panic resonated.

Brooke was taking too long to stand. Justine held her breath. She didn't know if Brooke had any broken ribs from the force of the assault, but her former teammate winced and pulled herself up sluggishly.

Gene took his time, swaggering toward Brooke with a triumphant smirk. "Pathetic. Once broken, so easy to break." He halted and snarled at Justine. "What are you doing here? For the last time, go find my mother. Be useful or you'll end up like Brooke."

Justine wasn't scared of much, but the twisted malice on Gene's face, the face of the devil, unnerved her. She ran out and the door closed behind her with a hiss.

Thump. Bang. Thud. Those sounds had her grimacing, her pulse skidding. Her imagination ran wild.

I don't want to hear it.

He was going to kill Brooke, and this time, there would be no returning.

Did Justine want this to happen?

No, she didn't. A week ago, she wouldn't have cared. But damn it, she did care. Justine missed her team. She could finally admit that. No matter how many arguments and disagreements she had with Brooke, the fact that they had each other's back, the trust they built in the field, bonded them in sisterhood whether Justine wanted it or not.

Whack. Crack.

Justine was a coward. Too cowardly to make the right decision. Too cowardly to make any difference. Too cowardly to disappoint her father. But what about her? What did she want?

Remember to do the right thing no matter how hard it is to do it. Can you remember that for me? Mitch's words to her. Had he guessed their fate all along?

Mitch might be dead. He *would* be dead if he didn't get out of here. Justine should help him, but that would mean betraying her father, betraying ISAN. She would be like Ava.

Justine couldn't believe her fate. Damned if she did, and damned if she didn't.

How do I do the right thing when I'm so scared, Mitch?

Ava. Brooke. Tamara. They had taken the leap to leave. They were the brave ones. For the first time, Justine wished she could be like them. How soon before her father decided she was expendable or disloyal? For these reasons, no matter the consequences, Justine made her decision to be brave.

Stronger in numbers. Do the right thing.

Justine pushed through the door with a new intensity and fury. Gene had Brooke pinned down on the ground by the table, his fingers like ropes around her vulnerable neck.

Brooke's body was limp, her face white as the floor beneath

her.

Please, don't let me be too late.

"Get off my friend, asshole." Justine gripped his shirt from behind and tossed him across the room. Effortless, light as a ragdoll. He skidded across the floor.

Sometimes, Justine loved her power.

"Brooke. Brooke. Are you okay?" She lightly patted Brooke's face and kept one eye on Gene.

Justine felt for Brooke's pulse and shook her a little. Thank God her eyes fluttered, color returning to her face. Brooke coughed relentlessly.

"Justine?" Brooke sounded surprised and she craned her neck to find Gene.

Gene snarled, standing. Any second now, he would charge toward them.

"I'll hold him off. Help the others." Justine rolled up her sleeves. "You have to hurry. This place is going to explode."

"Okay, but let me have the last blow," Brooke said, hoarse and still coughing.

Justine dodged a swing from Gene. He threw a second punch and missed. Justine delivered a roundhouse kick to his face, sending him soaring next to Tamara's cell.

Tamara whooped and threw an air punch. Brooke was at the far end of the room, releasing Reyna.

"Is that all you've got, *half brother*?" Justine said to distract him, giving Reyna time to go around Gene.

He scoffed. "I'm just getting started, traitor. I don't know what Father sees in you. He should have gotten rid of you. You're just like the rest. Incompetent. Whiny. And such a girl. You have no business in ISAN. It's a man's world."

Justine snarled. "Then you should leave. You're not a man. Mark my words. ISAN will fall. And you are looking at all the women who will bring it down."

Gene roared, the veins on his neck protruding. He sprang on Justine so fast she didn't see his fist connect with her chin. She slid across the floor, her back burning from the friction and pain shooting down her spine.

Gene went for Brooke. He swung at her, but his fist froze in midair. Reyna had raised both of her hands and created an invisible barrier. While Gene was distracted, Justine knocked the TABs and monitors off the table with one fast swipe of her arm and threw the table at him. He dove over it, somersaulted, and landed on all fours.

Brooke slapped the ground with an open palm by Ozzie's cell.

The ground splintered in a crooked line from Gene to where she stood, and the earth cracked open about twelve feet apart. It extended to Tamara's cell, shattering the barrier. Justine leaped to avoid falling in and stood by scattered monitors.

Holy mother. Justine had never seen such power from Brooke.

"Finally." Tamara jumped out and stood next to Brooke, who was working on getting Ozzie out.

"You're going to stop me with your little tremor?" Gene barked a laugh.

Justine expected Brooke to say something, but she had cocked her head to listen to something, not from this room. There must have been an explosion. Brooke went to go help the others and… Nina?

Justine had thought she was dead or had been captured by… It dawned on her then that Mitch had helped Nina and Cora escape ISAN.

But where was Cora?

Boom! The ground rattled. Another explosion, closer and louder.

Brooke's senses were incredible, especially her hearing, Justine believed Brooke had heard the blast before it happened because Brooke had halted a second before and turned to the direction the blast had come from.

"We need to get out of here," Ozzie said. "This place is going to blow."

"Watch out!" Reyna shouted.

Gene had withdrawn a gun from a secret storage compartment by the door and began shooting at them.

"You guys get out of here. I'll be right behind you." Brooke leaped over the table and jumped to Gene's side.

"No. Brooke." Ozzie reached for her, but too late.

"Just can't stay away from me, can you?" Gene aimed the weapon at Brooke.

Brooke dodged every single bullet, moving toward him, occasionally twisting from her waist or arching her back to avoid the assault. Justine had expected her to punch his throat or do something physical, but instead, she wrung her fingers around the wrist that held the gun.

On contact, Gene froze like a marble statue. The only part of him that could move was his eyes, which darted frantically from left to right as he whimpered.

"Now you know how I felt," Brooke said, her voice soothing, but so venomous. "As you broke all my ribs, I'm doing the same to you. Can you hear the cracks of your bones, snapping one by one? Do you feel the pain slicing through your muscles? It hurts like a mother, doesn't it? This is for all the people you killed at the rebel base, for every bit of harm you did. Revenge is sweet, especially on someone like you."

Gene whimpered again and tears trickled down his cheeks.

Justine thought, if given a chance, Brooke could blow up his body from the inside out. Such magnitude of power she held. Justine was never going to piss her off again.

"Brooke, let's go," Ozzie hollered. "He's not worth it."

Parts of the ceiling collapsed, falling into the gaping hole Brooke had created. It had widened after the explosions that shook the floor.

When Brooke let go, Gene collapsed.

"I just wanted you to have a taste of your own medicine," Brooke said. "I'm no murderer. Let ISAN be your downfall."

Another bomb exploded, rocking the ground again. The gap in the floor widened farther, and the exit on Brooke's side crumbled. They had no way out.

"Brooke. Jump. I'll catch you," Ozzie said.

The other half of the ceiling dropped. Reyna extended her arms outward and held the broken parts in midair.

"Hurry. I can't hold it much longer." Reyna heaved, her knees buckling.

"Jump, Brooke," Ozzie demanded.

Brooke backed as far as she could. Boosted by a running start, she jumped and soared across the chasm.

She wasn't going to make it. The ground had shifted again. Ozzie knew it too. If he reached for her, he would likely fall with her, but he did it anyway. That boy cared about her more than as a teammate.

Justine had to do something.

After Justine anchored her foot around the table leg, she

grabbed Ozzie's shirt. He didn't brush her off. He welcomed her help. Just as she welcomed Tamara holding her from behind, and Reyna and Nina behind her.

Because of the team effort, Ozzie caught Brooke's outreached hand. He yanked her up and folded her in his arms just for a second.

"Let's get the hell out of here." Brooke's eyes were set on Justine with a smile.

"I know the way out. This way," Justine said.

One decision had changed Justine's life forever.

CHAPTER FORTY-ONE – DISASTER

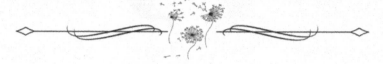

JOSEPHINE CHANG

Josephine met Vince at the given location. They surrounded a dome-shaped entrance and knocked out the two soldiers on duty.

Strange. She had expected more of a challenge. Sloppy of Novak not to have more guards by the entrance, but perhaps a handful waited inside.

"You should wait here, Councilor," Vince said, standing in front of the metal door with his gun aimed. "We don't know what awaits us inside."

Josephine had always listened to Vince's advice, and it had worked in her favor. Today shouldn't be any different, but she needed to see with her own eyes the horrific things Novak had been doing to the people she swore to protect.

"Not this time, Vince. I'm going in with you." Josephine readied her Taser in front of her chest and gave him a little shove.

Vince, built like a boulder, didn't budge. He paused for a second, his eyes roaming Josephine's face. She might have blushed, and thought he would tell her to stay behind, but he said, "Fine. Just stay close to me."

"Don't I always?" She jerked a shoulder.

He scowled. "You get yourself killed and I'll never forgive you."

"The same to you." She searched for her courage and positioned herself behind him.

Vince put up a fist to the sky, rallying his men. He yanked the cool metal handle and marched inside after the thirty or so men he had with him filed in.

Footsteps shuffled down the stairs and across the dimly lit hallway. A group of men rushed ahead and rounded the corner. Gunshots echoed. The frontline of their team went down. Vince tugged Josephine against the wall and hid in the shadows.

Just as she'd expected. ISAN wanted to lure them inside. They had the upper hand in this maze-like underground structure.

"Stay right here," Vince said. "I'll be right back. I'm going to split up my team."

Gunfire continued in a near-constant barrage. Josephine peeked out with her Taser readied. She couldn't see where the teams fought as *whack, thump*, and *thud* reverberated down the hall. The gunfire stopped and footsteps pounded toward her.

"What part of *stay right there* did you not understand?" Vince pulled her back and used his body to cover hers, her back against the wall and his chest inches from hers.

"I only moved three feet." She peered up, her gaze piercing his. Even in danger, she had to force herself to look away from those beautiful eyes she had always admired.

"Exactly." He cleared his throat, his eyes softening, but not his tone. "You moved. You could have gotten shot."

"I can protect myself, thank you very much. And I'm wearing a bulletproof shirt under my suit."

Vince pulled back. "You do recall the bulletproof shirt Verlot wore as well, don't you? Come on, let's go."

Josephine did recall. She was the one that had given the girl the bullet. Vince had been with her when she had set up the meeting. He was the only other person who knew besides Mr. San. Vince had sworn he wouldn't tell Zen and he hadn't.

They hustled stealthily down the long corridors and rested at an intersection.

"Which way?" Josephine whispered harshly.

The decision was made for them when the end of the hallway blasted open and threw them like bouncing balls. Josephine's back smacked the wall to her right and she collapsed. Her bones had been tossed and rattled inside her.

"Are you okay?"

Vince's frenzied voice echoed in her ear.

As his face came into focus, he cupped her cheek, the room stopped rotating, but the sounds of gunfire and Tasers pinging continued.

"I'm alive," she groaned. "Unless we're both dead and in hell together."

"I'd rather be in hell with you than here. Come, on. Up you go. No time for a nap, Councilor." Vince hefted her. Her feet found stable ground before she could register they were moving.

Vince's men flanked and covered them as they entered a larger room. Another bomb exploded, farther out.

"I thought ANS gave you twenty-four hours?" Vince said, surveying the room.

"They're not here. These explosions aren't from them."

Vince bristled, the tautness on his expression harder. He answered a call on his chip, then said, "Councilor. My men have already circled once, but if we don't find the rebels, we're getting out of here. This structure could blow up like the rebel base. You saw the photos I sent you. There was nothing left."

Josephine nodded, devastation rising to the surface. This place was their only hope for finding Zen and his crew. What then?

They pushed toward the back, entering through another room. The other entrance had collapsed, concrete piling on top of concrete. Smoke whooshed past them like a swift breeze over the ocean, only not as fresh and clean.

They passed through another door, and Vince shoved Josephine to the side as more bullets were exchanged. ISAN guards went down.

Josephine's prayers were answered, but what she saw was a nightmare. Three people had been shot, blood pooling around their bodies. Russ seemed unconscious, but unharmed.

Cleo's eyes went wild with happiness to see Josephine. She wiped away tears and shot up. "Councilor Chang. Thank God you're here."

Cleo had been dutifully watching over Mitch, Russ, her father, and—*no*. Lydia had been shot too. She was like a daughter. *Oh, dear, God. No!* She had to get everyone out now.

Josephine dropped to her knees and checked for Lydia's pulse, then to Russ and Zen. Their chests still rose and fell, though the movement was shallow. They lived.

"Councilor… Cha…" Mitch raised a hand weakly, his voice low. "Ly… dia."

"Mitch, don't talk. Save your energy. I'm getting you all out. Cleo." Josephine placed a gentle hand on her shoulder. "Do you know where Rhett and Ava are?"

Cleo shook her head, her fingers trembling as she pointed behind her. "They took them both. Novak is going to do horrible things to them. You have to help them."

Josephine instructed Vince's men to help carry the wounded

and told Cleo to follow.

"Councilor, I'll sweep around," Vince said. "You need to go with Cleo. You have a Dr. Machine in your glider and only your handprint can unlock it. You're going to have to go."

She nodded. "I'm not taking off without you, so you better hurry or you'll kill us all."

"Stubborn." Vince shook his head.

"Just in case." Josephine kissed his cheek. "Be safe. You've been my angel. If something were to happen to you, I don't know what I'd do."

Vince's eyes rounded in surprise. "Then let's not find out. A reminder what you'll be missing if you don't make it back to the glider."

He pressed his lips on hers. He kissed her hard, filled with passion and longing. When he let go, he bolted out the door.

Well, that was pleasantly unexpected.

Councilor Josephine Chang rushed off, gun at the ready, to fight and defend with all her heart and soul.

CHAPTER FORTY-TWO – PIVOTAL POINT

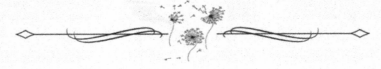

AVA

With Rhett's arm slung over my shoulder and my own snaked around his back, I dragged my feet across the floor.

I stumbled to the side when a bomb rocked the structure.

I pulled out the Taser from my pocket and aimed at a shadowy figure running down the hallway.

She halted. "Ava, don't shoot. It's me, Tamara."

It was so good to see her. "I need your help. I've got Rhett." I passed Rhett over to her when she reached me.

Rhett groaned, fighting to keep his eyes open.

"Where's everyone? Do you—" I never got to finish.

"Ava. Your eyes. Your body. You're glowing." Tamara marveled at me.

"I'll explain later. Get everyone out to safety. This place is going to blow. I'll meet you outside."

Fingers wrung my shirt. "Where... going." Rhett's voice was low and rough.

Even though he couldn't form words, he was aware of me.

My heart breaking, I cupped my hand over his. "I have to find my mother. I promise to meet you outside." I kissed Rhett's drooping head. "Take him out, Tamara. Take everyone out, now."

She nodded and turned.

"Ava. No!" Rhett's voice echoed down the hall, reminding me

of the day of the escape.

I felt his words like a dagger to my heart. I recalled how much I'd hurt him, how much he had suffered when I hadn't escaped with him. This time, it would be different. *I promise, Rhett.*

I sprinted to the garden. No sign of Mother. I dashed to her bedroom. No sign of her there either. When I came out, ISAN guards raised their weapons at me. Frightened faces replaced their confident ones. They had noticed how I glowed. Even their voices sounded feeble.

"Stay right there, Ava."

"I don't think so," I snarled.

With a flick of my finger, the luminous tendrils shot out of me. The energy wrapped around their weapons and slammed them against the wall. With another twitch of my finger, the soldiers flew every which direction. Some hit the ceiling and dropped. Others hit the wall and collided with each other.

Oh, the power. So glorious.

Novak was right. I was special. It had taken me a while to realize what I was truly meant to be, but my gift had blossomed at the right time.

More guards came at me from both sides. I used my power to fling their weapons. The soldiers who didn't run away, stood their ground.

"Come and get me, boys," I said.

Heavy fists flew at me and I dodged every single blow. Uppercut. Jab. High swing. Low blow. Ten men against me. They still didn't have a chance.

Time was running out and I needed to find my mother. I crouched low to duck a swing and swept my legs around the guards. Two guards dropped to the ground, and I gave them both a quick, hard jab to their guts. Some guards fled, but about five of them gave a brave front.

"This place is going down," I said. "Do you want to waste your time trying to bring me in, or is your life worth saving?"

They ran when the earth shook again and explosions rattled the very foundations.

Good choice.

"Mom?" I yelled, running down the corridors.

"Ava." Payton's voice.

"Payton?" I hollered.

"Ava." The voice came closer.

"Payton. Where are you?" I shouted over another blast.

"Ava. Here. I have your mother."

"Keep saying my name. I'm coming."

When I turned a final corner and found them, Payton looked relieved. Mother was still the same—dazed and confused—but she held an infant, tucked inside a pink blanket with a matching cap.

The CODE baby Novak had shown me.

"Do you know another way out?" I asked Payton. "This place is going to blow."

"Yes. Follow me."

I gathered my arms around Mother and guided her behind Payton. When she fidgeted, I thought she was trying to bail, but instead, her fingers intertwined with mine. Her gaze upon me was warm and tender. It reminded me of our past time together. Something wet prickled my eyes.

In that moment, I knew Mother existed, somewhere in her wild mind that had been plucked and twisted by Novak's doing. I wanted to cry with happiness. My time here had been worth it. In time, she might have a chance to recover and we would regain what we lost.

Dust filtered through as the hairline fractures in the wall lengthened and spread. Each section of the wall began to crumble.

"Hurry, Payton," I barked like an order.

We ran faster and faster for what felt like eternity. Every crack on the rumbling ground brought us closer to our demise.

"There it is." Payton's voice rose with exhilaration, his long legs sprinting quicker.

A light filtered through. Not a door but a gap in the ceiling, an exit nevertheless. For a moment, the light penetrated like heaven's ray. Holy and celestial in its beauty. I felt, if I stood there, an angel would pull me up to safety. Then it was gone.

Novak and a few nominal guards materialized out of the shadows as if waiting for us.

"I think you have something of mine," Novak said, blood trickling from the side of his skull.

Mother recoiled, holding the infant tighter. "No. No. No."

"Give her to me, Avary, and I'll let everyone go." Novak took a calculated step, slow but determined.

Mother gripped the back of my shirt, tugging me along with her.

"I'm afraid you don't have a choice," Novak said. "This place will be nothing but dirt and dust. If you want Ava to live, give the child to me."

I thought about using my power, but within the small space, I wasn't sure if I could control it. Mother backed farther away, shaking her head in a frenzy.

"Mom. Come back." I looked over my shoulder for a heartbeat, and Novak and his team were gone when I returned my gaze.

"Where did they go?" I demanded at Payton, who should have kept watch.

He opened his mouth to speak, but I answered my own question. Novak and his team were holograms, a distraction. I should have known. Mother had been yanked away from me.

Damn it.

I should have been prepared. But I hadn't thought Novak would revive so quickly. I had hoped he would die with the crumbling compound.

"Let her go, Novak," I said while dashing toward them.

Novak and Mom were a good distance away but I could stop him. He was alone. Until bullets whizzed by my ears.

My feet contacted the wall with the running momentum and I flipped over to evade all the bullets. I landed with a skidding halt. The building had rocked again and the ground fissured between me and my parents.

No, no, no. It's okay. I can jump.

Before I could make my move, Mother kneed Novak between his legs and ran. She couldn't jump the distance. No matter, I had to find a way to make a path for her to me.

"Ava. Baby," she said with all the love in her eyes and threw the stiffly bundled infant at me.

"Mom," I screamed as I caught the baby, cushioning her landing as best I could.

There was no way out for my mother.

Think, Ava. Do something.

The ceiling began to fall.

"Ava." Payton placed a gentle hand on my arm. "I'm sorry about your mom, but we have to go. This is it. It's done."

I passed the baby to Payton and told him to go first. Tears

streamed down my mother's face.

"Mom." I clapped to get her attention. "Go back and run and jump. I'll catch you."

Mother looked behind her. The other side had sunken. This was it. She knew it and I knew it. But I would never give up.

Never.

Mother clasped her hands together and said with clarity as if her mind had never been warped. "Ava. Run. Live."

"Mom, no!"

I had found my mother only to watch her be taken from me again. So many things I wanted to tell her. I'd thought we would have more time. I had planned to take her with me when we escaped. She would tell me everything that had happened. Questions would be answered. She would meet Rhett and my friends at the mountain base. But fate had other plans.

Mother ran toward Novak, who fought through the pain to stand. I'd thought she would punch him, but instead, she tackled him.

"Mom!" I screamed, watching in horror as they both fell off the edge into the gaping pit of rubble.

She wanted to ensure his death. My mother had killed Novak. No, not Novak. Her husband and my father.

I never thought I would be saddened by his death, but when he'd tried to take away my memories, all the happy ones had resurfaced. Something went wrong, and that had benefited me. I'd felt his love, and felt the love I'd had for him as a child.

It hurt. It hurt so much to see both of them gone.

Science had taken my father. He had buried himself in the dark work of ISAN and become someone else. A monster. But my mom… I had just found her.

CODE

I trembled, tears falling too fast to wipe away. In ISAN I learned how to control my emotions, but this was different. This was my life. They were my parents.

The ground shook. I stumbled to the side. I had to go now. Tears burned my eyes as I ran, carrying my mother's love with me.

CHAPTER FORTY-THREE – ESCAPE

AVA

I ran. Light as the wind, swift as a hummingbird, my feet barely touched the ground. Behind me was a giant, ravenous hole expanding, catching up to me, as white powdery dust coated the air.

Ava. Run. Live. My mother's voice boomed inside my head. *Faster. Faster. Faster.*

The walls punched out from the sides, knocking me off balance. Dust billowed in clouds, blinding my view. I went in circles to avoid being hit or sucked under. I wasn't sure where my exit was anymore, but I ran toward the tiny beacon of light and prayed I was going the right way.

If I died, I would die happy knowing everyone I loved was safe, and I'd gotten the chance to see my mother again.

No, you will not die today. As if my mother was still with me, her words pounded through me. *Run. Live.*

The encroaching ceiling forced me lower, my movement clumsier as I pushed my way through mud and walls caving inward. Then I felt no land beneath me.

Oh, God. Death had found me.

In the years I had been an assassin and known I might not make it back from a mission, I'd never thought being buried alive would be the way I would die. Rhett and the faces of my friends flashed in my mind, then my father and mother, and even Gene. The life I wished I had, the life I wished Rhett and I could've had together after bringing down ISAN was gone.

I had accepted my fate until…

A light burst through the darkness. Wind rushed in and wrapped around me like a net. I gravitated in air, held by someone's power. I pushed through the mud and dirt. Then strong hands gripped my arms.

"I've got you."

I knew that voice like my own heartbeat.

I blinked and dusted the dirt away from my face as he pulled me up. Rhett embraced me with all of him, then let go.

Brooke, Ozzie, Reyna, Tamara, Naomi, Mia, Payton with the baby, Justine, and the new girl with the nose ring, put their hands on my shoulders, my arms, and my back. They hadn't left me. They'd never given up on me. They'd stayed with me until the end. My eyes pooled with tears and I wanted to hug them, but we had no time.

Wordlessly, Rhett gripped my hand and we ran for our lives, our friends beside us. We just ran as the earth shook and land fissured behind us. We had no escape. ISAN gliders had been sucked under. We sprinted past the circle of destruction, but the land began to crumble farther out. And then I realized we had left people behind and my heart caved in again.

I didn't think I could handle more hurt and more bad news.

"What about Mitch, Russ—"

Before I could finish, Rhett hollered over the loud roar, his feet pounding on earth beside me. "Tamara ran into Vince. They're all with Councilor Chang."

I teared up again, but this time with joy.

A sleek glider hovered over us in the clearing, revealed as the heavy smoke blew away. Violent wind pushed me back. When the aircraft landed, a person came into view.

"Zeke?" Tamara sounded as excited as I felt as she ran toward him.

"Hurry," Zeke's voice hollered from the ramp.

Never had I been so happy to see him. I waited behind with Rhett until everyone was on board.

"You." Zeke pointed at my chest. A curl escaped over his forehead from his sleeked-back hair. "I never wanted to see you again, but I'm glad you're okay."

"You might change your mind later." I winked. "Now, get us out of here."

"Aye, aye, Captain." He placed his index and middle finger to the side of his forehead and dashed to his seat.

While everyone belted in, Rhett and I remained standing in the back. He held me in his arms as we peered down at our horrific view. The earth continued to rattle while the last bit of the ISAN facility caved inward.

Metal falling on metal screeched in a deafening cacophony. Like in quicksand, the sand sucked everything in its giant maw, taking my parents' bodies with it. A column of fire exploded and puffed out a titanic cloud above. Finally, it was all gone.

Tears dampened my cheeks. My chest felt hollow with loss. *Damn you, Novak, for making me remember my father.* It would be easier to see him dead without those memories, but the feeling, our happy times together ate through my soul. And then my mother.

It hurt. Damn, it hurt.

Then there was Gene... What had happened to him?

"I'm so sorry, babe." Rhett squeezed me tighter, kissing my

forehead, caressing my back.

No words were needed between Rhett and me. I sobbed in his arms, pouring out all my pain and regret for my mother, for my father—or who he had once been. Things I should have said. Things I could have done.

"What about your dad?" I pulled away and dabbed my eyes.

Rhett dipped his head. "He was there, but he'd been moved."

"I'm so sorry, Rhett."

Rhett kissed my cheek. "I'm going to find him."

"I'm going to help you," I said, hearing footsteps behind me.

Brooke and Tamara placed a hand on my shoulder with "I'm here for you" smiles. They knew my pain. I smiled too, but it took some effort. The three of us hugged and sobbed.

I wept from missing them. Cried knowing how much Brooke had been though, how she'd almost died and I hadn't been there for her. It felt so damn good to cry.

The infant crying got my attention, and Brooke and Tamara went back to their seats. I wiped my tears and wondered what I was going to do with the baby. Who would take care of her?

Payton unbuckled his seat and brought her to me, the tightly wrapped pink blanket had loosened, revealing a pink onesie to match her cap.

"Here. The baby won't stop crying," Payton said. "She fell asleep for a while, but now she's awake and I don't know what to do with her."

"She needs to be fed, I think, or a diaper change," Justine said, then shrank back in her seat when everyone stared at her.

Justine would need time to get used to all the new faces, and we would need time to get used to her. She had tried to kill us countless times. But she had proved her loyalty and she was my half sister.

I had to accept that and try to fix us. She was the only family I had, since Gene was no brother of mine. And unless he'd escaped before the building had fallen, there was no way he could have survived.

The baby stopped crying as soon as she was in my arms. I took her farther back to the corner where it was quieter. When she'd been inside the hub, she'd had her eyes closed and I hadn't bothered to look at her face. But now that I held her in my arms... So precious. Cute nose, small lips, and her beautiful amber eyes, like Rhett's, stared back at me.

"She must like you," Rhett said.

"Maybe. She smells like heaven." I pressed my nose to her pink cap with dark strands sticking out, I inhaled a deep breath. "She smells like my mother, like all the flowers in her garden."

"What is that?" Rhett pulled out the silver chain necklace sticking out by her shoulder.

My lips spread and I felt happy with disbelief. "My necklace. Novak took it from me and my mom... she knew it was mine."

It was the dandelion necklace Rhett had gifted me at Hope City.

Rhett locked the chain around my neck. "There. Where it belongs." He reached for something white poking out from the blanket. "It's addressed to you. Your mom?"

"I don't know. I don't think my mother was well enough to write a letter."

"Why don't you read it? I'll hold this girl." Rhett snatched the baby out of my arms before I could protest.

When I knew they were both fine, I sat in the back seat, secluded from others, and ripped the seal.

CODE

Dearest Ava,

If you're reading this letter then it means I have passed on and I wasn't able to go with you. I had to write this letter before I lost my mind. There are many things I want to tell you, but I don't have enough time and paper. You must have tons of questions and hopefully I'll be able to answer them in this letter.

When you turned thirteen, your father told me I had a son, your twin. I didn't believe him at first, but when he told me he had separated us and showed me a picture of the son I'd never known, I had to meet him.

I agreed to visit Gene, but didn't anticipate your father would kidnap me by faking my death. Know that I would have never left you. I tried to get back to you, but your father wouldn't allow it. Many times I tried, but failed. I even tried to kill him with a dinner knife, which is why only spoons were allowed.

I continued to rebel. I had to get back to you, for I knew how much you would suffer. How does a mother pretend her child doesn't exist? So he tried to erase my memory of you. In the process, I had a stroke and lost my ability to speak. Some of my motor skills were deteriorating, but he didn't know that I could write my thoughts down. I made him believe I couldn't remember you.

I used this situation to my advantage and wandered in the facility alone whenever I had the chance. I studied the layout and memorized every room, every escape route.

In the lab is where I found out your father is Mr. Novak, the head of ISAN, and about the serum. And all the horrible things Novak is doing. I needed to learn more and prepare for you. He told me he would bring you to me, and we would be a family again.

Knowing his plan, I stopped trying to escape. I kept myself busy in the garden. Gene and I got to know each other, but I didn't love him the same as I loved you. How do you love a monster Novak created? He is not the boy I would have raised. He is not my son.

Years have passed, but I knew all about you. Novak's workers would talk among themselves when he was gone and I engulfed every word. Almost nine months ago, I learned a CODE pod was brought here. Inside was a fetus. What I learned brought me to my knees.

The infant's name is Ava, like you. Her initials stand for Advance Variant Ability. She was taken from the mother's womb before the mother knew she was pregnant. Novak knew this baby was special, believes she will become more powerful than you.

Girls in ISAN can't get pregnant because of the serum and the protein drink called CHB20, but you are not like them, are you? You were told you couldn't get pregnant, right? Had it been someone else, this would have been true. But they were wrong. There's no easy way to tell you. Ava, you're the mother. The baby is yours and Rhett's.

Novak found out you were pregnant through routine blood work about ten months ago; it must have been just after she was conceived. He wanted that baby more than anything, so he took her from you. For this reason, I was protective of the baby. She is my granddaughter.

I know that this is much to take in, but your baby needs you. Take good care of her as I tried to do for you. Teach her to own her powers. To be resilient. But also teach her to be humble. Nurture her. Love her. Embrace her. Tell her you love her every day. Most of all, teach her to be kind and gentle, and that she can make a difference in the world, just like her mother.

I had thirteen glorious years with you. Those were the best years of my life. I only wish I had more, and with my granddaughter. I wish I'd gotten to know Rhett. I knew whoever my daughter loved would be special.

I'm so proud of you, Ava. You have to know that I've missed you so much. I cried every night, wishing I was with you. I never stopped thinking of you even after all these years. It killed me that you had to become an assassin because you felt you had no choice when they locked you up in juvie.

I am so sorry, Ava. I should have been there for you. Not a day goes by I wished I could have done things differently. Please forgive me for not being there for you when you needed me the most. I only hope I've done right by you by giving your baby back to you.

Promise me you'll not shed sad tears over me. Instead, keep me close to your heart and always remember the happy times. I'm thankful I got to see you again and give you this closure.

There is one more thing. There are more CODE babies. One site is stationed in Sokcho, South Korea, but I don't know where the rest are. These kids deserve a better future. Please save them.

Remember me not for how I died, but how I lived.

Forever in your heart,

Mom

It was a good thing I was sitting or I would have fallen on my knees. I put a hand to my chest as breath escaped me in quick spurts. I couldn't believe it. How? I knew how I'd gotten pregnant but... I dropped my head between my legs and puffed out air, panicking.

Oh, God. Oh, God. Oh, God. I'm a mother. Holy mother of all mothers, something Ozzie would say.

I could barely take care of myself. How was I going to take care of an infant? How was I going to tell Rhett? Rhett and I were parents! How would we raise a child in the middle of ISAN's war?

Oh, Mom. I wish you were here with me. As tears slid down my cheeks, it dawned on me. The two words—baby and letter—Mother had written on her wrist had been so she wouldn't forget.

The letter gave me some closure, but I was furious with Novak. If it hadn't been for my mother, I would have never known about my baby. Rhett's and my child.

CODE

When you have children of your own, you will understand. And I have a feeling you will one day. Novak had said to me. He showed me my child and never said a word.

If not for my mother, our baby might have died in the blast, or Novak would have raised her as his own. The thought repulsed me. He could have escaped, but he'd risked his life to take *my* baby.

How dare Novak take away the fetus growing inside me? He'd robbed me of the pregnancy experience. He'd taken away my bonding with my baby, all the months I should have carried her inside me. Not just my experience, but Rhett's as well. Listening for the baby's heartbeat. The first kick. Finding out the sex. All the experiences we should have shared together.

I had to stop thinking of what should have been and be thankful that our baby was safe and with us. We had faced death in the eye and had escaped with few deaths. Everything else seemed inconsequential.

CHAPTER FORTY-FOUR— AVARY

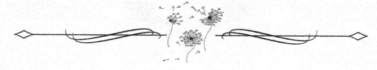

AVA

R hett had flashed a worried glance at me a couple of times while I was reading, but he went back to cooing at the baby. Our baby.

He didn't know she was ours, yet he already seemed to have fallen in love with her. Spellbound, he held her tiny fingers, and his eyes were full of hope and wonder.

Rhett's lips spread with joy, his face relaxing into a happy place. He had forgotten the world around him. I wondered if he wished she was his.

"Rhett," I said, as tears streamed down my face. Two emotions twisting and conflicting, overwhelming me. Sorrow for the loss of my parents, and the joy of knowing he and I had a child.

"Babe. What is it? Are you okay?" His gaze lowered to the letter in my hand.

"You should read this." I exchanged the letter for our baby and gave him space, while I waited for him by the back window.

When he was done, wordlessly he wrapped his arms around us and tears spilled from his eyes. I had never seen Rhett cry before, but I understood. He kissed my forehead with reverence, and he did the same to our daughter.

Our daughter. I still couldn't believe the miracle in my arms.

"Everything is going to be fine," Rhett said. "We're going to love her the best we can. She will be loved by all her uncles and aunties. We'll give her the best of everything."

"I know." I smiled and stared at my little girl's closed eyes. "I can't believe she's ours."

And to think we would have never known if it hadn't been for my mother.

"I can't either." Rhett caressed her cheek and kissed her curled fingers. "What shall we name her?"

"How about after my mom? Avary."

"Avary it is. I think it's a wonderful idea. So, when should we tell our friends, Mom?"

Mom... such a foreign word.

"How about now?" I said. "We have much to discuss any way."

Zeke put the aircraft to autopilot and joined our circle of friends when Rhett and I asked for their attention. While everyone remained in their seats, Rhett and I stood side by side at the rear so they could see us.

I told them what I had seen and experienced when I first arrived at ISAN's secret facility. I also told them that Novak was my father, Dr. Hunt. Gene was my twin, and Justine, my half sister.

Everyone wore shocked expressions but said nothing. Justine kept her head down while I explained. At last, Rhett and I told them the baby in my arms was ours. They were stunned to silence, then finally congratulated us. Though their excitement rang true, I detected some concern.

Rhett and I didn't know the first thing about raising a child, but we would figure it out together. After all, didn't all parents feel the same? There was no manual. Babies didn't come with instructions. We would learn as we went along and take guidance from the elders.

Ozzie cleared his throat. "Believe or not, we have infant formulas and baby bottles."

Reyna twisted in her seat. "We have a box of diapers, too, in the storage room."

"Perfect," I said. "We're set for now."

A message came through Rhett's chip and broke up our meeting. Councilor Chang confirmed they were safe, heading to her headquarters. Mitch, Lydia, and Zen had been shot by Novak, which we already knew. Mitch and Zen were in recovery, but Lydia was in critical condition and it didn't look good for her.

We all took a moment of silence.

I had admired Lydia for her strength and for her bravery. She was one of the silent heroes. She *had* to recover.

"Where to?" Zeke asked, taking the driver's seat again.

"To our mountain base." Rhett carefully slid into the passenger seat while holding Avary in his arms.

I loved watching him stare at our child. He would probably never let her out of his sight.

"Then what's next?" Ozzie asked, leaning over Rhett's shoulder to get a better look at Avary. "I'm your uncle Ozzie, but you can call me Oz. You have so many uncles and aunties. They're going to spoil you like crazy. Aren't we, Payton?"

"Uh—yes, of course," Payton said, startled by Oz's clap on his back.

I laughed. Payton was going to have the shock of his life at the base. Where ISAN was orderly, we were chaos. Beautiful chaos. Family chaos.

We had many things to consider when we got to the base. One thing for sure—we would set up a team to search for the missing parents, and locate the CODE children as my mother had requested. As for my team, we would head for South Korea. My gut told me we would find more answers there.

While the boys fell into conversation about strategy, I sat between Brooke and Reyna. I looked behind me to Tamara, Naomi, Mia, Nina, and Justine. But Cleo was missing. She unknowingly had cracked the sonic barrier and had helped me, too. She must have tons of questions.

I smiled at all of them, and they in returned a smile to me, and each other. No words were needed. There was a mutual understanding of respect and loyalty.

How strong we were when we worked as a team. Each beautiful in their own gifts. Each strong woman with a mind of her own. Each of them my friend. My family.

We would fight for justice.

We would fight for peace.

We would bring the rest of ISAN down.

When Rhett walked to the back window, I left my friends and sat beside him. He placed an arm around me, his other arm around Avary, who was fast asleep. While we exchanged loving glances, he kissed my lips, then we stared at our daughter all the way home.

ABOUT THE AUTHOR

Mary is an international bestselling, award-winning author. She writes soulful, spellbinding stories that excite the imagination and captivate readers around the world. Her books span a wide range of genres, and her storytelling talents have earned a devoted legion of fans, as well as garnered critical praise.

Becoming an author happened by chance. It was a way to grieve the death of her beloved grandmother, and inspired by a dream she had in high school. After realizing she wanted to become a full-time author, Mary retired from teaching after twenty years. She also had the privileged of touring with the Magic Johnson Foundation to promote literacy and her children's chapter book: *No Bullies Allowed*.

Mary resides in Southern California with her husband, two children, and two little dogs, Mochi and Mocha. She enjoys oil painting and making jewelry.

WWW.ISAN.AGENCY
WWW.TANGLEDTALESOFTING.COM